PENGUIN BOOKS

The Catcher in the Rye

J. D. Salinger (1919–2010) was bo [illegible] appeared in many magazines [illegible] 1951 and 1963 he published fo [illegible] *Catcher in the Rye*; *For Esmé – w* [illegible] and *Raise High the Roof Beam, Ca* [illegible] – that have been embraced and cele [illegible] world, and have been credited with instilling in [illegible] long love of reading.

[illegible] born in New York City. His stories [illegible] most notably the *New Yorker*. Between [illegible] four book-length works of fiction – *The* [illegible] and Squalor, *Franny and Zooey*, [illegible] *Carpenters* and *Seymour: An Introduction* [illegible] and translated throughout the [illegible] many [illegible]

The Catcher in the Rye

J. D. SALINGER

PENGUIN BOOKS

PENGUIN BOOKS

UK | USA | Canada | Ireland | Australia
India | New Zealand | South Africa

Penguin Books is part of the Penguin Random House group of companies
whose addresses can be found at global.penguinrandomhouse.com.

Penguin Random House UK

First published in serial form in the United States of America 1945–6
First published in book form in the United States of America 1951
First published in Great Britain by Hamish Hamilton 1951
Published in Penguin Books 1958
This original American edition first published in Great Britain in Penguin Books
and simultaneously by Hamish Hamilton 1994
Reissued in this hardback edition by Penguin Books 2018
Published in Penguin Books 2019
023

Typeset by Jouve (UK), Milton Keynes
Printed and bound in Great Britain by Clays Ltd, Elcograf S.p.A.

A CIP catalogue record for this book is available from the British Library

ISBN: 978–0–241–95043–2

www.greenpenguin.co.uk

MIX
Paper from
responsible sources
FSC® C018179
FSC www.fsc.org

Penguin Random House is committed to a sustainable future for our business, our readers and our planet. This book is made from Forest Stewardship Council® certified paper.

To My Mother

I

If you really want to hear about it, the first thing you'll probably want to know is where I was born, and what my lousy childhood was like, and how my parents were occupied and all before they had me, and all that David Copperfield kind of crap, but I don't feel like going into it, if you want to know the truth. In the first place, that stuff bores me, and in the second place, my parents would have about two hemorrhages apiece if I told anything pretty personal about them. They're quite touchy about anything like that, especially my father. They're *nice* and all – I'm not saying that – but they're also touchy as hell. Besides, I'm not going to tell you my whole goddam autobiography or anything. I'll just tell you about this madman stuff that happened to me around last Christmas just before I got pretty run-down and had to come out here and take it easy. I mean that's all I told D.B. about, and he's my *brother* and all. He's in Hollywood. That isn't too far from this crumby place, and he comes over and visits me practically every week end. He's going to drive me home when I go home next month maybe. He just got a Jaguar. One of those little English jobs that can do around two hundred miles an hour. It cost him damn near four thousand bucks. He's got a lot of dough, now. He didn't *use* to. He used to be just a regular writer, when he was home. He wrote this terrific book of short stories, *The Secret Goldfish*, in case you never heard of him. The best one in it was 'The Secret Goldfish.' It was about this little kid that wouldn't let anybody look at his goldfish because he'd bought it with his own money. It killed me. Now he's out in Hollywood, D.B., being a prostitute. If there's one thing I hate, it's the movies. Don't even mention them to me.

Where I want to start telling is the day I left Pencey Prep. Pencey Prep is this school that's in Agerstown, Pennsylvania. You probably heard of it. You've probably seen the ads, anyway. They advertise in about a thousand magazines, always showing some hot-shot guy on a horse jumping over a fence. Like as if all you ever did at Pencey was play polo all the time. I never even once saw a horse anywhere *near* the place. And underneath the guy on the horse's picture, it always says: 'Since 1888 we have been molding boys into splendid, clear-thinking young men.' Strictly for the birds. They don't do any damn more *mold*ing at Pencey than they do at any other school. And I didn't know anybody there that was splendid and clear-thinking and all. Maybe two guys. If that many. And they probably *came* to Pencey that way.

Anyway, it was the Saturday of the football game with Saxon Hall. The game with Saxon Hall was supposed to be a very big deal around Pencey. It was the last game of the year, and you were supposed to commit suicide or something if old Pencey didn't win. I remember around three o'clock that afternoon I was standing way the hell up on top of Thomsen Hill, right next to this crazy cannon that was in the Revolutionary War and all. You could see the whole field from there, and you could see the two teams bashing each other all over the place. You couldn't see the grandstand too hot, but you could hear them all yelling, deep and terrific on the Pencey side, because practically the whole school except me was there, and scrawny and faggy on the Saxon Hall side, because the visiting team hardly ever brought many people with them.

There were never many girls at all at the football games. Only seniors were allowed to bring girls with them. It was a terrible school, no matter how you looked at it. I like to be somewhere at least where you can see a few girls around once in a while, even if they're only scratching their arms or blowing their noses or even just giggling or something. Old Selma Thurmer – she was the headmaster's daughter – showed up at the games quite often, but she wasn't exactly the type that drove you mad with desire. She was a pretty nice girl, though. I sat next to her once in the bus from Agerstown and we sort of struck up a conversation. I liked her. She had a big nose and her nails were all bitten down and bleedy-looking and she had on those damn falsies that point all over the place, but you felt sort of sorry for her. What I liked about her, she didn't give you a lot of horse manure about what a great guy her father was. She probably knew what a phony slob he was.

The reason I was standing way up on Thomsen Hill, instead of down at the game, was because I'd just got back from New York with the fencing team. I was the goddam manager of the fencing team. Very big deal. We'd gone in to New York that morning for this fencing meet with McBurney School. Only, we didn't have the meet. I left all the foils and equipment and stuff on the goddam subway. It wasn't all my fault. I had to keep getting up to look at this map, so we'd know where to get off. So we got back to Pencey around two-thirty instead of around dinnertime. The whole team ostracized me the whole way back on the train. It was pretty funny, in a way.

The other reason I wasn't down at the game was because I was on my way to say good-by to old Spencer, my history teacher. He had the grippe, and I figured I probably wouldn't see him again till Christmas vacation started. He wrote me this note saying he wanted to see me before I went home. He knew I wasn't coming back to Pencey.

I forgot to tell you about that. They kicked me out. I wasn't supposed to come back after Christmas vacation, on account of I was flunking four subjects and not applying myself and all. They gave me frequent warning to start applying myself – especially around mid-terms, when my parents came up for a conference with old Thurmer – but I didn't do it. So I got the ax. They give guys the ax quite frequently at Pencey. It has a very good academic rating, Pencey. It really does.

Anyway, it was December and all, and it was cold as a witch's teat, especially on top of that stupid hill. I only had on my reversible and no gloves or anything. The week before that, somebody'd stolen my camel's-hair coat right out of my room, with my fur-lined gloves right in the pocket and all. Pencey was full of crooks. Quite a few guys came from these very wealthy families, but it was full of crooks anyway. The more expensive a school is, the more crooks it has – I'm not kidding. Anyway, I kept standing next to that crazy cannon, looking down at the game and freezing my ass off. Only, I wasn't watching the game too much. What I was really hanging around for, I was trying to feel some kind of a good-by. I mean I've left schools and places I didn't even know I was leaving them. I hate that. I don't care if it's a sad good-by or a bad good-by, but when I leave a place I like to *know* I'm leaving it. If you don't, you feel even worse.

I was lucky. All of a sudden I thought of something that helped make me know I was getting the hell out. I suddenly remembered this time, in around October, that I and Robert Tichener and Paul Campbell were chucking a football around, in front of the academic building. They were nice guys, especially Tichener. It was just before dinner and it was getting pretty dark out, but we kept chucking the ball around anyway. It kept getting darker and darker, and we could hardly *see* the ball any more, but we didn't want to stop doing what we were doing. Finally we had to. This teacher that taught biology, Mr Zambesi, stuck his head out of this window in the academic building and told us to go back to the dorm and get ready for dinner. If I get a chance to remember that kind of stuff, I can get a good-by when I need one – at least, most of the time I can. As soon as I got it, I turned around and started running down the other side of the hill, toward old Spencer's house. He didn't live on the campus. He lived on Anthony Wayne Avenue.

I ran all the way to the main gate, and then I waited a second till I got my breath. I have no wind, if you want to know the truth. I'm quite a heavy smoker, for one thing – that is, I used to be. They made me cut it out. Another thing, I *grew* six and a half inches last year. That's also how I practically got t.b. and came out here for all these goddam checkups and stuff. I'm pretty healthy, though.

Anyway, as soon as I got my breath back I ran across Route 204. It was icy as hell and I damn near fell down. I don't even know what I was running for – I guess I just felt like it. After I got across the road, I felt like I was sort of disappearing. It was that kind of a crazy afternoon, terrifically cold, and no sun out or anything, and you felt like you were disappearing every time you crossed a road.

Boy, I rang that doorbell fast when I got to old Spencer's house. I was really frozen. My ears were hurting and I could hardly move my fingers at all. 'C'mon, c'mon,' I said right out loud, almost, 'somebody open the *door*.' Finally old Mrs Spencer opened it. They didn't have a maid or anything, and they always opened the door themselves. They didn't have too much dough.

'Holden!' Mrs Spencer said. 'How lovely to see you! Come in, dear! Are you frozen to death?' I think she was glad to see me. She liked me. At least, I think she did.

Boy, did I get in that house fast. 'How are you, Mrs Spencer?' I said. 'How's Mr Spencer?'

'Let me take your coat, dear,' she said. She didn't hear me ask her how Mr Spencer was. She was sort of deaf.

She hung up my coat in the hall closet, and I sort of brushed my hair back with my hand. I wear a crew cut quite frequently and I never have to comb it much. 'How've you been, Mrs Spencer?' I said again, only louder, so she'd hear me.

'I've been just fine, Holden.' She closed the closet door. 'How have *you* been?' The way she asked me, I knew right away old Spencer'd told her I'd been kicked out.

'Fine,' I said. 'How's Mr Spencer? He over his grippe yet?'

'Over it! Holden, he's behaving like a perfect – I don't know *what* . . . He's in his room, dear. Go right in.'

2

They each had their own room and all. They were both around seventy years old, or even more than that. They got a bang out of things, though – in a half-assed way, of course. I know that sounds mean to say, but I don't mean it mean. I just mean that I used to think about old Spencer quite a lot, and if you thought about him *too* much, you wondered what the heck he was still living for. I mean he was all stooped over, and he had very terrible posture, and in class, whenever he dropped a piece of chalk at the blackboard, some guy in the first row always had to get up and pick it up and hand it to him. That's awful, in my opinion. But if you thought about him just enough and not *too* much, you could figure it out that he wasn't doing too bad for himself. For instance, one Sunday when some other guys and I were over there for hot chocolate, he showed us this old beat-up Navajo blanket that he and Mrs Spencer'd bought off some Indian in Yellowstone Park. You could tell old Spencer'd got a big bang out of buying it. That's what I mean. You take somebody old as hell, like old Spencer, and they can get a big bang out of buying a blanket.

His door was open, but I sort of knocked on it anyway, just to be polite and all. I could see where he was sitting. He was sitting in a big leather chair, all wrapped up in that blanket I just told you about. He looked over at me when I knocked. 'Who's that?' he yelled. 'Caulfield? Come in, boy.' He was always yelling, outside class. It got on your nerves sometimes.

The minute I went in, I was sort of sorry I'd come. He was reading the *Atlantic Monthly*, and there were pills and medicine all over the place, and everything smelled like Vicks Nose Drops. It was pretty depressing. I'm not too crazy about sick people, anyway. What made it even more depressing, old Spencer had on this very sad, ratty old bathrobe that he was probably born in or something. I don't much like to see old guys in their pajamas and bathrobes anyway. Their bumpy old chests are always showing. And their legs. Old guys' legs, at beaches and places, always look so white and unhairy. 'Hello, sir,' I said. 'I got your note. Thanks a lot.' He'd written me this note asking me to stop by and say good-by before vacation started, on account of I wasn't coming back. 'You didn't have to do all that. I'd have come over to say good-by anyway.'

'Have a seat there, boy,' old Spencer said. He meant the bed.

I sat down on it. 'How's your grippe, sir?'

'M'boy, if I felt any better I'd have to send for the doctor,' old Spencer said. That knocked him out. He started chuckling like a madman. Then he finally straightened himself out and said, 'Why aren't you down at the game? I thought this was the day of the big game.'

'It is. I was. Only, I just got back from New York with the fencing team,' I said. Boy, his bed was like a rock.

He started getting serious as hell. I knew he would. 'So you're leaving us, eh?' he said.

'Yes, sir. I guess I am.'

He started going into this nodding routine. You never saw anybody nod as much in your life as old Spencer did. You never knew if he was nodding a lot because he was thinking and all, or just because he was a nice old guy that didn't know his ass from his elbow.

'What did Dr Thurmer say to you, boy? I understand you had quite a little chat.'

'Yes, we did. We really did. I was in his office for around two hours, I guess.'

'What'd he say to you?'

'Oh . . . well, about Life being a game and all. And how you should play it according to the rules. He was pretty nice about it. I mean he didn't hit the ceiling or anything. He just kept talking about Life being a game and all. You know.'

'Life *is* a game, boy. Life *is* a game that one plays according to the rules.'

'Yes, sir. I know it is. I know it.'

Game, my ass. Some game. If you get on the side where all the hot-shots are, then it's a game, all right – I'll admit that. But if you get on the *other* side, where there aren't any hot-shots, then what's a game about it? Nothing. No game. 'Has Dr Thurmer written to your parents yet?' old Spencer asked me.

'He said he was going to write them Monday.'

'Have you yourself communicated with them?'

'No, sir, I haven't communicated with them, because I'll probably see them Wednesday night when I get home.'

'And how do you think they'll take the news?'

'Well . . . they'll be pretty irritated about it,' I said. 'They really will. This is about the fourth school I've gone to.' I shook my head. I shake my head quite a lot. 'Boy!' I said. I also say 'Boy!' quite a lot. Partly because I have a lousy vocabulary and partly because I act quite young for my age sometimes. I was sixteen then, and I'm seventeen now, and sometimes I act like I'm about thirteen. It's really ironical, because I'm six foot two and a half and I have gray hair. I really do. The one side of my head – the right side – is full of millions of gray hairs. I've had them ever since I was a kid. And yet I still act sometimes like I was only about twelve. Everybody says that, especially my father. It's partly true, too, but it isn't *all* true. People always think something's *all* true. I don't give a damn, except that I get bored sometimes when people tell me to act my age. Sometimes I act a lot older than I am – I really do – but people never notice it. People never notice anything.

Old Spencer started nodding again. He also started picking his nose. He made out like he was only pinching it, but he was really getting the old thumb right in there. I guess he thought it was all right to do because it was only me that was in the room. I didn't *care*, except that it's pretty disgusting to watch somebody pick their nose.

Then he said, 'I had the privilege of meeting your mother and dad when they had their little chat with Dr Thurmer some weeks ago. They're grand people.'

'Yes, they are. They're very nice.'

Grand. There's a word I really hate. It's a phony. I could puke every time I hear it.

Then all of a sudden old Spencer looked like he had something very good, something sharp as a tack, to say to me. He sat up more in his chair and sort of moved around. It was a false alarm, though. All he did was lift the *Atlantic Monthly* off his lap and try to chuck it on the bed, next to me. He missed. It was only about two inches away, but he missed anyway. I got up and picked it up and put it down on the bed. All of a sudden then, I wanted to get the hell out of the room. I could feel a terrific lecture coming on. I didn't mind the idea so much, but I didn't feel like being lectured to and smell Vicks Nose Drops and look at old Spencer in his pajamas and bathrobe all at the same time. I really didn't.

It started, all right. 'What's the matter with you, boy?' old Spencer said. He said it pretty tough, too, for him. 'How many subjects did you carry this term?'

'Five, sir.'

'Five. And how many are you failing in?'

'Four.' I moved my ass a little bit on the bed. It was the hardest bed I ever sat on. 'I passed English all right,' I said, 'because I had all that Beowulf and Lord Randal My Son stuff when I was at the Whooton School. I mean I didn't have to do any work in English at all hardly, except write compositions once in a while.'

He wasn't even listening. He hardly ever listened to you when you said something.

'I flunked you in history because you knew absolutely nothing.'

'I know that, sir. Boy, I know it. You couldn't help it.'

'Absolutely nothing,' he said over again. That's something that drives me crazy. When people say something twice that way, after you *admit* it the first time. Then he said it *three* times. 'But absolutely nothing. I doubt very much if you opened your textbook even once the whole term. Did you? Tell the truth, boy.'

'Well, I sort of glanced through it a couple of times,' I told him. I didn't want to hurt his feelings. He was mad about history.

'You glanced through it, eh?' he said – very sarcastic. 'Your, ah, *exam* paper is over there on top of my chiffonier. On top of the pile. Bring it here, please.'

It was a very dirty trick, but I went over and brought it over to him – I didn't have any alternative or anything. Then I sat down on his cement bed again. Boy, you can't imagine how sorry I was getting that I'd stopped by to say good-by to him.

He started handling my exam paper like it was a turd or something. 'We studied the Egyptians from November 4th to December 2nd,' he said. 'You *chose* to write about them for the optional essay question. Would you care to hear what you had to say?'

'No, sir, not very much,' I said.

He read it anyway, though. You can't stop a teacher when they want to do something. They just *do* it.

> The Egyptians were an ancient race of Caucasians residing in one of the northern sections of Africa. The latter as we all know is the largest continent in the Eastern Hemisphere.

I had to sit there and *listen* to that crap. It certainly was a dirty trick.

> The Egyptians are extremely interesting to us today for various reasons. Modern science would still like to know what the secret ingredients were that the Egyptians used when they wrapped up dead people so that their faces would not rot for innumerable centuries. This interesting riddle is still quite a challenge to modern science in the twentieth century.

He stopped reading and put my paper down. I was beginning to sort of hate him. 'Your *es*say, shall we say, ends there,' he said in this very sarcastic voice. You wouldn't think such an old guy would be so sarcastic and all. 'However, you dropped me a little note, at the bottom of the page,' he said.

'I know I did,' I said. I said it very fast because I wanted to stop him before he started reading *that* out loud. But you couldn't stop him. He was hot as a firecracker.

> DEAR MR SPENCER [he read out loud]. That is all I know about the Egyptians. I can't seem to get very interested in them

although your lectures are very interesting. It is all right with me if you flunk me though as I am flunking everything else except English anyway. Respectfully yours, HOLDEN CAULFIELD.

He put my goddam paper down then and looked at me like he'd just beaten hell out of me in ping-pong or something. I don't think I'll ever forgive him for reading me that crap out loud. I wouldn't've read it out loud to *him* if *he'd* written it – I really wouldn't. In the first place, I'd only *writ*ten that damn note so that he wouldn't feel too bad about flunking me.

'Do you blame me for flunking you, boy?' he said.

'No, sir! I certainly don't,' I said. I wished to hell he'd stop calling me 'boy' all the time.

He tried chucking my exam paper on the bed when he was through with it. Only, he missed again, naturally. I had to get up again and pick it up and put it on top of the *Atlantic Monthly*. It's *boring* to do that every two minutes.

'What would you have done in my place?' he said. 'Tell the truth, boy.'

Well, you could see he really felt pretty lousy about flunking me. So I shot the bull for a while. I told him I was a real moron, and all that stuff. I told him how I would've done exactly the same thing if I'd been in his place, and how most people didn't appreciate how tough it is being a teacher. That kind of stuff. The old bull.

The funny thing is, though, I was sort of thinking of something else while I shot the bull. I live in New York, and I was thinking about the lagoon in Central Park, down near Central Park South. I was wondering if it would be frozen over when I got home, and if it was, where did the ducks go. I was wondering where the ducks went when the lagoon got all icy and frozen over. I wondered if some guy came in a truck and took them away to a zoo or something. Or if they just flew away.

I'm lucky, though. I mean I could shoot the old bull to old Spencer and think about those ducks at the same time. It's funny. You don't have to think too hard when you talk to a teacher. All of a sudden, though, he interrupted me while I was shooting the bull. He was always interrupting you.

'How do you *feel* about all this, boy? I'd be very interested to know. Very interested.'

'You mean about my flunking out of Pencey and all?' I said. I sort of wished he'd cover up his bumpy chest. It wasn't such a beautiful view.

'If I'm not mistaken, I believe you also had some difficulty at the Whooton School and at Elkton Hills.' He didn't say it just sarcastic, but sort of nasty, too.

'I didn't have too much difficulty at Elkton Hills,' I told him. 'I didn't exactly flunk out or anything. I just quit, sort of.'

'Why, may I ask?'

'Why? Oh, well it's a long story, sir. I mean it's pretty complicated.' I didn't feel like going into the whole thing with him. He wouldn't have understood it anyway. It wasn't up his alley at all. One of the biggest reasons I left Elkton Hills was because I was surrounded by phonies. That's all. They were coming in the goddam window. For instance, they had this headmaster, Mr Haas, that was the phoniest bastard I ever met in my life. Ten times worse than old Thurmer. On Sundays, for instance, old Haas went around shaking hands with everybody's parents when they drove up to school. He'd be charming as hell and all. Except if some boy had little old funny-looking parents. You should've seen the way he did with my roommate's parents. I mean if a boy's mother was sort of fat or corny-looking or something, and if somebody's father was one of those guys that wear those suits with very big shoulders and corny black-and-white shoes, then old Haas would just shake hands with them and give them a phony smile and then he'd go talk, for maybe a half an *hour*, with somebody else's parents. I can't stand that stuff. It drives me crazy. It makes me so depressed I go crazy. I hated that goddam Elkton Hills.

Old Spencer asked me something then, but I didn't hear him. I was thinking about old Haas. 'What, sir?' I said.

'Do you have any particular *qualms* about leaving Pencey?'

'Oh, I have a few qualms, all right. Sure . . . but not too many. Not yet, anyway. I guess it hasn't really hit me yet. It takes things a while to hit me. All I'm doing right now is thinking about going home Wednesday. I'm a moron.'

'Do you feel absolutely no concern for your future, boy?'

'Oh, I feel some concern for my future, all right. Sure. Sure, I do.' I thought about it for a minute. 'But not too much, I guess. Not too much, I guess.'

'You *will*,' old Spencer said. 'You will, boy. You will when it's too late.'

I didn't like hearing him say that. It made me sound dead or something. It was very depressing. 'I guess I will,' I said.

'I'd like to put some sense in that head of yours, boy. I'm trying to help you. I'm trying to *help* you, if I can.'

He really was, too. You could see that. But it was just that we were too much on opposite sides of the pole, that's all. 'I know you are, sir,' I said. 'Thanks a lot. No kidding. I appreciate it. I really do.' I got up from the bed then. Boy, I couldn't've sat there another ten minutes to save my life. 'The thing is, though, I have to get going now. I have quite a bit of equipment at the gym I have to get to take home with me. I really do.' He looked up at me and started nodding again, with this very serious look on his face. I felt sorry as hell for him, all of a sudden. But I just couldn't hang around there any longer, the way we were on opposite sides of the pole, and the way he kept missing the bed whenever he chucked something at it, and his sad old bathrobe with his chest showing, and that grippy smell of Vicks Nose Drops all over the place. 'Look, sir. Don't worry about me,' I said. 'I mean it. I'll be all right. I'm just going through a phase right now. Everybody goes through phases and all, don't they?'

'I don't know, boy. I don't know.'

I hate it when somebody answers that way. 'Sure. Sure, they do,' I said. 'I mean it, sir. Please don't worry about me.' I sort of put my hand on his shoulder. 'Okay?' I said.

'Wouldn't you like a cup of hot chocolate before you go? Mrs Spencer would be –'

'I would, I really would, but the thing is, I have to get going. I have to go right to the gym. Thanks, though. Thanks a lot, sir.'

Then we shook hands. And all that crap. It made me feel sad as hell, though.

'I'll drop you a line, sir. Take care of your grippe, now.'

'Good-by, boy.'

After I shut the door and started back to the living room, he yelled something at me, but I couldn't exactly hear him. I'm pretty sure he yelled 'Good luck!' at me. I hope not. I hope to hell not. I'd never yell 'Good luck!' at anybody. It sounds terrible, when you think about it.

3

I'm the most terrific liar you ever saw in your life. It's awful. If I'm on my way to the store to buy a magazine, even, and somebody asks me where I'm going, I'm liable to say I'm going to the opera. It's terrible. So when I told old Spencer I had to go to the gym to get my equipment and stuff, that was a sheer lie. I don't even keep my goddam equipment in the gym.

Where I lived at Pencey, I lived in the Ossenburger Memorial Wing of the new dorms. It was only for juniors and seniors. I was a junior. My roommate was a senior. It was named after this guy Ossenburger that went to Pencey. He made a pot of dough in the undertaking business after he got out of Pencey. What he did, he started these undertaking parlors all over the country that you could get members of your family buried for about five bucks apiece. You should see old Ossenburger. He probably just shoves them in a sack and dumps them in the river. Anyway, he gave Pencey a pile of dough, and they named our wing after him. The first football game of the year, he came up to school in this big goddam Cadillac, and we all had to stand up in the grandstand and give him a locomotive – that's a cheer. Then, the next morning, in chapel, he made a speech that lasted about ten hours. He started off with about fifty corny jokes, just to show us what a regular guy he was. Very big deal. Then he started telling us how he was never ashamed, when he was in some kind of trouble or something, to get right down on his knees and pray to God. He told us we should always pray to

God – talk to Him and all – wherever we were. He told us we ought to think of Jesus as our buddy and all. He said *he* talked to Jesus all the time. Even when he was driving his car. That killed me. I can just see the big phony bastard shifting into first gear and asking Jesus to send him a few more stiffs. The only good part of his speech was right in the middle of it. He was telling us all about what a swell guy he was, what a hot-shot and all, then all of a sudden this guy sitting in the row in front of me, Edgar Marsalla, laid this terrific fart. It was a very crude thing to do, in chapel and all, but it was also quite amusing. Old Marsalla. He damn near blew the roof off. Hardly anybody laughed out loud, and old Ossenburger made out like he didn't even hear it, but old Thurmer, the headmaster, was sitting right next to him on the rostrum and all, and you could tell *he* heard it. *Boy*, was he sore. He didn't say anything then, but the next night he made us have compulsory study hall in the academic building and he came up and made a speech. He said that the boy that had created the disturbance in chapel wasn't fit to go to Pencey. We tried to get old Marsalla to rip off another one, right while old Thurmer was making his speech, but he wasn't in the right mood. Anyway, that's where I lived at Pencey. Old Ossenburger Memorial Wing, in the new dorms.

It was pretty nice to get back to my room, after I left old Spencer, because everybody was down at the game, and the heat was on in our room, for a change. It felt sort of cosy. I took off my coat and my tie and unbuttoned my shirt collar, and then I put on this hat that I'd bought in New York that morning. It was this red hunting hat, with one of those very, very long peaks. I saw it in the window of this sports store when we got out of the subway, just after I noticed I'd lost all the goddam foils. It only cost me a buck. The way I wore it, I swung the old peak way around to the back – very corny, I'll admit, but I liked it that way. I looked good in it that way. Then I got this book I was reading and sat down in my chair. There were two chairs in every room. I had one and my roommate, Ward Stradlater, had one. The arms were in sad shape, because everybody was always sitting on them, but they were pretty comfortable chairs.

The book I was reading was this book I took out of the library by mistake. They gave me the wrong book, and I didn't notice it till I got back to my room. They gave me *Out of Africa*, by Isak Dinesen. I thought it was going to stink, but it didn't. It was a very good book. I'm quite illiterate, but I read a lot. My favorite author is my brother D.B., and my next favorite is Ring Lardner. My brother gave me a book by Ring Lardner for my birthday, just before I went to Pencey. It had these very funny, crazy plays in it, and then it had this one story about a traffic cop that falls in love with this very cute girl that's always speeding. Only, he's married, the cop, so he can't marry her or anything. Then this girl gets killed, because she's always speeding. That story just about killed me. What I like best is a book that's at least funny once in a while. I read a lot of classical books, like *The Return of the Native* and all, and I like them, and I read a lot of war books and mysteries and all, but they don't knock me out too much. What really knocks me out is a book that, when you're all done reading it, you wish the author that wrote it was a terrific friend of yours and you could call him up on the phone whenever you felt like it. That doesn't happen much, though. I wouldn't mind calling this Isak Dinesen up. And Ring Lardner, except that D.B. told me he's dead. You take that book *Of Human Bondage*, by Somerset Maugham, though. I read it last summer. It's a pretty good book and all, but I wouldn't want to call Somerset Maugham up. I don't know. He just isn't the kind of a guy I'd want to call up, that's all. I'd rather call old Thomas Hardy up. I like that Eustacia Vye.

Anyway, I put on my new hat and sat down and started reading that book *Out of Africa*. I'd read it already, but I wanted to read certain parts over again. I'd only read about three pages, though, when I heard somebody coming through the shower curtains. Even without looking up, I knew right away who it was. It was Robert Ackley, this guy that roomed right next to me. There was a shower right between every two rooms in our wing, and about eighty-five times a day old Ackley barged in on me. He was probably the only guy in the whole dorm, besides me, that wasn't down at the game. He hardly ever went *any*where. He was a very peculiar guy. He was a senior, and he'd been at Pencey the whole four years and all, but nobody ever called him anything except 'Ackley.' Not even Herb Gale, his own roommate, ever called him 'Bob' or even 'Ack.' If he ever gets married, his own wife'll probably call him 'Ackley.' He was one of these very, very tall, round-shouldered guys – he was about six four – with lousy teeth. The whole time he roomed next to me, I never even once saw him brush his teeth. They always looked mossy and awful, and he damn near made you sick if you saw him in the dining room with his mouth full of mashed potatoes and peas or something. Besides that, he had a lot of pimples. Not just on his forehead or his chin, like most guys, but all over his whole face. And not only that, he had a terrible personality. He was also sort of a nasty guy. I wasn't too crazy about him, to tell you the truth.

I could feel him standing on the shower ledge, right behind my chair, taking a look to see if Stradlater was around. He hated Stradlater's guts and he never came in the room if Stradlater was around. He hated *ev*erybody's guts, damn near.

He came down off the shower ledge and came in the room. 'Hi,' he said. He always said it like he was terrifically bored or terrifically tired. He didn't want you to think he was *vis*iting you or anything. He wanted you to think he'd come in by mis*take*, for God's sake.

'Hi,' I said, but I didn't look up from my book. With a guy like Ackley, if you looked up from your book you were a goner. You were a goner *any*way, but not as quick if you didn't look up right away.

He started walking around the room, very slow and all, the way he always did, picking up your personal stuff off your desk and chiffonier. He always picked up your personal stuff and looked at it. Boy, could he get on your nerves sometimes. 'How was the fencing?' he said. He just wanted me to quit reading and enjoying myself. He didn't give a damn about the fencing. 'We win, or what?' he said.

'Nobody won,' I said. Without looking up, though.

'What?' he said. He always made you say everything twice.

'Nobody won,' I said. I sneaked a look to see what he was fiddling around with on my chiffonier. He was looking at this picture of this girl I used to go around with in New York, Sally Hayes. He must've picked up that goddam picture and looked at it at least five thousand times since I got it. He always put it back in the wrong place, too, when he was finished. He did it on purpose. You could tell.

'*No*body won,' he said. 'How come?'

'I left the goddam foils and stuff on the subway.' I still didn't look up at him.

'On the *sub*way, for Chrissake! Ya *lost* them, ya mean?'

'We got on the wrong subway. I had to keep getting up to look at a goddam map on the wall.'

He came over and stood right in my light. 'Hey,' I said. 'I've read this same sentence about twenty times since you came in.'

Anybody else except Ackley would've taken the goddam hint. Not him, though. 'Think they'll make you pay for 'em?' he said.

'I don't know, and I don't give a damn. How 'bout sitting *down* or something, Ackley kid? You're right in my goddam light.' He didn't like it when you called him 'Ackley kid.' He was always telling me I was a goddam kid, because I was sixteen and he was eighteen. It drove him mad when I called him 'Ackley kid.'

He kept standing there. He was ex*act*ly the kind of a guy that wouldn't get out of your light when you asked him to. He'd *do* it, finally, but it took him a lot longer if you *asked* him to. 'What the hellya reading?' he said.

'Goddam book.'

He shoved my book back with his hand so that he could see the name of it. 'Any good?' he said.

'This *sen*tence I'm reading is terrific.' I can be quite sarcastic when I'm in the mood. He didn't get it, though. He started walking around the room again, picking up all my personal stuff, and Stradlater's. Finally, I put my book down on the floor. You couldn't read anything with a guy like Ackley around. It was impossible.

I slid way the hell down in my chair and watched old Ackley making himself at home. I was feeling sort of tired from the trip to New York and all, and I started yawning. Then I started horsing around a little bit. Sometimes I horse around quite a lot, just to keep from getting bored. What I did was, I pulled the old peak of my hunting hat around to the front, then pulled it way down over my eyes. That way, I couldn't see a goddam thing. 'I think I'm going blind,' I said in this very hoarse voice. 'Mother darling, everything's getting so *dark* in here.'

'You're nuts. I swear to God,' Ackley said.

'Mother darling, give me your *hand*. Why won't you give me your *hand*?'

'For Chrissake, grow up.'

I started groping around in front of me, like a blind guy, but without getting up or anything. I kept saying, 'Mother darling, why won't you give me your *hand*?' I was only horsing around, naturally. That stuff gives me a bang sometimes. Besides, I know it annoyed hell out of old Ackley. He always brought out the old sadist in me. I was pretty sadistic with him quite often. Finally, I quit, though. I pulled the peak around to the back again, and relaxed.

'Who belongsa this?' Ackley said. He was holding my roommate's knee supporter up to show me. That guy Ackley'd pick up *any*thing. He'd even pick up your jock strap or something. I told him it was Stradlater's. So he chucked it on Stradlater's bed. He got it off Stradlater's *chiffonier*, so he chucked it on the *bed*.

He came over and sat down on the arm of Stradlater's chair. He never sat down *in* a chair. Just always on the arm. 'Where the hellja get that hat?' he said.

'New York.'

'How much?'

'A buck.'

'You got robbed.' He started cleaning his goddam fingernails with the end of a match. He was always cleaning his fingernails. It was funny, in a way. His teeth were always mossy-looking, and his ears were always dirty as hell, but he was always cleaning his fingernails. I guess he thought that made him a very *neat* guy. He took another look at my hat while he was cleaning them. 'Up home we wear a hat like that to shoot *deer* in, for Chrissake,' he said. 'That's a deer shooting hat.'

'Like hell it is.' I took it off and looked at it. I sort of closed one eye, like I was taking aim at it. 'This is a people shooting hat,' I said. 'I shoot people in this hat.'

'Your folks know you got kicked out yet?'

'Nope.'

'Where the hell's Stradlater at, anyway?'

'Down at the game. He's got a date.' I yawned. I was yawning all over the place. For one thing, the room was too damn hot. It made you sleepy. At Pencey, you either froze to death or died of the heat.

'The great Stradlater,' Ackley said. '– Hey. Lend me your scissors a second, willya? Ya got 'em handy?'

'No. I packed them already. They're way in the top of the closet.'

'Get 'em a second, willya?' Ackley said. 'I got this hangnail I want to cut off.'

He didn't care if you'd packed something or not and had it way in the top of the closet. I got them for him though. I nearly got killed doing it, too. The second I opened the closet door, Stradlater's tennis racket – in its wooden press and all – fell right on my head. It made a big *clunk*, and it hurt like hell. It damn near killed old Ackley, though. He started laughing in this very high falsetto voice. He kept laughing the whole time I was taking down my suitcase and getting the scissors out for him. Something like that – a guy getting hit on the head with a rock or something – tickled the pants off Ackley. 'You have a damn good sense of humor, Ackley kid,' I told him. 'You know that?' I handed him the scissors. 'Lemme be your manager. I'll get you on the goddam radio.' I sat down in my chair again, and he started cutting his big horny-looking nails. 'How 'bout using the table or something?' I said. 'Cut 'em over the table, willya? I don't feel like walking on your crumby nails in my bare feet tonight.' He kept right on cutting them over the floor, though. What lousy manners. I mean it.

'Who's Stradlater's date?' he said. He was always keeping tabs on who Stradlater was dating, even though he hated Stradlater's guts.

'I don't know. Why?'

'No reason. Boy, I can't stand that sonuvabitch. He's one sonuvabitch I really can't stand.'

'He's crazy about *you*. He told me he thinks you're a goddam prince,' I said. I call people a 'prince' quite often when I'm horsing around. It keeps me from getting bored or something.

'He's got this superior *at*titude all the time,' Ackley said. 'I just can't stand the sonuvabitch. You'd think he –'

'Do you mind cutting your nails over the *table*, hey?' I said. 'I've asked you about fifty –'

'He's got this goddam superior attitude all the time,' Ackley said. 'I don't even think the sonuvabitch is intelligent. He *thinks* he is. He thinks he's about the most –'

'*Ack*ley! For Chrissake. Willya *please* cut your crumby nails over the table? I've asked you fifty times.'

He started cutting his nails over the table, for a change. The only way he ever did anything was if you yelled at him.

I watched him for a while. Then I said, 'The reason you're sore at Stradlater is because he said that stuff about brushing your teeth once in a while. He didn't mean to insult you, for cryin' out loud. He didn't *say* it right or anything, but he didn't mean anything insulting. All he meant was you'd look better and *feel* better if you sort of brushed your teeth once in a while.'

'I brush my teeth. Don't gimme *that*.'

'No, you don't. I've seen you, and you don't,' I said. I didn't say it nasty, though. I felt sort of sorry for him, in a way. I mean it isn't too nice, naturally, if somebody tells you you don't brush your teeth. 'Stradlater's all right. He's not too bad,' I said. 'You don't know him, that's the trouble.'

'I still say he's a sonuvabitch. He's a conceited sonuvabitch.'

'He's conceited, but he's very generous in some things. He really is,' I said. 'Look. Suppose, for instance, Stradlater was wearing a tie or something that you liked. Say he had a tie on that you liked a helluva lot – I'm just giving you an example, now. You know what he'd do? He'd probably take it off and give it to you. He really would. Or – you know what he'd do? He'd leave it on your bed or something. But he'd *give* you the goddam tie. Most guys would probably just –'

'*Hell*,' Ackley said. 'If I had his dough, I would, too.'

'No, you wouldn't.' I shook my head. 'No, you wouldn't, Ackley kid. If you had his dough, you'd be one of the biggest –'

'Stop calling me "Ackley kid," God damn it. I'm old enough to be your lousy father.'

'No, you're not.' Boy, he could really be aggravating sometimes. He never missed a chance to let you know you were sixteen and he was eighteen. 'In the first place, I wouldn't let you *in* my goddam family,' I said.

'Well, just cut out calling me –'

All of a sudden the door opened, and old Stradlater barged in, in a big hurry. He was always in a big hurry. Everything was a very big deal. He came over to me and gave me these two playful as hell slaps on both cheeks – which is something that can be very annoying. 'Listen,' he said. 'You going out anywheres special tonight?'

'I don't know. I might. What the hell's it doing out – snowing?' He had snow all over his coat.

'Yeah. Listen. If you're not going out anyplace special, how 'bout lending me your hound's-tooth jacket?'

'Who won the game?' I said.

'It's only the half. We're leaving,' Stradlater said. 'No kidding, you gonna use your hound's-tooth tonight or not? I spilled some crap all over my gray flannel.'

'No, but I don't want you stretching it with your goddam shoulders and all,' I said. We were practically the same height, but he weighed about twice as much as I did. He had these very broad shoulders.

'I won't stretch it.' He went over to the closet in a big hurry. 'How'sa boy, Ackley?' he said to Ackley. He was at least a pretty friendly guy, Stradlater. It was partly a phony kind of friendly, but at least he always said hello to Ackley and all.

Ackley just sort of grunted when he said 'How'sa boy?' He wouldn't *answer* him, but he didn't have guts enough not to at least grunt. Then he said to me, 'I think I'll get going. See ya later.'

'Okay,' I said. He never exactly broke your heart when he went back to his own room.

Old Stradlater started taking off his coat and tie and all. 'I think maybe I'll take a fast shave,' he said. He had a pretty heavy beard. He really did.

'Where's your date?' I asked him.

'She's waiting in the Annex.' He went out of the room with his toilet kit and towel under his arm. No shirt on or anything. He always walked around in his bare torso because he thought he had a damn good build. He did, too. I have to admit it.

4

I didn't have anything special to do, so I went down to the can and chewed the rag with him while he was shaving. We were the only ones in the can, because everybody was still down at the game. It was hot as hell and the windows were all steamy. There were about ten washbowls, all right against the wall. Stradlater had the middle one. I sat down on the one right next to him and started turning the cold water on and off – this nervous habit I have. Stradlater kept whistling 'Song of India' while he shaved. He had one of those very piercing whistles that are practically never in tune, and he always picked out some song that's hard to whistle even if you're a *good* whistler, like 'Song of India' or 'Slaughter on Tenth Avenue.' He could really mess a song up.

You remember I said before that Ackley was a slob in his personal habits? Well, so was Stradlater, but in a different way. Stradlater was more of a secret slob. He always *looked* all right, Stradlater, but for instance, you should've seen the razor he shaved himself with. It was always rusty as hell and full of lather and hairs and crap. He never cleaned it or anything. He always *looked* good when he was finished fixing himself up, but he was a secret slob anyway, if you knew him the way I did. The reason he fixed himself up to look good was because he was madly in love with himself. He thought he was the handsomest guy in the Western Hemisphere. He *was* pretty handsome, too – I'll admit it. But he was mostly the kind of a handsome guy that if your parents saw his picture in your Year Book, they'd right away say, 'Who's *this* boy?' I mean he was mostly a Year Book kind of handsome guy. I knew a lot of guys at Pencey I thought were a lot handsomer than Stradlater, but they wouldn't look handsome if you saw their pictures in the Year Book. They'd look like they had big noses or their ears stuck out. I've had that experience frequently.

Anyway, I was sitting on the washbowl next to where Stradlater was shaving, sort of turning the water on and off. I still had my red hunting hat on, with the peak around to the back and all. I really got a bang out of that hat.

'Hey,' Stradlater said. 'Wanna do me a big favor?'

'What?' I said. Not too enthusiastic. He was always asking you to do him a big favor. You take a very handsome guy, or a guy that thinks he's a real hot-shot, and they're always asking you to do them a big favor. Just because *they're* crazy about themself, they think *you're* crazy about them, too, and that you're just dying to do them a favor. It's sort of funny, in a way.

'You goin' out tonight?' he said.

'I might. I might not. I don't know. Why?'

'I got about a hundred pages to read for history for Monday,' he said. 'How 'bout writing a composition for me, for English? I'll be up the creek if I don't get the goddam thing in by Monday, the reason I ask. How 'bout it?'

It was very ironical. It really was.

'*I'm* the one that's flunking out of the goddam place, and *you're* asking me to write you a goddam composition,' I said.

'Yeah, I know. The thing is, though, I'll be up the creek if I don't get it in. Be a buddy. Be a buddyroo. Okay?'

I didn't answer him right away. Suspense is good for some bastards like Stradlater.

'What on?' I said.

'*Any*thing. Anything descriptive. A room. Or a house. Or something you once lived in or something – *you* know. Just as long as it's descriptive as hell.' He gave out a big yawn while he said that. Which is something that gives me a royal pain in the ass. I mean if somebody *yawns* right while they're asking you to do them a goddam favor. 'Just don't do it *too* good, is all,' he said. 'That sonuvabitch Hartzell thinks you're a hot-shot in English, and he knows you're my roommate. So I mean don't stick all the commas and stuff in the right place.'

That's something else that gives me a royal pain. I mean if you're good at writing compositions and somebody starts talking about commas. Stradlater was always doing that. He wanted you to think that the only reason *he* was lousy at writing compositions was because he stuck all the commas in the wrong place. He was a little bit like Ackley, that way. I once sat next to Ackley at this basketball game. We had a terrific guy on the team, Howie Coyle, that could sink them from the middle of the floor, without even touching the backboard or anything. Ackley kept saying, the whole goddam game, that Coyle had a perfect *build* for basketball. God, how I hate that stuff.

I got bored sitting on that washbowl after a while, so I backed up a few feet and started doing this tap-dance, just for the hell of it. I was just amusing myself. I can't really tap-dance or anything, but it was a stone floor in the can, and it was good for tap-dancing. I started imitating one of those guys in the movies. In one of those *musicals*. I hate the movies like poison, but I get a bang imitating them. Old Stradlater watched me in the mirror while he was shaving. All I need's an audience. I'm an exhibitionist. 'I'm the goddam Governor's son,' I said. I was knocking myself out. Tap-dancing all over the place. 'He doesn't want me to be a tap-dancer. He wants me to go to Oxford. But it's in my goddam blood, tap-dancing.' Old Stradlater laughed. He didn't have too bad a sense of humor. 'It's the opening night of the *Ziegfeld Follies*.' I was getting out of breath. I have hardly any wind at all. 'The leading man can't go on. He's drunk as a bastard. So who do they get to take his place? Me, that's who. The little ole goddam Governor's son.'

'Where'dja get that hat?' Stradlater said. He meant my hunting hat. He'd never seen it before.

I was out of breath anyway, so I quit horsing around. I took off my hat and looked at it for about the ninetieth time. 'I got it in New York this morning. For a buck. Ya like it?'

Stradlater nodded. 'Sharp,' he said. He was only flattering me, though, because right away he said, 'Listen. Are ya gonna write that composition for me? I have to know.'

'If I get the time, I will. If I don't, I won't,' I said. I went over and sat down on the washbowl next to him again. 'Who's your date?' I asked him. 'Fitzgerald?'

'Hell, no! I told ya, I'm through with that pig.'

'Yeah? Give her to me, boy. No kidding. She's my type.'

'Take her . . . She's too old for you.'

All of a sudden – for no good reason, really, except that I was sort of in the mood for horsing around – I felt like jumping off the washbowl and getting old Stradlater in a half nelson. That's a wrestling hold, in case you don't know, where you get the other guy around the neck and choke him to death, if you feel like it. So I did it. I landed on him like a goddam panther.

'Cut it out, Holden, for Chrissake!' Stradlater said. He didn't feel like horsing around. He was shaving and all. 'Wuddaya wanna make me do – cut my goddam head off?'

I didn't let go, though. I had a pretty good half nelson on him. 'Liberate yourself from my viselike grip,' I said.

'Je-sus *Christ*.' He put down his razor, and all of a sudden jerked his arms up and sort of broke my hold on him. He was a very strong guy. I'm a very weak guy. 'Now, cut out the crap,' he said. He started shaving himself all over again. He always shaved himself twice, to look gorgeous. With his crumby old razor.

'Who *is* your date if it isn't Fitzgerald?' I asked him. I sat down on the washbowl next to him again. 'That Phyllis Smith babe?'

'No. It was supposed to be, but the arrangements got all screwed up. I got Bud Thaw's girl's roommate now . . . Hey. I almost forgot. She knows *you*.'

'Who does?' I said.

'My date.'

'Yeah?' I said. 'What's her name?' I was pretty interested.

'I'm thinking . . . Uh. Jean Gallagher.'

Boy, I nearly dropped *dead* when he said that.

'*Jane* Gallagher,' I said. I even got up from the washbowl when he said that. I damn near dropped dead. 'You're damn right I know her. She practically lived right next *door* to me, the summer before last. She had this big damn Doberman pinscher. That's how I met her. Her dog used to keep coming over in our –'

'You're right in my light, Holden, for Chrissake,' Stradlater said. 'Ya have to stand right there?'

Boy, was I excited, though. I really was.

'Where is she?' I asked him. 'I oughta go down and say hello to her or something. Where is she? In the Annex?'

'Yeah.'

'How'd she happen to mention me? Does she go to B.M. now? She said she might go there. She said she might go to Shipley, too. I thought she went to Shipley. How'd she happen to mention me?' I was pretty excited. I really was.

'*I* don't know, for Chrissake. Lift up, willya? You're on my towel,' Stradlater said. I was sitting on his stupid towel.

'Jane Gallagher,' I said. I couldn't get over it. 'Jesus H. Christ.'

Old Stradlater was putting Vitalis on his hair. *My* Vitalis.

'She's a dancer,' I said. 'Ballet and all. She used to practice about two hours every day, right in the middle of the hottest weather and all. She was worried that it might make her legs lousy – all thick and all. I used to play checkers with her all the time.'

'You used to play *what* with her all the time?'

'Checkers.'

'*Checkers*, for Chrissake!'

'Yeah. She wouldn't move any of her kings. What she'd do, when she'd get a king, she wouldn't move it. She'd just leave it in the back row. She'd get them all lined up in the back row. Then she'd never use them. She just liked the way they looked when they were all in the back row.'

Stradlater didn't say anything. That kind of stuff doesn't interest most people.

'Her mother belonged to the same club we did,' I said. 'I used to caddy once in a while, just to make some dough. I caddy'd for her mother a couple of times. She went around in about a hundred and seventy, for nine holes.'

Stradlater wasn't hardly listening. He was combing his gorgeous locks.

'I oughta go down and at least say hello to her,' I said.

'Why don'tcha?'

'I will, in a minute.'

He started parting his hair all over again. It took him about an hour to comb his hair.

'Her mother and father were divorced. Her mother was married again to some booze hound,' I said. 'Skinny guy with hairy legs. I remember him. He wore shorts all the time. Jane said he was supposed to be a playwright or some goddam thing, but all *I* ever saw him do was booze all the time and listen to every single goddam mystery program on the radio. And run around the goddam house, naked. With *Jane* around, and all.'

'Yeah?' Stradlater said. That really interested him. About the booze hound running around the house naked, with Jane around. Stradlater was a very sexy bastard.

'She had a lousy childhood. I'm not kidding.'

That didn't interest Stradlater, though. Only very sexy stuff interested him.

'Jane Gallagher. Jesus.' I couldn't get her off my mind. I really couldn't. 'I oughta go down and say hello to her, at least.'

'Why the hell *don't*cha, instead of keep saying it?' Stradlater said.

I walked over to the window, but you couldn't see out of it, it was so steamy from all the heat in the can. 'I'm not in the mood right now,' I said. I wasn't, either. You have to be in the mood for those things. 'I thought she went to Shipley. I could've sworn she went to Shipley.' I walked around the can for a little while. I didn't have anything else to do. 'Did she enjoy the game?' I said.

'Yeah, I guess so. I don't know.'

'Did she tell you we used to play checkers all the time, or anything?'

'I don't know. For Chrissake, I only just *met* her,' Stradlater said. He was finished combing his goddam gorgeous hair. He was putting away all his crumby toilet articles.

'Listen. Give her my regards, willya?'

'Okay,' Stradlater said, but I knew he probably wouldn't. You take a guy like Stradlater, they never give your regards to people.

He went back to the room, but I stuck around in the can for a while, thinking about old Jane. Then I went back to the room, too.

Stradlater was putting on his tie, in front of the mirror, when I got there. He spent around half his goddam life in front of the mirror. I sat down in my chair and sort of watched him for a while.

'Hey,' I said. 'Don't tell her I got kicked out, willya?'

'Okay.'

That was one good thing about Stradlater. You didn't have to explain every goddam little thing with him, the way you had to do with Ackley. Mostly, I guess, because he wasn't too interested. That's really why. Ackley, it was different. Ackley was a very nosy bastard.

He put on my hound's-tooth jacket.

'Jesus, now, try not to stretch it all over the place,' I said. I'd only worn it about twice.

'I won't. Where the hell's my cigarettes?'

'On the desk.' He never knew where he left anything. 'Under your muffler.' He put them in his coat pocket – *my* coat pocket.

I pulled the peak of my hunting hat around to the front all of a sudden, for a change. I was getting sort of nervous, all of a sudden. I'm quite a nervous guy. 'Listen, where ya going on your date with her?' I asked him. 'Ya know yet?'

'I don't know. New York, if we have time. She only signed out for nine-thirty, for Chrissake.'

I didn't like the way he said it, so I said, 'The reason she did that, she probably just didn't know what a handsome, charming bastard you are. If she'd *known*, she probably would've signed out for nine-thirty in the *morning*.'

'Goddam right,' Stradlater said. You couldn't rile him too easily. He was too conceited. 'No kidding, now. Do that composition for me,' he said. He had his coat on, and he was all ready to go. 'Don't knock yourself out or anything, but just make it descriptive as hell. Okay?'

I didn't answer him. I didn't feel like it. All I said was, 'Ask her if she still keeps all her kings in the back row.'

'Okay,' Stradlater said, but I knew he wouldn't. 'Take it easy, now.' He banged the hell out of the room.

I sat there for about a half hour after he left. I mean I just sat in my chair, not doing anything. I kept thinking about Jane, and about Stradlater having a date with her and all. It made me so nervous I nearly went crazy. I already told you what a sexy bastard Stradlater was.

All of a sudden, Ackley barged back in again, through the damn shower curtains, as usual. For once in my stupid life, I was really glad to see him. He took my mind off the other stuff.

He stuck around till around dinnertime, talking about all the guys at Pencey that he hated their guts, and squeezing this big pimple on his chin. He didn't even use his handkerchief. I don't even think the bastard *had* a handkerchief, if you want to know the truth. I never saw him use one, anyway.

5

We always had the same meal on Saturday nights at Pencey. It was supposed to be a big deal, because they gave you steak. I'll bet a thousand bucks the reason they did that was because a lot of guys' parents came up to school on Sunday, and old Thurmer probably figured everybody's mother would ask their darling boy what he had for dinner last night, and he'd say, 'Steak.' What a racket. You should've seen the steaks. They were these little hard, dry jobs that you could hardly even cut. You always got these very lumpy mashed potatoes on steak night, and for dessert you got Brown Betty, which nobody ate, except maybe the little kids in the lower school that didn't know any better – and guys like Ackley that ate *ev*erything.

It was nice, though, when we got out of the dining room. There were about three inches of snow on the ground, and it was still coming down like a madman. It looked pretty as hell, and we all started throwing snowballs and horsing around all over the place. It was very childish, but everybody was really enjoying themselves.

I didn't have a date or anything, so I and this friend of mine, Mal Brossard, that was on the wrestling team, decided we'd take a bus into Agerstown and have a hamburger and maybe see a lousy movie. Neither of us felt like sitting around on our ass all night. I asked Mal if he minded if Ackley came along with us. The reason I asked was because Ackley never did *any*thing on Saturday night, except stay in his room and squeeze his pimples or something. Mal said he didn't *mind* but that he wasn't too crazy about the idea. He didn't like Ackley much. Anyway, we both went to our rooms to get ready and all, and while I was putting on my galoshes and crap, I yelled over and asked old Ackley if he wanted to go to the movies. He could hear me all right through the shower curtains, but he didn't answer me right away. He was the kind of a guy that hates to answer you right away. Finally he came over, through the goddam curtains, and stood on the shower ledge and asked who was going besides me. He always had to know who was going. I swear, if that guy was shipwrecked somewhere, and you rescued him in a goddam boat, he'd want to know who the guy was that was rowing it before he'd even get in. I told him Mal Brossard was going. He said, '*That* bastard . . . All right. Wait a second.' You'd think he was doing you a big favor.

It took him about five hours to get ready. While he was doing it, I went over to my window and opened it and packed a snowball with my bare hands. The snow was very good for packing. I didn't throw it at anything, though. I *start*ed to throw it. At a car that was parked across the street. But I changed my mind. The car looked so nice and white. Then I started to throw it at a hydrant, but that looked too nice and white, too. Finally I didn't throw it at anything. All I did was close the window and walk around the room with the snowball, packing it harder. A little while later, I still had it with me when I and Brossard and Ackley got on the bus. The bus driver opened the doors and made me throw it out. I *told* him I wasn't going to chuck it at anybody, but he wouldn't believe me. People never believe you.

Brossard and Ackley both had seen the picture that was playing, so all we did, we just had a couple of hamburgers and played the pinball machine for a little while, then took the bus back to Pencey. I didn't care about not seeing the movie, anyway. It was supposed to be a comedy, with Cary Grant in it, and all that crap. Besides, I'd been to the movies with Brossard and Ackley before. They both laughed like hyenas at stuff that wasn't even funny. I didn't even enjoy sitting next to them in the movies.

It was only about a quarter to nine when we got back to the dorm. Old Brossard was a bridge fiend, and he started looking around the dorm for a game. Old Ackley parked himself in my room, just for a change. Only, instead of sitting on the arm of Stradlater's chair, he laid down on my bed, with his face right on my pillow and all. He started talking in this very monotonous voice, and picking at all his pimples. I dropped about a thousand hints, but I couldn't get rid of him. All he did was keep talking in this very monotonous voice about some babe he was supposed to have had sexual intercourse with the summer before. He'd already told me about it about a hundred times. Every time he told it, it was different. One minute he'd be giving it to her in his cousin's Buick, the next minute he'd be giving it to her under some boardwalk. It was all a lot of crap, naturally. He was a virgin if ever I saw one. I doubt if he ever even gave anybody a feel. Anyway, finally I had to come right out and tell him that I had to write a composition for Stradlater, and that he had to clear the hell out, so I could concentrate. He finally did, but he took his time about it, as usual. After he left, I put on my pajamas and bathrobe and my old hunting hat, and started writing the composition.

The thing was, I couldn't think of a room or a house or anything to describe the way Stradlater said he had to have. I'm not too crazy about describing rooms and houses anyway. So what

I did, I wrote about my brother Allie's baseball mitt. It was a very descriptive subject. It really was. My brother Allie had this left-handed fielder's mitt. He was left-handed. The thing that was descriptive about it, though, was that he had poems written all over the fingers and the pocket and everywhere. In green ink. He wrote them on it so that he'd have something to read when he was in the field and nobody was up at bat. He's dead now. He got leukemia and died when we were up in Maine, on July 18, 1946. You'd have liked him. He was two years younger than I was, but he was about fifty times as intelligent. He was terrifically intelligent. His teachers were always writing letters to my mother, telling her what a pleasure it was having a boy like Allie in their class. And they weren't just shooting the crap. They really meant it. But it wasn't just that he was the most intelligent member in the family. He was also the nicest, in lots of ways. He never got mad at anybody. People with red hair are supposed to get mad very easily, but Allie never did, and he had very red hair. I'll tell you what kind of red hair he had. I started playing golf when I was only ten years old. I remember once, the summer I was around twelve, teeing off and all, and having a hunch that if I turned around all of a sudden, I'd see Allie. So I did, and sure enough, he was sitting on his bike outside the fence – there was this fence that went all around the course – and he was sitting there, about a hundred and fifty yards behind me, watching me tee off. That's the kind of red hair he had. God, he was a nice kid, though. He used to laugh so hard at something he thought of at the dinner table that he just about fell off his chair. I was only thirteen, and they were going to have me psychoanalyzed and all, because I broke all the windows in the garage. I don't blame them. I really don't. I slept in the garage the night he died, and I broke all the goddam windows with my fist, just for the hell of it. I even tried to break all the windows on the station wagon we had that summer, but my hand was already broken and everything by that time, and I couldn't do it. It was a very stupid thing to do, I'll admit, but I hardly didn't even know I was doing it, and you didn't know Allie. My hand still hurts me once in a while, when it rains and all, and I can't make a real fist any more – not a tight one, I mean – but outside of that I don't care much. I mean I'm not going to be a goddam surgeon or a violinist or anything *any*-way.

Anyway, that's what I wrote Stradlater's composition about. Old Allie's baseball mitt. I happened to have it with me, in my suitcase, so I got it out and copied down the poems that were written on it. All I had to do was change Allie's name so that nobody would know it was my brother and not Stradlater's. I wasn't too crazy about doing it, but I couldn't think of anything else descriptive. Besides, I sort of liked writing about it. It took me about an hour, because I had to use Stradlater's lousy typewriter, and it kept jamming on me. The reason I didn't use my own was because I'd lent it to a guy down the hall.

It was around ten-thirty, I guess, when I finished it. I wasn't tired, though, so I looked out the window for a while. It wasn't snowing out any more, but every once in a while you could hear a car somewhere not being able to get started. You could also hear old Ackley snoring. Right through the goddam shower curtains you could hear him. He had sinus trouble and he couldn't breathe too hot when he was asleep. That guy had just about everything. Sinus trouble, pimples, lousy teeth, halitosis, crumby fingernails. You had to feel a little sorry for the crazy sonuvabitch.

6

Some things are hard to remember. I'm thinking now of when Stradlater got back from his date with Jane. I mean I can't remember exactly what I was doing when I heard his goddam stupid footsteps coming down the corridor. I probably was still looking out the window, but I swear I can't remember. I was so damn worried, that's why. When I really worry about something, I don't just fool around. I even have to go to the bathroom when I worry about something. Only, I don't go. I'm too worried to go. I don't want to interrupt my worrying to go. If you knew Stradlater, you'd have been worried, too. I'd double-dated with that bastard a couple of times, and I know what I'm talking about. He was unscrupulous. He really was.

Anyway, the corridor was all linoleum and all, and you could hear his goddam footsteps coming right towards the room. I don't even remember where I was sitting when he came in – at the window, or in my chair or his. I swear I can't remember.

He came in griping about how cold it was out. Then he said, 'Where the hell is everybody? It's like a goddam morgue around here.' I didn't even bother to answer him. If he was so goddam stupid not to realize it was Saturday night and everybody was out or asleep or home for the week end, I wasn't going to break my neck telling him. He started getting undressed. He didn't say one goddam word about Jane. Not one. Neither did I. I just watched him. All he did was thank me for letting him wear my hound's-tooth. He hung it up on a hanger and put it in the closet.

Then, when he was taking off his tie, he asked me if I'd written his goddam composition for him. I told him it was over on his goddam bed. He walked over and read it while he was unbuttoning his shirt. He stood there, reading it, and sort of stroking his bare chest and stomach, with this very stupid expression on his face. He was always stroking his stomach or his chest. He was mad about himself.

All of a sudden, he said, 'For Chris*sake*, Holden. This is about a goddam *base*ball glove.'

'So what?' I said. Cold as hell.

'Wuddaya mean *so what*? I told ya it had to be about a goddam *room* or a house or something.'

'You said it had to be descriptive. What the hell's the difference if it's about a baseball glove?'

'God damn it.' He was sore as hell. He was really furious. 'You always do everything backasswards.' He looked at me. 'No wonder you're flunking the hell out of here,' he said. 'You don't do *one damn thing* the way you're supposed to. I mean it. Not one damn thing.'

'All right, give it back to me, then,' I said. I went over and pulled it right out of his goddam hand. Then I tore it up.

'What the hellja do *that* for?' he said.

I didn't even answer him. I just threw the pieces in the wastebasket. Then I lay down on my bed, and we both didn't say anything for a long time. He got all undressed, down to his shorts, and I lay on my bed and lit a cigarette. You weren't allowed to smoke in the dorm, but you could do it late at night when everybody was asleep or out and nobody could smell the smoke. Besides, I did it to annoy Stradlater. It drove him crazy when you broke any rules. He never smoked in the dorm. It was only me.

He still didn't say one single solitary word about Jane. So finally I said, 'You're back pretty goddam late if she only signed out for nine-thirty. Did you make her be late signing in?'

He was sitting on the edge of his bed, cutting his goddam toenails, when I asked him that. 'Coupla minutes,' he said. 'Who the hell signs out for nine-thirty on a Saturday night?' *God*, how I hated him.

'Did you go to New York?' I said.

'Ya crazy? How the hell could we go to New York if she only signed out for nine-thirty?'

'That's tough.'

He looked up at me. 'Listen,' he said, 'if you're gonna smoke in the room, how 'bout going down to the can and do it? *You* may be getting the hell out of here, but I have to stick around long enough to graduate.'

I ignored him. I really did. I went right on smoking like a madman. All I did was sort of turn over on my side and watched him cut his damn toenails. What a school. You were always watching somebody cut their damn toenails or squeeze their pimples or something.

'Did you give her my regards?' I asked him.

'Yeah.'

The hell he did, the bastard.

'What'd she say?' I said. 'Did you ask her if she still keeps all her kings in the back row?'

'*No*, I didn't ask her. What the hell ya think we did all night – play checkers, for Chrissake?'

I didn't even answer him. God, how I hated him.

'If you didn't go to New York, where'd ya go with her?' I asked him, after a little while. I could hardly keep my voice from shaking all over the place. Boy, was I getting nervous. I just had a *feeling* something had gone funny.

He was finished cutting his damn toenails. So he got up from the bed, in just his damn shorts and all, and started getting very damn playful. He came over to my bed and started leaning over me and taking these playful as hell socks at my shoulder. 'Cut it out,' I said. 'Where'd you go with her if you didn't go to New York?'

'Nowhere. We just sat in the goddam car.' He gave me another one of those playful stupid little socks on the shoulder.

'Cut it *out*,' I said. 'Whose car?'

'Ed Banky's.'

Ed Banky was the basketball coach at Pencey. Old Stradlater was one of his pets, because he was the center on the team, and Ed Banky always let him borrow his car when he wanted it. It wasn't allowed for students to borrow faculty guys' cars, but all the athletic bastards stuck together. In every school I've gone to, all the athletic bastards stick together.

Stradlater kept taking these shadow punches down at my shoulder. He had his toothbrush in his hand, and he put it in his mouth. 'What'd you do?' I said. 'Give her the time in Ed Banky's goddam car?' My voice was shaking something awful.

'What a thing to say. Want me to wash your mouth out with soap?'

'*Did* you?'

'That's a professional secret, buddy.'

This next part I don't remember so hot. All I know is I got up from the bed, like I was going down to the can or something, and then I tried to sock him, with all my might, right smack in the toothbrush, so it would split his goddam throat open. Only, I missed. I didn't connect. All I did was sort of get him on the side of the head or something. It probably hurt him a little bit, but not as much as I wanted. It probably would've hurt him a lot, but I did it with my right hand, and I can't make a good fist with that hand. On account of that injury I told you about.

Anyway, the next thing I knew, I was on the goddam floor and he was sitting on my chest, with his face all red. That is, he had his goddam *knees* on my chest, and he weighed about a ton. He had hold of my wrists, too, so I couldn't take another sock at him. I'd've killed him.

'What the hell's the matter with you?' he kept saying, and his stupid face kept getting redder and redder.

'Get your lousy *knees* off my *chest*,' I told him. I was almost bawling. I really was. 'Go on, get *offa* me, ya crumby bastard.'

He wouldn't do it, though. He kept holding onto my wrists and I kept calling him a sonuvabitch and all, for around ten hours. I can hardly even remember what all I said to him. I told him he thought he could give the time to anybody he felt like. I told him he didn't even care if a girl kept all her kings in the back row or not, and the reason he didn't care was because he was a goddam stupid moron. He hated it when you called him a moron. All morons hate it when you call them a moron.

'Shut up, now, Holden,' he said with his big stupid red face. 'Just shut up, now.'

'You don't even know if her first name is Jane or *Jean*, ya goddam moron!'

'Now, *shut up*, Holden, God damn it – I'm *warn*ing ya,' he said – I really had him going. 'If you don't shut up, I'm gonna slam ya one.'

'Get your dirty stinking moron knees off my chest.'

'If I letcha up, will you keep your mouth shut?'

I didn't even answer him.

He said it over again. 'Holden. If I letcha up, willya keep your mouth shut?'

'Yes.'

He got up off me, and I got up, too. My chest hurt like hell from his dirty knees. 'You're a dirty stupid sonuvabitch of a moron,' I told him.

That got him *really* mad. He shook his big stupid finger in my face. 'Holden, God damn it, I'm *warning* you, now. For the last time. If you don't keep your yap shut, I'm gonna –'

'Why should I?' I said – I was practically yelling. 'That's just the trouble with all you morons. You never want to discuss anything. That's the way you can always tell a moron. They never want to discuss anything intellig –'

Then he really let one go at me, and the next thing I knew I was on the goddam floor again. I don't remember if he knocked me out or not, but I don't think so. It's pretty hard to knock a guy out, except in the goddam movies. But my nose was bleeding all over the place. When I looked up, old Stradlater was standing practically right on top of me. He had his goddam toilet kit under his arm. 'Why the hell don'tcha shut *up* when I tellya to?' he said. He sounded pretty nervous. He probably was scared he'd fractured my skull or something when I hit the floor. It's too bad I didn't. 'You asked for it, God damn it,' he said. Boy, did he look worried.

I didn't even bother to get up. I just lay there on the floor for a while, and kept calling him a moron sonuvabitch. I was so mad, I was practically bawling.

'Listen. Go wash your face,' Stradlater said. 'Ya hear me?'

I told him to go wash his own moron face – which was a

pretty childish thing to say, but I was mad as hell. I told him to stop off on the way to the can and give Mrs Schmidt the time. Mrs Schmidt was the janitor's wife. She was around sixty-five.

I kept sitting there on the floor till I heard old Stradlater close the door and go down the corridor to the can. Then I got up. I couldn't find my goddam hunting hat anywhere. Finally I found it. It was under the bed. I put it on, and turned the old peak around to the back, the way I liked it, and then I went over and took a look at my stupid face in the mirror. You never saw such gore in your life. I had blood all over my mouth and chin and even on my pajamas and bathrobe. It partly scared me and it partly fascinated me. All that blood and all sort of made me look tough. I'd only been in about two fights in my life, and I lost *both* of them. I'm not too tough. I'm a pacifist, if you want to know the truth.

I had a feeling old Ackley'd probably heard all the racket and was awake. So I went through the shower curtains into his room, just to see what the hell he was doing. I hardly ever went over to his room. It always had a funny stink in it, because he was so crumby in his personal habits.

7

A tiny bit of light came through the shower curtains and all from our room, and I could see him lying in bed. I knew damn well he was wide awake. 'Ackley?' I said. 'Y'awake?'

'Yeah.'

It was pretty dark, and I stepped on somebody's shoe on the floor and damn near fell on my head. Ackley sort of sat up in bed and leaned on his arm. He had a lot of white stuff on his face, for his pimples. He looked sort of spooky in the dark. 'What the hellya doing, anyway?' I said.

'Wuddaya mean what the hell am I doing? I was tryna *sleep* before you guys started making all that noise. What the hell was the fight about, anyhow?'

'Where's the light?' I couldn't find the light. I was sliding my hand all over the wall.

'Wuddaya want the light for? . . . Right next to your hand.'

I finally found the switch and turned it on. Old Ackley put his hand up so that the light wouldn't hurt his eyes.

'*Je*sus!' he said. 'What the hell happened to *you*?' He meant all the blood and all.

'I had a little goddam tiff with Stradlater,' I said. Then I sat down on the floor. They never had any chairs in their room. I don't know what the hell they did with their chairs. 'Listen,' I said, 'do you feel like playing a little Canasta?' He was a Canasta fiend.

'You're still *bleed*ing, for Chrissake. You better put something on it.'

'It'll stop. Listen. Ya wanna play a little Canasta or don'tcha?'

'Ca*nas*ta, for Chrissake. Do you know what time it is, by any chance?'

'It isn't late. It's only around eleven, eleven-thirty.'

'*On*ly around!' Ackley said. 'Listen. I gotta get up and go to *Mass* in the morning, for Chrissake. You guys start hollering and fighting in the middle of the goddam – What the hell was the fight about, anyhow?'

'It's a long story. I don't wanna bore ya, Ackley. I'm thinking of your welfare,' I told him. I never discussed my personal life with him. In the first place, he was even more stupid than Stradlater. Stradlater was a goddam genius next to Ackley. 'Hey,' I said, 'is it okay if I sleep in Ely's bed tonight? He won't be back till tomorrow night, will he?' I knew damn well he wouldn't. Ely went home damn near every week end.

'*I* don't know when the hell he's coming back,' Ackley said.

Boy, did that annoy me. 'What the hell do you mean you don't know when he's coming back? He never comes back till Sunday *night*, does he?'

'No, but for Chrissake, I can't just tell somebody they can sleep in his goddam *bed* if they want to.'

That killed me. I reached up from where I was sitting on the floor and patted him on the goddam shoulder. 'You're a prince, Ackley kid,' I said. 'You know that?'

'No, I mean it – I can't just tell somebody they can sleep in –'

'You're a real prince. You're a gentleman and a scholar, kid,' I said. He really was, too. 'Do you happen to have any cigarettes, by any chance? – Say "no" or I'll drop dead.'

'No, I don't, as a matter of fact. Listen, what the hell was the fight about?'

I didn't answer him. All I did was, I got up and went over and looked out the window. I felt so lonesome, all of a sudden. I almost wished I was dead.

'What the hell was the fight about, anyhow?' Ackley said, for about the fiftieth time. He certainly was a bore about that.

'About you,' I said.

'About *me*, for Chrissake?'

'Yeah. I was defending your goddam honor. Stradlater said you had a lousy personality. I couldn't let him get away with that stuff.'

That got him excited. 'He did? No kidding? He did?'

I told him I was only kidding, and then I went over and laid down on Ely's bed. Boy, did I feel rotten. I felt so damn lonesome.

'This room stinks,' I said. 'I can smell your socks from way over here. Don'tcha ever send them to the laundry?'

'If you don't like it, you know what you can do,' Ackley said. What a witty guy. 'How 'bout turning off the goddam light?'

I didn't turn it off right away, though. I just kept laying there on Ely's bed, thinking about Jane and all. It just drove me stark staring mad when I thought about her and Stradlater parked somewhere in that fat-assed Ed Banky's car. Every time I thought about it, I felt like jumping out the window. The thing is, you didn't know Stradlater. I knew him. Most guys at Pencey just *talked* about having sexual intercourse with girls all the time – like Ackley, for instance – but old Stradlater really did it. I was personally acquainted with at least two girls he gave the time to. That's the truth.

'Tell me the story of your fascinating life, Ackley kid,' I said.

'How 'bout turning off the goddam light? I gotta get up for Mass in the morning.'

I got up and turned it off, if it made him happy. Then I laid down on Ely's bed again.

'What're ya gonna do – sleep in Ely's bed?' Ackley said. He was the perfect host, boy.

'I may. I may not. Don't worry about it.'

'I'm not *wor*ried about it. Only, I'd hate like hell if Ely came in all of a sudden and found some guy –'

'Relax. I'm not gonna sleep here. I wouldn't abuse your goddam hospitality.'

A couple of minutes later, he was snoring like mad. I kept laying there in the dark anyway, though, trying not to think about old Jane and Stradlater in that goddam Ed Banky's car. But it was almost impossible. The trouble was, I knew that guy Stradlater's technique. That made it even worse. We once double-dated, in Ed Banky's car, and Stradlater was in the back, with his date, and I was in the front with mine. What a technique that guy had. What he'd do was, he'd start snowing his date in this very quiet, *sincere* voice – like as if he wasn't only a very handsome guy but a nice, *sincere* guy, too. I damn near puked, listening to him. His date kept saying, 'No – *please*. Please, don't. *Please*.' But old Stradlater kept snowing her in this Abraham Lincoln, sincere voice, and finally there'd be this terrific silence in the back of the car. It was really embarrassing. I don't think he gave that girl the time that night – but damn near. *Damn* near.

While I was laying there trying not to think, I heard old Stradlater come back from the can and go in our room. You could hear him putting away his crumby toilet articles and all, and opening the window. He was a fresh-air fiend. Then, a little while later, he turned off the light. He didn't even look around to see where I was at.

It was even depressing out in the street. You couldn't even hear any cars any more. I got feeling so lonesome and rotten, I even felt like waking Ackley up.

'Hey, Ackley,' I said, in sort of a whisper, so Stradlater couldn't hear me through the shower curtain.

Ackley didn't hear me, though.

'Hey, Ackley!'

He still didn't hear me. He slept like a rock.

'Hey, *Ackley*!'

He heard that, all right.

'What the hell's the matter with you?' he said. 'I was asleep, for Chrissake.'

'Listen. What's the routine on joining a monastery?' I asked him. I was sort of toying with the idea of joining one. 'Do you have to be a Catholic and all?'

'*Cert*ainly you have to be a Catholic. You bastard, did you wake me just to ask me a dumb ques–'

'Aah, go back to sleep. I'm not gonna join one anyway. The kind of luck I have, I'd probably join one with all the wrong kind of monks in it. All stupid bastards. Or just bastards.'

When I said that, old Ackley sat way the hell up in bed. 'Listen,' he said, 'I don't care what you say about *me* or anything, but if you start making cracks about my goddam re*lig*ion, for Chrissake –'

'Relax,' I said. 'Nobody's making any cracks about your goddam religion.' I got up off Ely's bed, and started toward the door. I didn't want to hang around in that stupid atmosphere any more. I stopped on the way, though, and picked up Ackley's hand, and gave him a big phony handshake. He pulled it away from me. 'What's the idea?' he said.

'No idea. I just want to thank you for being such a goddam

prince, that's all,' I said. I said it in this very sincere voice. 'You're aces, Ackley kid,' I said. 'You know that?'

'Wise guy. Someday somebody's gonna bash your –'

I didn't even bother to listen to him. I shut the damn door and went out in the corridor.

Everybody was asleep or out or home for the week end, and it was very, very quiet and depressing in the corridor. There was this empty box of Kolynos toothpaste outside Leahy and Hoffman's door, and while I walked down toward the stairs, I kept giving it a boot with this sheep-lined slipper I had on. What I thought I'd do, I thought I might go down and see what old Mal Brossard was doing. But all of a sudden, I changed my mind. All of a sudden, I decided what I'd really do, I'd get the hell out of Pencey – right that same night and all. I mean not wait till Wednesday or anything. I just didn't want to hang around any more. It made me too sad and lonesome. So what I decided to do, I decided I'd take a room in a hotel in New York – some very inexpensive hotel and all – and just take it easy till Wednesday. Then, on Wednesday, I'd go home all rested up and feeling swell. I figured my parents probably wouldn't get old Thurmer's letter saying I'd been given the ax till maybe Tuesday or Wednesday. I didn't want to go home or anything till they got it and thoroughly digested it and all. I didn't want to be around when they *first* got it. My mother gets very hysterical. She's not too bad after she gets something thoroughly digested, though. Besides, I sort of needed a little vacation. My nerves were shot. They really were.

Anyway, that's what I decided I'd do. So I went back to the room and turned on the light, to start packing and all. I already had quite a few things packed. Old Stradlater didn't even wake up. I lit a cigarette and got all dressed and then I packed these two Gladstones I have. It only took me about two minutes. I'm a very rapid packer.

One thing about packing depressed me a little. I had to pack these brand-new ice skates my mother had practically just sent me a couple of days before. That depressed me. I could see my mother going in Spaulding's and asking the salesman a million dopey questions – and here I was getting the ax again. It made me feel pretty sad. She bought me the wrong kind of skates – I wanted racing skates and she bought hockey – but it made me sad anyway. Almost every time somebody gives me a present, it ends up making me sad.

After I got all packed, I sort of counted my dough. I don't remember exactly how much I had, but I was pretty loaded. My grandmother'd just sent me a wad about a week before. I have this grandmother that's quite lavish with her dough. She doesn't have all her marbles any more – she's old as hell – and she keeps sending me money for my birthday about four times a year. Anyway, even though I was pretty loaded, I figured I could always use a few extra bucks. You never know. So what I did was, I went down the hall and woke up Frederick Woodruff, this guy I'd lent my typewriter to. I asked him how much he'd give me for it. He was a pretty wealthy guy. He said he didn't know. He said he didn't much want to buy it. Finally he bought it, though. It cost about ninety bucks, and all he bought it for was twenty. He was sore because I'd woke him up.

When I was all set to go, when I had my bags and all, I stood for a while next to the stairs and took a last look down the goddam corridor. I was sort of crying. I don't know why. I put my red hunting hat on, and turned the peak around to the back, the way I liked it, and then I yelled at the top of my goddam voice, '*Sleep tight, ya morons!*' I'll bet I woke up every bastard on the whole floor. Then I got the hell out. Some stupid guy had thrown peanut shells all over the stairs, and I damn near broke my crazy neck.

8

It was too late to call up for a cab or anything, so I walked the whole way to the station. It wasn't too far, but it was cold as hell, and the snow made it hard for walking, and my Gladstones kept banging hell out of my legs. I sort of enjoyed the air and all, though. The only trouble was, the cold made my nose hurt, and right under my upper lip, where old Stradlater'd laid one on me. He'd smacked my lip right on my teeth, and it was pretty sore. My ears were nice and warm, though. That hat I bought had earlaps in it, and I put them on – I didn't give a damn how I looked. Nobody was around anyway. Everybody was in the sack.

I was quite lucky when I got to the station, because I only had to wait about ten minutes for a train. While I waited, I got some snow in my hand and washed my face with it. I still had quite a bit of blood on.

Usually I like riding on trains, especially at night, with the lights on and the windows so black, and one of those guys coming up the aisle selling coffee and sandwiches and magazines. I usually buy a ham sandwich and about four magazines. If I'm on a train at night, I can usually even read one of those dumb stories in a magazine without puking. You know. One of those stories with a lot of phony, lean-jawed guys named David in it, and a lot of phony girls named Linda or Marcia that are always lighting all the goddam Davids' pipes for them. I can even read one of those lousy stories on a train at night, usually. But this time, it was different. I just didn't feel like it. I just sort of sat and not did anything. All I did was take off my hunting hat and put it in my pocket.

All of a sudden, this lady got on at Trenton and sat down next to me. Practically the whole car was empty, because it was pretty late and all, but she sat down next to me, instead of an empty seat, because she had this big bag with her and I was sitting in the front seat. She stuck the bag right out in the middle of the aisle, where the conductor and everybody could trip over it. She had these orchids on, like she'd just been to a big party or something. She was around forty or forty-five, I guess, but she was very good-looking. Women kill me. They really do. I don't mean I'm oversexed or anything like that – although I am quite sexy. I just like them, I mean. They're always leaving their goddam bags out in the middle of the aisle.

Anyway, we were sitting there, and all of a sudden she said to me, 'Excuse me, but isn't that a Pencey Prep sticker?' She was looking up at my suitcases, up on the rack.

'Yes, it is,' I said. She was right. I did have a goddam Pencey sticker on one of my Gladstones. Very corny, I'll admit.

'Oh, do you go to Pencey?' she said. She had a nice voice. A nice telephone voice, mostly. She should've carried a goddam telephone around with her.

'Yes, I do,' I said.

'Oh, how lovely! Perhaps you know my son, then. Ernest Morrow? He goes to Pencey.'

'Yes, I do. He's in my class.'

Her son was doubtless the biggest bastard that ever went to Pencey, in the whole crumby history of the school. He was always going down the corridor, after he'd had a shower, snapping his soggy old wet towel at people's asses. That's exactly the kind of a guy he was.

'Oh, how nice!' the lady said. But not corny. She was just nice and all. 'I must tell Ernest we met,' she said. 'May I ask your name, dear?'

'Rudolf Schmidt,' I told her. I didn't feel like giving her my whole life history. Rudolf Schmidt was the name of the janitor of our dorm.

'Do you like Pencey?' she asked me.

'Pencey? It's not too bad. It's not *para*dise or anything, but it's as good as most schools. Some of the faculty are pretty conscientious.'

'Ernest just adores it.'

'I know he does,' I said. Then I started shooting the old crap around a little bit. 'He adapts himself very well to things. He really does. I mean he really knows how to adapt himself.'

'Do you think so?' she asked me. She sounded interested as hell.

'Ernest? Sure,' I said. Then I watched her take off her gloves. Boy, was she lousy with rocks.

'I just broke a nail, getting out of a cab,' she said. She looked up at me and sort of smiled. She had a terrifically nice smile. She really did. Most people have hardly any smile at all, or a lousy one. 'Ernest's father and I sometimes worry about him,' she said. 'We sometimes feel he's not a terribly good mixer.'

'How do you mean?'

'Well. He's a very sensitive boy. He's really never been a terribly good mixer with other boys. Perhaps he takes things a little more seriously than he should at his age.'

Sensitive. That killed me. That guy Morrow was about as sensitive as a goddam toilet seat.

I gave her a good look. She didn't look like any dope to me. She looked like she might have a pretty damn good idea what a bastard she was the mother of. But you can't always tell – with somebody's mother, I mean. Mothers are all slightly insane. The thing is, though, I liked old Morrow's mother. She was all right. 'Would you care for a cigarette?' I asked her.

She looked all around. 'I don't believe this is a smoker, Rudolf,' she said. Rudolf. That killed me.

'That's all right. We can smoke till they start screaming at us,' I said. She took a cigarette off me, and I gave her a light.

She looked nice, smoking. She inhaled and all, but she didn't *wolf* the smoke down, the way most women around her age do. She had a lot of charm. She had quite a lot of sex appeal, too, if you really want to know.

She was looking at me sort of funny. 'I may be wrong, but I believe your nose is bleeding, dear,' she said, all of a sudden.

I nodded and took out my handkerchief. 'I got hit with a snowball,' I said. 'One of those very icy ones.' I probably would've told her what really happened, but it would've taken too long. I liked her, though. I was beginning to feel sort of sorry I'd told her my name was Rudolf Schmidt. 'Old Ernie,' I said. 'He's one of the most popular boys at Pencey. Did you know that?'

'No, I didn't.'

I nodded. 'It really took everybody quite a long time to get to know him. He's a funny guy. A *strange* guy, in lots of ways – know what I mean? Like when I first met him. When I first met him, I thought he was kind of a snobbish person. That's what I thought. But he isn't. He's just got this very original personality that takes you a little while to get to know him.'

Old Mrs Morrow didn't say anything, but boy, you should've seen her. I had her glued to her seat. You take somebody's mother, all they want to hear about is what a hot-shot their son is.

Then I *real*ly started chucking the old crap around. 'Did he tell you about the elections?' I asked her. 'The class elections?'

She shook her head. I had her in a trance, like. I really did.

'Well, a bunch of us wanted old Ernie to be president of the class. I mean he was the unanimous choice. I mean he was the only boy that could really handle the job,' I said – boy, was I chucking it. 'But this other boy – Harry Fencer – was elected. And the *reason* he was elected, the simple and obvious reason, was because Ernie wouldn't let us nominate him. Because he's so darn shy and modest and all. He re*fused* . . . Boy, he's *really* shy. You oughta make him try to get over that.' I looked at her. 'Didn't he tell you about it?'

'No, he didn't.'

I nodded. 'That's Ernie. He wouldn't. That's the one fault with him – he's too shy and modest. You really oughta get him to try to relax occasionally.'

Right that minute, the conductor came around for old Mrs Morrow's ticket, and it gave me a chance to quit shooting it. I'm glad I shot it for a while, though. You take a guy like Morrow that's always snapping their towel at people's asses – really trying to *hurt* somebody with it – they don't just stay a rat while they're a kid. They stay a rat their whole life. But I'll bet, after all the crap I shot, Mrs Morrow'll keep thinking of him now as this very shy, modest guy that wouldn't let us nominate him for president. She might. You can't tell. Mothers aren't too sharp about that stuff.

'Would you care for a cocktail?' I asked her. I was feeling in the mood for one myself. 'We can go in the club car. All right?'

'Dear, are you allowed to order drinks?' she asked me. Not snotty, though. She was too charming and all to be snotty.

'Well, no, not exactly, but I can usually get them on account of my height,' I said. 'And I have quite a bit of gray hair.' I turned sideways and showed her my gray hair. It fascinated hell out of her. 'C'mon, join me, why don't you?' I said. I'd've enjoyed having her.

'I really don't think I'd better. Thank you so much, though, dear,' she said. 'Anyway, the club car's most likely closed. It's quite late, you know.' She was right. I'd forgotten all about what time it was.

Then she looked at me and asked me what I was afraid she was going to ask me. 'Ernest wrote that he'd be home on Wednesday, that Christmas vacation would start on *Wednes*day,' she said. 'I hope you weren't called home suddenly because of illness in the family.' She really looked worried about it. She wasn't just being nosy, you could tell.

'No, everybody's fine at home,' I said. 'It's me. I have to have this operation.'

'Oh! I'm *so* sorry,' she said. She really was, too. I was right away sorry I'd said it, but it was too late.

'It isn't very serious. I have this tiny little tumor on the brain.'

'Oh, *no*!' She put her hand up to her mouth and all.

'Oh, I'll be all right and everything! It's right near the outside. And it's a very tiny one. They can take it out in about two minutes.'

Then I started reading this timetable I had in my pocket. Just to stop lying. Once I get started, I can go on for hours if I feel like it. No kidding. *Hours*.

We didn't talk too much after that. She started reading this *Vogue* she had with her, and I looked out the window for a while. She got off at Newark. She wished me a lot of luck with the operation and all. She kept calling me Rudolf. Then she invited me to visit Ernie during the summer, at Gloucester, Massachusetts. She said their house was right on the beach, and they had a tennis court and all, but I just thanked her and told her I was going to South America with my grandmother. Which was really a hot one, because my grandmother hardly ever even goes out of the *house*, except maybe to go to a goddam matinee or something. But I wouldn't visit that sonuvabitch Morrow for all the dough in the world, even if I was desperate.

9

The first thing I did when I got off at Penn Station, I went into this phone booth. I felt like giving somebody a buzz. I left my bags right outside the booth so that I could watch them, but as soon as I was inside, I couldn't think of anybody to call up. My brother D.B. was in Hollywood. My kid sister Phoebe goes to bed around nine o'clock – so I couldn't call *her* up. She wouldn't've cared if I'd woke her up, but the trouble was, she wouldn't've been the one that answered the phone. My parents would be the ones. So that was out. Then I thought of giving Jane Gallagher's mother a buzz, and find out when Jane's vacation started, but I didn't feel like it. Besides, it was pretty late to call up. Then I thought of calling this girl I used to go around with quite frequently, Sally Hayes, because I knew her Christmas vacation had started already – she'd written me this long, phony letter, inviting me over to help her trim the Christmas tree Christmas Eve and all – but I was afraid her mother'd answer the phone. Her mother knew my mother, and I could picture her breaking a goddam leg to get to the phone and tell my mother I was in New York. Besides, I wasn't crazy about talking to old Mrs Hayes on the phone. She once told Sally I was wild. She said I was wild and that I had no direction in life. Then I thought of calling up this guy that went to the Whooton School when I was there, Carl Luce, but I didn't like him much. So I ended up not calling anybody. I came out of the booth, after about twenty minutes or so, and got my bags and walked over to that tunnel where the cabs are and got a cab.

I'm so damn absent-minded, I gave the driver my regular address, just out of habit and all – I mean I completely forgot I was going to shack up in a hotel for a couple of days and not go home till vacation started. I didn't think of it till we were halfway through the park. Then I said, 'Hey, do you mind turning around when you get a chance? I gave you the wrong address. I want to go back downtown.'

The driver was sort of a wise guy. 'I can't turn around here, Mac. This here's a one-way. I'll have to go all the way to Ninedieth Street now.'

I didn't want to start an argument. 'Okay,' I said. Then I thought of something, all of a sudden. 'Hey, listen,' I said. 'You know those ducks in that lagoon right near Central Park South? That little lake? By any chance, do you happen to know where they go, the ducks, when it gets all frozen over? Do you happen to know, by any chance?' I realized it was only one chance in a million.

He turned around and looked at me like I was a madman. 'What're ya tryna do, bud?' he said. 'Kid me?'

'*No* – I was just interested, that's all.'

He didn't say anything more, so I didn't either. Until we came out of the park at Ninetieth Street. Then he said, 'All right, buddy. Where to?'

'Well, the thing is, I don't want to stay at any hotels on the East Side where I might run into some acquaintances of mine. I'm traveling incognito,' I said. I hate saying corny things like 'traveling incognito.' But when I'm with somebody that's corny, I always act corny too. 'Do you happen to know whose band's at the Taft or the New Yorker, by any chance?'

'No idear, Mac.'

'Well – take me to the Edmont, then,' I said. 'Would you care to stop on the way and join me for a cocktail? On me. I'm loaded.'

'Can't do it, Mac. Sorry.' He certainly was good company. Terrific personality.

We got to the Edmont Hotel, and I checked in. I'd put on my red hunting cap when I was in the cab, just for the hell of it, but I took it off before I checked in. I didn't want to look like a screwball or something. Which is really ironic. I didn't *know* then that the goddam hotel was full of perverts and morons. Screwballs all over the place.

They gave me this very crumby room, with nothing to look out of the window at except the other side of the hotel. I didn't care much. I was too depressed to care whether I had a good view or not. The bellboy that showed me to the room was this very old guy around sixty-five. He was even more depressing than the room was. He was one of those bald guys that comb all their hair over from the side to cover up the baldness. I'd rather be bald than do that. Anyway, what a gorgeous job for a guy around sixty-five years old. Carrying people's suitcases and waiting around for a tip. I suppose he wasn't too intelligent or anything, but it was terrible anyway.

After he left, I looked out the window for a while, with my coat on and all. I didn't have anything else to do. You'd be surprised what was going on on the other side of the hotel. They didn't even bother to pull their shades down. I saw one guy, a gray-haired, very distinguished-looking guy with only his shorts on, do something you wouldn't believe me if I told you. First he put his suitcase on the bed. Then he took out all these women's clothes, and put them on. Real women's clothes – silk stockings, high-heeled shoes, brassière, and one of those corsets with the straps hanging down and all. Then he put on this very tight black evening dress. I swear to God. Then he started walking up and down the room, taking these very small steps, the way a woman does, and smoking a cigarette and looking at himself in the mirror. He was all alone, too. Unless somebody was in the bathroom – I couldn't see that much. Then, in the window almost right over his, I saw a man and a woman squirting water out of their mouths at each other. It probably was highballs, not water, but I couldn't see what they had in their glasses. Anyway, first he'd take a swallow and squirt it all over *her*, then she did it to *him* – they took *turns*, for God's sake. You should've seen them. They were in hysterics the whole time, like it was the funniest thing that ever happened. I'm not kidding, that hotel was lousy with perverts. I was probably the only normal bastard in the whole place – and that isn't saying much. I damn near sent a telegram to old Stradlater telling him to take the first train to New York. He'd have been the king of the hotel.

The trouble was, that kind of junk is sort of fascinating to watch, even if you don't want it to be. For instance, that girl that was getting water squirted all over her face, she was pretty good-looking. I mean that's my big trouble. In my *mind*, I'm probably the biggest sex maniac you ever saw. Sometimes I can think of *very* crumby stuff I wouldn't mind doing if the opportunity came up. I can even see how it might be quite a lot of fun, in a crumby way, and if you were both sort of drunk and all, to get a girl and squirt water or something all over each other's face. The thing is, though, I don't *like* the idea. It stinks, if you analyze it. I think if you don't really like a girl, you shouldn't horse around with her at all, and if you *do* like her, then you're supposed to like her face, and if you like her face, you ought to be careful about doing crumby stuff to it, like squirting water all over it. It's really too bad that so much crumby stuff is a lot of fun sometimes. Girls aren't too much help, either, when you start trying not to get *too* crumby, when you start trying not to spoil anything really good. I knew this one girl, a couple of years ago, that was even crumbier than I was. Boy, was she crumby! We had a lot of fun, though, for a while, in a crumby way. Sex is something I really don't understand too hot. You never know *where* the hell you are. I keep making up these sex rules for myself, and then I break them right away. Last year I made a rule that I was going to quit horsing around with girls that, deep down, gave me a pain in the ass. I broke it, though, the same week I made it – the same *night*, as a matter of fact. I spent the whole night necking with a terrible phony named Anne Louise Sherman. Sex is something I just don't understand. I swear to God I don't.

I started toying with the idea, while I kept standing there, of giving old Jane a buzz – I mean calling her long distance at B.M., where she went, instead of calling up her mother to find out when she was coming home. You weren't supposed to call students up late at night, but I had it all figured out. I was going to tell whoever answered the phone that I was her uncle. I was going to say her aunt had just got killed in a car accident and I had to speak to her immediately. It would've worked, too. The only reason I didn't do it was because I wasn't in the mood. If you're not in the mood, you can't do that stuff right.

After a while I sat down in a chair and smoked a couple of cigarettes. I was feeling pretty horny. I have to admit it. Then, all of a sudden, I got this idea. I took out my wallet and started looking for this address a guy I met at a party last summer, that went to Princeton, gave me. Finally I found it. It was all a funny color from my wallet, but you could still read it. It was the address of this girl that wasn't exactly a whore or anything but that didn't mind doing it once in a while, this Princeton guy told me. He brought her to a dance at Princeton once, and they nearly kicked him out for bringing her. She used to be a burlesque stripper or something. Anyway, I went over to the phone and gave her a buzz. Her name was Faith Cavendish, and she lived at the Stanford Arms Hotel on Sixty-fifth and Broadway. A dump, no doubt.

For a while, I didn't think she was home or something. Nobody kept answering. Then, finally, somebody picked up the phone.

'Hello?' I said. I made my voice quite deep so that she wouldn't suspect my age or anything. I have a pretty deep voice anyway.

'Hello,' this woman's voice said. None too friendly, either.

'Is this Miss Faith Cavendish?'

'Who's *this*?' she said. 'Who's calling me up at this crazy goddam hour?'

That sort of scared me a little bit. 'Well, I know it's quite late,' I said, in this very mature voice and all. 'I hope you'll forgive me, but I was very anxious to get in touch with you.' I said it suave as hell. I really did.

'Who *is* this?' she said.

'Well, you don't know me, but I'm a friend of Eddie Birdsell's. He suggested that if I were in town sometime, we ought to get together for a cocktail or two.'

'*Who?* You're a friend of *who*?' Boy, she was a real tigress over the phone. She was damn near yelling at me.

'Edmund Birdsell. Eddie Birdsell,' I said. I couldn't remember if his name was Edmund or Edward. I only met him once, at a goddam stupid party.

'I don't know anybody by that name, Jack. And if you think I en*joy* bein' woke up in the middle –'

'Eddie *Bird*sell? From Princeton?' I said.

You could tell she was running the name over in her mind and all.

'Birdsell, Birdsell . . . from Princeton . . . Princeton College?'

'That's right,' I said.

'You from Princeton College?'

'Well, approximately.'

'Oh . . . How *is* Eddie?' she said. 'This is certainly a peculiar time to call a person up, though. Jesus Christ.'

'He's fine. He asked to be remembered to you.'

'Well, thank you. Remember me to *him*,' she said. 'He's a grand person. What's he doing now?' She was getting friendly as hell, all of a sudden.

'Oh, you know. Same old stuff,' I said. How the hell did *I* know what he was doing? I hardly knew the guy. I didn't even know if he was still at Princeton. 'Look,' I said. 'Would you be interested in meeting me for a cocktail somewhere?'

'By any chance do you have any idea what *time* it is?' she said. 'What's your name, anyhow, may I ask?' She was getting an English accent, all of a sudden. 'You sound a little on the young side.'

I laughed. 'Thank you for the compliment,' I said – suave as hell. 'Holden Caulfield's my name.' I should've given her a phony name, but I didn't think of it.

'Well, look, Mr Cawffle. I'm not in the habit of making engagements in the middle of the night. I'm a working gal.'

'Tomorrow's Sunday,' I told her.

'Well, *any*way. I gotta get my beauty sleep. You know how it is.'

'I thought we might have just one cocktail together. It isn't too late.'

'Well. You're very sweet', she said. 'Where ya callin' from? Where ya at now, anyways?'

'Me? I'm in a phone booth.'

'Oh,' she said. Then there was this very long pause. 'Well, I'd like awfully to get together with you sometime, Mr Cawffle. You sound very attractive. You sound like a very attractive person. But it *is* late.'

'I could come up to your place.'

'Well, ordinary, I'd say grand. I mean I'd love to have you drop up for a cocktail, but my roommate happens to be ill. She's been laying here all night without a wink of sleep. She just this minute closed her eyes and all. I mean.'

'Oh. That's too bad.'

'Where ya stopping at? Perhaps we could get together for cocktails tomorrow.'

'I can't make it tomorrow,' I said. 'Tonight's the only time I can make it.' What a dope I was. I shouldn't've said that.

'Oh. Well, I'm awfully sorry.'

'I'll say hello to Eddie for you.'

'Willya do that? I hope you enjoy your stay in New York. It's a grand place.'

'I know it is. Thanks. Good night,' I said. Then I hung up.

Boy, I *real*ly fouled that up. I should've at least made it for cocktails or something.

10

It was still pretty early. I'm not sure what time it was, but it wasn't too late. The one thing I hate to do is go to bed when I'm not even tired. So I opened my suitcases and took out a clean shirt, and then I went in the bathroom and washed and changed my shirt. What I thought I'd do, I thought I'd go downstairs and see what the hell was going on in the Lavender Room. They had this night club, the Lavender Room, in the hotel.

While I was changing my shirt, I damn near gave my kid sister Phoebe a buzz, though. I certainly felt like talking to her on the phone. Somebody with sense and all. But I couldn't take a chance on giving her a buzz, because she was only a little kid and she wouldn't have been up, let alone anywhere near the phone. I thought of maybe hanging up if my parents answered, but that wouldn't've worked, either. They'd know it was me. My mother always knows it's me. She's psychic. But I certainly wouldn't have minded shooting the crap with old Phoebe for a while.

You should see her. You never saw a little kid so pretty and smart in your whole life. She's really smart. I mean she's had all *A*'s ever since she started school. As a matter of fact, I'm the only dumb one in the family. My brother D.B.'s a writer and all, and my brother Allie, the one that died, that I told you about, was a wizard. I'm the only really dumb one. But you ought to see old Phoebe. She has this sort of red hair, a little bit like Allie's was, that's very short in the summertime. In the summertime, she sticks it behind her ears. She has nice, pretty little ears. In the wintertime, it's pretty long, though. Sometimes my mother braids it and sometimes she doesn't. It's really nice, though. She's only ten. She's quite skinny, like me, but nice skinny. Roller-skate skinny. I watched her once from the window when she was crossing over Fifth Avenue to go to the park, and that's what she is, roller-skate skinny. You'd like her. I mean if you tell old Phoebe something, she knows exactly what the hell you're talking about. I mean you can even take her anywhere with you. If you take her to a lousy movie, for instance, she knows it's a lousy movie. If you take her to a pretty good movie, she knows it's a pretty good movie. D.B. and I took her to see this French movie, *The Baker's Wife*, with Raimu in it. It killed her. Her favorite is *The 39 Steps*, though, with Robert Donat. She knows the whole goddam movie by heart, because I've taken her to see it about ten times. When old Donat comes up to this Scotch farmhouse, for instance, when he's running away from the cops and all, Phoebe'll say right out loud in the movie – right when the Scotch guy in the picture says it –'Can you eat the herring?' She knows all the talk by heart. And when this professor in the picture, that's really a German spy, sticks up his little finger with part of the middle joint missing, to show Robert Donat, old Phoebe beats him to it – she holds up *her* little finger at me in the dark, right in front of my face. She's all right. You'd like her. The only trouble is, she's a little too affectionate sometimes. She's very emotional, for a child. She really is. Something else she does, she writes books all the time. Only, she doesn't finish them. They're all about some kid named Hazel Weatherfield – only old Phoebe spells it 'Hazle.' Old Hazle Weatherfield is a girl detective. She's supposed to be an orphan, but her old man keeps showing up. Her old man's always a 'tall attractive gentleman about 20 years of age.' That kills me. Old Phoebe. I swear to God you'd like her. She was smart even when she was a very tiny little kid. When she was a very tiny little kid, I and Allie used to take her to the park with us, especially on Sundays. Allie had this sailboat he used to like to fool around with on Sundays, and we used to take old Phoebe with us. She'd wear white gloves and walk right between us, like a lady and all. And when Allie and I were having some conversation about things in general, old Phoebe'd be listening. Sometimes you'd forget she was around, because she was such a little kid, but *she'd* let you know. She'd interrupt you all the time. She'd give Allie or I a push or something, and say, '*Who?* Who said that? Bobby or the lady?' And we'd tell her who said it, and she'd say, 'Oh,' and go right on listening and all. She killed Allie, too. I mean he liked her, too. She's ten now, and not such a tiny little kid any more, but she still kills everybody – everybody with any sense, anyway.

Anyway, she was somebody you always felt like talking to on the phone. But I was too afraid my parents would answer, and then they'd find out I was in New York and kicked out of Pencey and all. So I just finished putting on my shirt. Then I got all ready and went down in the elevator to the lobby to see what was going on.

Except for a few pimpy-looking guys, and a few whory-looking blondes, the lobby was pretty empty. But you could hear the band playing in the Lavender Room, and so I went in there. It wasn't very crowded, but they gave me a lousy table anyway – way in the back. I should've waved a buck under the head-waiter's nose. In New York, boy, money really talks – I'm not kidding.

The band was putrid. Buddy Singer. Very brassy, but not

good brassy – corny brassy. Also, there were very few people around my age in the place. In fact, nobody was around my age. They were mostly old, show-offy-looking guys with their dates. Except at the table right next to me. At the table right next to me, there were these three girls around thirty or so. The whole three of them were pretty ugly, and they all had on the kind of hats that you knew they didn't really live in New York, but one of them, the blonde one, wasn't too bad. She was sort of cute, the blonde one, and I started giving her the old eye a little bit, but just then the waiter came up for my order. I ordered a Scotch and soda, and told him not to mix it – I said it fast as hell, because if you hem and haw, they think you're under twenty-one and won't sell you any intoxicating liquor. I had trouble with him anyway, though. 'I'm sorry, sir,' he said, 'but do you have some verification of your age? Your driver's license, perhaps?'

I gave him this very cold stare, like he'd insulted the hell out of me, and asked him, 'Do I look like I'm under twenty-one?'

'I'm sorry, sir, but we have our –'

'Okay, okay,' I said. I figured the hell with it. 'Bring me a Coke.' He started to go away, but I called him back. 'Can'tcha stick a little rum in it or something?' I asked him. I asked him very nicely and all. 'I can't sit in a corny place like this cold *sober*. Can'tcha stick a little rum in it or something?'

'I'm very sorry, sir . . . ' he said, and beat it on me. I didn't hold it against him, though. They lose their jobs if they get caught selling to a minor. I'm a goddam minor.

I started giving the three witches at the next table the eye again. That is, the blonde one. The other two were strictly from hunger. I didn't do it crudely, though. I just gave all three of them this very cool glance and all. What they did, though, the three of them, when I did it, they started giggling like morons.

They probably thought I was too young to give anybody the once-over. That annoyed hell out of me – you'd've thought I wanted to *marry* them or something. I should've given them the freeze, after they did that, but the trouble was, I really felt like dancing. I'm very fond of dancing, sometimes, and that was one of the times. So all of a sudden, I sort of leaned over and said, 'Would any of you girls care to dance?' I didn't ask them crudely or anything. Very suave, in fact. But God damn it, they thought *that* was a panic, too. They started giggling some more. I'm not kidding, they were three real morons. 'C'mon,' I said. 'I'll dance with you one at a time. All right? How 'bout it? C'mon!' I really felt like dancing.

Finally, the blonde one got up to dance with me, because you could tell I was really talking to *her*, and we walked out to the dance floor. The other two grools nearly had hysterics when we did. I certainly must've been very hard up to even bother with any of them.

But it was worth it. The blonde was some dancer. She was one of the best dancers I ever danced with. I'm not kidding, some of these very stupid girls can really knock you out on a dance floor. You take a really smart girl, and half the time she's trying to lead *you* around the dance floor, or else she's such a lousy dancer, the best thing to do is stay at the table and just get drunk with her.

'You really can dance,' I told the blonde one. 'You oughta be a pro. I mean it. I danced with a pro once, and you're twice as good as she was. Did you ever hear of Marco and Miranda?'

'What?' she said. She wasn't even listening to me. She was looking all around the place.

'I said did you ever hear of Marco and Miranda?'

'I don't know. No. I don't know.'

'Well, they're dancers, she's a dancer. She's not too hot, though. She does everything she's sup*posed* to, but she's not so hot anyway. You know when a girl's really a terrific dancer?'

'Wudga say?' she said. She wasn't listening to me, even. Her mind was wandering all over the place.

'I said do you know when a girl's really a terrific dancer?'

'Uh-uh.'

'Well – where I have my hand on your back. If I think there isn't anything underneath my hand – no can, no legs, no feet, no *any*thing – then the girl's really a terrific dancer.'

She wasn't listening, though. So I ignored her for a while. We just danced. God, could that dopey girl dance. Buddy Singer and his stinking band was playing 'Just One of Those Things' and even *they* couldn't ruin it entirely. It's a swell song. I didn't try any trick stuff while we danced – I hate a guy that does a lot of show-off tricky stuff on the dance floor – but I was moving her around plenty, and she stayed right with me. The funny thing is, I thought she was enjoying it, too, till all of a sudden she came out with this very dumb remark. 'I and my girl friends saw Peter Lorre last night,' she said. 'The movie actor. In person. He was buyin' a newspaper. He's *cute*.'

'You're lucky,' I told her. 'You're really lucky. You know that?' She was really a moron. But what a dancer. I could hardly stop myself from sort of giving her a kiss on the top of her dopey head – you know – right where the part is, and all. She got sore when I did it.

'Hey! What's the idea?'

'Nothing. No idea. You really can dance,' I said. 'I have a kid sister that's only in the goddam fourth grade. You're about as good as she is, and she can dance better than anybody living or dead.'

'Watch your language, if you don't mind.'

What a lady, boy. A *queen*, for Chrissake.

'Where you girls from?' I asked her.

She didn't answer me, though. She was busy looking around for old Peter Lorre to show up, I guess.

'Where you girls from?' I asked her again.

'What?' she said.

'Where you girls from? Don't answer if you don't feel like it. I don't want you to strain yourself.'

'Seattle, Washington,' she said. She was doing me a big favor to tell me.

'You're a very good conversationalist,' I told her. 'You know that?'

'What?'

I let it drop. It was over her head, anyway. 'Do you feel like jitterbugging a little bit, if they play a fast one? Not corny jitterbug, not jump or anything – just nice and easy. Everybody'll all sit down when they play a fast one, except the old guys and the fat guys, and we'll have plenty of room. Okay?'

'It's immaterial to me,' she said. 'Hey – how old are you, anyhow?'

That annoyed me, for some reason. 'Oh, Christ. Don't spoil it,' I said. 'I'm twelve, for Chrissake. I'm big for my age.'

'*Lis*ten. I toleja about that. I don't like that type language,' she said. 'If you're gonna use that type language, I can go sit down with my girl friends, you know.'

I apologized like a madman, because the band was starting a fast one. She started jitterbugging with me – but just very nice and easy, not corny. She was really good. All you had to do was touch her. And when she turned around, her pretty little butt twitched so nice and all. She knocked me out. I mean it. I was about half in love with her by the time we sat down. That's the thing about girls. Every time they do something pretty, even if they're not much to look at, or even if they're sort of stupid, you fall half in love with them, and then you never know *where* the hell you are. Girls. Jesus Christ. They can drive you crazy. They really can.

They didn't invite me to sit down at their table – mostly because they were too ignorant – but I sat down anyway. The blonde I'd been dancing with's name was Bernice something – Crabs or Krebs. The two ugly ones' names were Marty and Laverne. I told them my name was Jim Steele, just for the hell of it. Then I tried to get them in a little intelligent conversation, but it was practically impossible. You had to twist their arms. You could hardly tell which was the stupidest of the three of them. And the whole three of them kept looking all around the goddam room, like as if they expected a flock of goddam *movie stars* to come in any minute. They probably thought movie stars always hung out in the Lavender Room when they came to New York, instead of the Stork Club or El Morocco and all. Anyway, it took me about a half hour to find out where they all worked and all in Seattle. They all worked in the same insurance office. I asked them if they liked it, but do you think you could get an intelligent answer out of those three dopes? I thought the two ugly ones, Marty and Laverne, were sisters, but they got very insulted when I asked them. You could tell neither one of them wanted to look like the other one, and you couldn't blame them, but it was very amusing anyway.

I danced with them all – the whole three of them – one at a time. The one ugly one, Laverne, wasn't too bad a dancer, but the other one, old Marty, was murder. Old Marty was like dragging the Statue of Liberty around the floor. The only way

I could even half enjoy myself dragging her around was if I amused myself a little. So I told her I just saw Gary Cooper, the movie star, on the other side of the floor.

'*Where?*' she asked me – excited as hell. '*Where?*'

'Aw, you just missed him. He just went out. Why didn't you look when I told you?'

She practically stopped dancing, and started looking over everybody's heads to see if she could see him. 'Oh, shoot!' she said. I'd just about broken her heart – I really had. I was sorry as hell I'd kidded her. Some people you shouldn't kid, even if they deserve it.

Here's what was very funny, though. When we got back to the table, old Marty told the other two that Gary Cooper had just gone out. Boy, old Laverne and Bernice nearly committed suicide when they heard that. They got all excited and asked Marty if she'd seen him and all. Old Mart said she'd only caught a glimpse of him. That killed me.

The bar was closing up for the night, so I bought them all two drinks apiece quick before it closed, and I ordered two more Cokes for myself. The goddam table was lousy with glasses. The one ugly one, Laverne, kept kidding me because I was only drinking Cokes. She had a sterling sense of humor. She and old Marty were drinking Tom Collinses – in the middle of December, for God's sake. They didn't know any better. The blonde one, old Bernice, was drinking bourbon and water. She was really putting it away, too. The whole three of them kept looking for movie stars the whole time. They hardly talked – even to each other. Old Marty talked more than the other two. She kept saying these very corny, boring things, like calling the can the 'little girls' room,' and she thought Buddy Singer's poor old beat-up clarinet player was really terrific when he stood up and took a couple of ice-cold hot licks. She called his clarinet a 'licorice stick.' Was she corny. The other ugly one, Laverne, thought she was a very witty type. She kept asking me to call up my father and ask him what he was doing tonight. She kept asking me if my father had a date or not. *Four times* she asked me that – she was certainly witty. Old Bernice, the blonde one, didn't say hardly anything at all. Every time I'd ask her something, she said 'What?' That can get on your nerves after a while.

All of a sudden, when they finished their drink, all three of them stood up on me and said they had to get to bed. They said they were going to get up early to see the first show at Radio City Music Hall. I tried to get them to stick around for a while, but they wouldn't. So we said good-by and all. I told them I'd look them up in Seattle sometime, if I ever got there, but I doubt if I ever will. Look them up, I mean.

With cigarettes and all, the check came to about thirteen bucks. I think they should've at least *of*fered to pay for the drinks they had before I joined them – I wouldn't've *let* them, naturally, but they should've at least offered. I didn't care much, though. They were so ignorant, and they had those sad, fancy hats on and all. And that business about getting up early to see the first show at Radio City Music Hall depressed me. If somebody, some girl in an awful-looking hat, for instance, comes all the way to New York – from Seattle, *Wash*ington, for God's sake – and ends up getting up early in the morning to see the goddam first show at Radio City Music Hall, it makes me so depressed I can't stand it. I'd've bought the whole three of them a *hundred* drinks if only they hadn't told me that.

I left the Lavender Room pretty soon after they did. They were closing it up anyway, and the band had quit a long time ago. In the first place, it was one of those places that are very terrible to be in unless you have somebody good to dance with, or unless the waiter lets you buy real drinks instead of just Cokes. There isn't any night club in the world you can sit in for a long time unless you can at least buy some liquor and get drunk. Or unless you're with some girl that really knocks you out.

11

All of a sudden, on my way out to the lobby, I got old Jane Gallagher on the brain again. I got her on, and I couldn't get her off. I sat down in this vomity-looking chair in the lobby and thought about her and Stradlater sitting in that goddam Ed Banky's car, and though I was pretty damn sure old Stradlater hadn't given her the time – I know old Jane like a book – I still couldn't get her off my brain. I knew her like a book. I really did. I mean, besides checkers, she was quite fond of all athletic sports, and after I got to know her, the whole summer long we played tennis together almost every morning and golf almost every afternoon. I really got to know her quite intimately. I don't mean it was anything *physical* or anything – it wasn't – but we saw each other all the time. You don't always have to get too sexy to get to know a girl.

The way I met her, this Doberman pinscher she had used to come over and relieve himself on our lawn, and my mother got very irritated about it. She called up Jane's mother and made a big stink about it. My mother can make a very big stink about that kind of stuff. Then what happened, a couple of days later I saw Jane laying on her stomach next to the swimming pool, at the club, and I said hello to her. I knew she lived in the house next to ours, but I'd never conversed with her before or anything. She gave me the big freeze when I said hello that day, though. I had a helluva time convincing her that *I* didn't give a good goddam *where* her dog relieved himself. He could do it in the living room, for all I cared. Anyway, after that, Jane and I got to be friends and all. I played golf with her that same afternoon. She lost eight balls, I remember. *Eight*. I had a terrible time getting her to at least open her eyes when she took a swing at the ball. I improved her game immensely, though. I'm a very good golfer. If I told you what I go around in, you probably wouldn't believe me. I almost was once in a movie short, but I changed my mind at the last minute. I figured that anybody that hates the movies as much as I do, I'd be a phony if I let them stick me in a movie short.

She was a funny girl, old Jane. I wouldn't exactly describe her as strictly beautiful. She knocked me out, though. She was sort of muckle-mouthed. I mean when she was talking and she got excited about something, her mouth sort of went in about fifty directions, her lips and all. That killed me. And she never really closed it all the way, her mouth. It was always just a little bit open, especially when she got in her golf stance, or when she was reading a book. She was always reading, and she read very good books. She read a lot of poetry and all. She was the only one, outside my family, that I ever showed Allie's baseball mitt to, with all the poems written on it. She'd never met Allie or anything, because that was her first summer in Maine – before that, she went to Cape Cod – but I told her quite a lot about him. She was interested in that kind of stuff.

My mother didn't like her too much. I mean my mother always thought Jane and her mother were sort of snubbing her or something when they didn't say hello. My mother saw them in the village a lot, because Jane used to drive to market with her mother in this LaSalle convertible they had. My mother didn't think Jane was pretty, even. I did, though. I just liked the way she looked, that's all.

I remember this one afternoon. It was the only time old Jane and I ever got close to necking, even. It was a Saturday and it was raining like a bastard out, and I was over at her house, on the porch – they had this big screened-in porch. We were playing checkers. I used to kid her once in a while because she wouldn't take her kings out of the back row. But I didn't kid her much, though. You never wanted to kid Jane too much. I think I really like it best when you can kid the pants off a girl when the opportunity arises, but it's a funny thing. The girls I like best are the ones I never feel much like kidding. Sometimes I think they'd *like* it if you kidded them – in fact, I *know* they would – but it's hard to get started, once you've known them a pretty long time and never kidded them. Anyway, I was telling you about that afternoon Jane and I came close to necking. It was raining like hell and we were out on her porch, and all of a sudden this booze hound her mother was married to came out on the porch and asked Jane if there were any cigarettes in the house. I didn't know him too well or anything, but he looked like the kind of a guy that wouldn't talk to you much unless he wanted something off you. He had a lousy personality. Anyway, old Jane wouldn't answer him when he asked her if she knew where there was any cigarettes. So the guy asked her again, but she still wouldn't answer him. She didn't even look up from the game. Finally the guy went inside the house. When he did, I asked Jane what the hell was going on. She wouldn't even answer *me*, then. She made out like she was concentrating on her next move in the game and all. Then all of a sudden, this tear plopped down on the checkerboard. On one of the red squares – boy, I can still see it. She just rubbed it into the board with her finger. I don't know why, but it bothered hell out of me. So what I did was, I went over and made her move over on the glider so that I could sit down next to her – I practically sat down in her *lap*, as a matter of fact. Then she *really* started to cry, and the next thing I knew, I was kissing her all over – *any*where – her eyes, her *nose*, her forehead, her eyebrows and all, her *ears* – her whole face except her mouth and all. She sort of wouldn't let me get to her mouth. Anyway, it was the closest we ever got to necking. After a while, she got up and went in and put on this red and white sweater she had, that knocked me out, and we went to a goddam movie. I asked her, on the way, if Mr Cudahy – that was the booze hound's name – had ever tried to get wise with her. She was pretty young, but she had this terrific figure, and I wouldn't've put it past that Cudahy bastard. She said no, though. I never did find out what the hell was the matter. Some girls you practically never find out what's the matter.

I don't want you to get the idea she was a goddam *icicle* or something, just because we never necked or horsed around much. She wasn't. I held hands with her all the time, for instance. That doesn't sound like much, I realize, but she was terrific to hold hands with. Most girls if you hold hands with them, their goddam hand *dies* on you, or else they think they have to keep *moving* their hand all the time, as if they were afraid they'd bore you or something. Jane was different. We'd get into a goddam movie or something, and right away we'd start holding hands, and we wouldn't quit till the movie was over. And without changing the position or making a big deal out of it. You never even worried, with Jane, whether your hand was sweaty or not. All you knew was, you were happy. You really were.

One other thing I just thought of. One time, in this movie, Jane did something that just about knocked me out. The newsreel was on or something, and all of a sudden I felt this hand on the back of my neck, and it was Jane's. It was a funny thing to do. I mean she was quite young and all, and most girls if you see them putting their hand on the back of somebody's neck, they're around twenty-five or thirty and usually they're doing it to their husband or their little kid – I do it to my kid sister Phoebe once in a while, for instance. But if a girl's quite young and all and she does it, it's so pretty it just about kills you.

Anyway, that's what I was thinking about while I sat in that vomity-looking chair in the lobby. Old Jane. Every time I got to the part about her out with Stradlater in that damn Ed Banky's car, it almost drove me crazy. I knew she wouldn't let him get to first base with her, but it drove me crazy anyway. I don't even like to talk about it, if you want to know the truth.

There was hardly anybody in the lobby any more. Even all the whory-looking blondes weren't around any more, and all of a sudden I felt like getting the hell out of the place. It was too depressing. And I wasn't tired or anything. So I went up to my room and put on my coat. I also took a look out the window to see if all the perverts were still in action, but the lights and all were out now. I went down in the elevator again and got a cab and told the driver to take me down to Ernie's. Ernie's is this night club in Greenwich Village that my brother D.B. used to go to quite frequently before he went out to Hollywood and prostituted himself. He used to take me with him once in a while. Ernie's a big fat colored guy that plays the piano. He's a terrific snob and he won't hardly even talk to you unless you're a big shot or a celebrity or something, but he can really play the piano. He's so good he's almost corny, in fact. I don't exactly know what I mean by that, but I mean it. I certainly like to hear him play, but sometimes you feel like turning his goddam piano over. I think it's because sometimes when he plays, he *sounds* like the kind of a guy that won't talk to you unless you're a big shot.

12

The cab I had was a real old one that smelled like someone'd just tossed his cookies in it. I always get those vomity kind of cabs if I go anywhere late at night. What made it worse, it was so quiet and lonesome out, even though it was Saturday night. I didn't see hardly anybody on the street. Now and then you just saw a man and a girl crossing a street, with their arms around each other's waists and all, or a bunch of hoodlumy-looking guys and their dates, all of them laughing like hyenas at something you could bet wasn't funny. New York's terrible when somebody laughs on the street very late at night. You can hear it for miles. It makes you feel so lonesome and depressed. I kept wishing I could go home and shoot the bull for a while with old Phoebe. But finally, after I was riding a while, the cab driver and I sort of struck up a conversation. His name was Horwitz. He was a much better guy than the other driver I'd had. Anyway, I thought maybe he might know about the ducks.

'Hey, Horwitz,' I said. 'You ever pass by the lagoon in Central Park? Down by Central Park South?'

'The *what*?'

'The lagoon. That little lake, like, there. Where the ducks are. You know.'

'Yeah, what about it?'

'Well, you know the ducks that swim around in it? In the springtime and all? Do you happen to know where they go in the wintertime, by any chance?'

'Where *who* goes?'

'The ducks. Do you know, by any chance? I mean does somebody come around in a truck or something and take them away, or do they fly away by themselves – go south or something?'

Old Horwitz turned all the way around and looked at me. He was a very impatient-type guy. He wasn't a bad guy, though. 'How the hell should I know?' he said. 'How the hell should I know a stupid thing like that?'

'Well, don't get *sore* about it,' I said. He was sore about it or something.

'Who's sore? Nobody's sore.'

I stopped having a conversation with him, if he was going to get so damn touchy about it. But he started it up again himself. He turned all the way around again, and said, 'The *fish* don't go no place. They stay right where they are, the fish. Right in the goddam lake.'

'The fish – that's different. The fish is different. I'm talking about the *ducks*,' I said.

'What's *dif*ferent about it? Nothin's *dif*ferent about it,' Horwitz said. Everything he said, he sounded sore about something. 'It's tougher for the *fish*, the winter and all, than it is for the ducks, for Chrissake. Use your head, for Chrissake.'

I didn't say anything for about a minute. Then I said, 'All right. What do they do, the fish and all, when that whole little lake's a solid block of ice, people *skating* on it and all?'

Old Horwitz turned around again. 'What the hellaya mean what do they do?' he yelled at me. 'They stay right where they are, for Chrissake.'

'They can't just ignore the ice. They can't just ig*nore* it.'

'Who's ignoring it? Nobody's ig*nor*ing it!' Horwitz said. He got so damn excited and all, I was afraid he was going to drive the cab right into a lamppost or something. 'They live right *in* the goddam ice. It's their nature, for Chrissake. They get frozen right in one position for the whole winter.'

'Yeah? What do they eat, then? I mean if they're frozen *solid*, they can't swim around looking for *food* and all.'

'Their *bodies*, for Chrissake – what'sa matter with ya? Their bodies take in nutrition and all, right through the goddam sea-weed and crap that's in the ice. They got their *pores* open the whole time. That's their *nature*, for Chrissake. See what I mean?' He turned way the hell around again to look at me.

'Oh,' I said. I let it drop. I was afraid he was going to crack the damn taxi up or something. Besides, he was such a touchy guy, it wasn't any pleasure discussing anything with him. 'Would you care to stop off and have a drink with me somewhere?' I said.

He didn't answer me, though. I guess he was still thinking. I asked him again, though. He was a pretty good guy. Quite amusing and all.

'I ain't got no time for no liquor, bud,' he said. 'How the hell old are you, anyways? Why ain'tcha home in bed?'

'I'm not tired.'

When I got out in front of Ernie's and paid the fare, old Horwitz brought up the fish again. He certainly had it on his mind. 'Listen,' he said. 'If you was a fish, Mother Nature'd take care of *you*, wouldn't she? Right? You don't think them fish just *die* when it gets to be winter, do ya?'

'No, but –'

'You're goddam right they don't,' Horwitz said, and drove off like a bat out of hell. He was about the touchiest guy I ever met. Everything you said made him sore.

Even though it was so late, old Ernie's was jam-packed. Mostly with prep school jerks and college jerks. Almost every damn school in the world gets out earlier for Christmas vacation than the schools *I* go to. You could hardly check your coat, it was so crowded. It was pretty quiet, though, because Ernie was playing the piano. It was supposed to be something *holy*, for God's sake, when he sat down at the piano. Nobody's *that* good. About three couples, besides me, were waiting for tables, and they were all shoving and standing on tiptoes to get a look at old Ernie while he played. He had a big damn mirror in front of the piano, with this big spotlight on him, so that everybody could watch his face while he played. You couldn't see his *fingers* while he played – just his big old face. Big deal. I'm not too sure what the name of the song was that he was playing when I came in, but whatever it was, he was really stinking it up. He was putting all these dumb, showoffy ripples in the high notes, and a lot of other very tricky stuff that gives me a pain in the ass. You should've heard the crowd, though, when he was finished. You would've puked. They went mad. They were exactly the same morons that laugh like hyenas in the movies at stuff that isn't funny. I swear to God, if I were a piano player or an actor or something and all those dopes thought I was terrific, I'd hate it. I wouldn't even want them to *clap* for me. People always clap for the wrong things. If I were a piano player, I'd play it in the goddam closet. Anyway, when he was finished, and everybody was clapping their heads off, old Ernie turned around on his stool and gave this very phony, *humble* bow. Like as if he was a helluva humble guy, besides being a terrific piano player. It was very phony – I mean him being such a big snob and all. In a funny way, though, I felt sort of sorry for him when he was finished. I don't even think he *knows* any more when he's playing right or not. It isn't all his fault. I partly blame all those dopes that clap their heads off – they'd foul up *any*body, if you gave them a chance. Anyway, it made me feel depressed and lousy again, and I damn near got my coat back and went back to the hotel, but it was too early and I didn't feel much like being all alone.

They finally got me this stinking table, right up against a wall and behind a goddam post, where you couldn't see anything. It was one of those tiny little tables that if the people at the next table don't get up to let you by – and they never *do*, the bastards – you practically have to *climb* into your chair. I ordered a Scotch and soda, which is my favorite drink, next to frozen Daiquiris. If you were only around six years old, you could get liquor at Ernie's, the place was so dark and all, and besides, nobody cared how old you were. You could even be a dope fiend and nobody'd care.

I was surrounded by jerks. I'm not kidding. At this other tiny table, right to my left, practically on *top* of me, there was this funny-looking guy and this funny-looking girl. They were around my age, or maybe just a little older. It was funny. You could see they were being careful as hell not to drink up the minimum too fast. I listened to their conversation for a while, because I didn't have anything else to do. He was telling her about some pro football game he'd seen that afternoon. He gave her every single goddam play in the whole game – I'm not kidding. He was the most boring guy I ever listened to. And you could tell his date wasn't even interested in the goddam game, but she was even funnier-looking than *he* was, so I guess she *had* to listen. Real ugly girls have it tough. I feel so sorry for them sometimes. Sometimes I can't even look at them, especially if they're with some dopey guy that's telling them all about a goddam football game. On my *right*, the conversation was even worse, though. On my right there was this very Joe Yale-looking guy, in a gray flannel suit and one of those flitty-looking Tattersall vests. All those Ivy League bastards look alike. My father wants me to go to Yale, or maybe Princeton, but I swear, I wouldn't go to one of those Ivy League colleges if I was *dy*ing, for God's sake. Anyway, this Joe Yale-looking guy had a terrific-looking girl with him. Boy, she was good-looking. But you should've heard the conversation they were having. In the first place, they were both slightly crocked. What he was doing, he was giving her a feel under the table, and at the same time telling her all about some guy in his dorm that had eaten a whole bottle of aspirin and nearly committed suicide. His date kept saying to him, 'How *hor*rible . . . Don't, darling. Please, don't. Not here.' Imagine giving somebody a feel and telling them about a guy committing suicide at the same time! They killed me.

I certainly began to feel like a prize horse's ass, though, sitting there all by myself. There wasn't anything to do except smoke and drink. What I did do, though, I told the waiter to ask old Ernie if he'd care to join me for a drink. I told him to tell him I was D.B.'s brother. I don't think he ever even gave him my message, though. Those bastards never give your message to anybody.

All of a sudden, this girl came up to me and said, 'Holden Caulfield!' Her name was Lillian Simmons. My brother D.B. used to go around with her for a while. She had very big knockers.

'Hi,' I said. I tried to get up, naturally, but it was some job getting up, in a place like that. She had some Navy officer with her that looked like he had a poker up his ass.

'How marvelous to see you!' old Lillian Simmons said. Strictly a phony. 'How's your big brother?' That's all she really wanted to know.

'He's fine. He's in Hollywood.'

'In *Hol*lywood! How *marv*elous! What's he *do*ing?'

'I don't know. Writing,' I said. I didn't feel like discussing it. You could tell she thought it was a big deal, his being in Hollywood. Almost everybody does. Mostly people who've never read any of his stories. It drives me crazy, though.

'How ex*cit*ing,' old Lillian said. Then she introduced me to the Navy guy. His name was Commander Blop or something. He was one of those guys that think they're being a pansy if they don't break around forty of your fingers when they shake hands with you. God, I hate that stuff. 'Are you all alone, baby?' old Lillian asked me. She was blocking up the *whole goddam traffic* in the aisle. You could tell she liked to block up a lot of traffic. This waiter was waiting for her to move out of the way, but she didn't even notice him. It was funny. You could tell the waiter didn't like her much, you could tell even the Navy guy didn't like her much, even though he was dating her. And *I* didn't like her much. Nobody did. You had to feel sort of sorry for her, in a way. 'Don't you have a date, baby?' she asked me. I was standing up now, and she didn't even tell me to sit down. She was the type that keeps you standing up for hours. 'Isn't he handsome?' she said to the Navy guy. 'Holden, you're getting handsomer by the minute.' The Navy guy told her to come on. He told her they were blocking up the whole aisle. 'Holden, come join us,' old Lillian said. 'Bring your drink.'

'I was just leaving,' I told her. 'I have to meet somebody.' You could tell she was just trying to get in good with me. So that I'd tell old D.B. about it.

'Well, you little so-and-so. All right for you. Tell your big brother I hate him, when you see him.'

Then she left. The Navy guy and I told each other we were

glad to've met each other. Which always kills me. I'm always saying 'Glad to've met you' to somebody I'm not at *all* glad I met. If you want to stay alive, you have to say that stuff, though.

After I'd told her I had to meet somebody, I didn't have any goddam choice except to *leave*. I couldn't even stick around to hear old Ernie play something halfway decent. But I certainly wasn't going to sit down at a table with old Lillian Simmons and that Navy guy and be bored to death. So I left. It made me mad, though, when I was getting my coat. People are always ruining things for you.

13

I walked all the way back to the hotel. Forty-one gorgeous blocks. I didn't do it because I felt like walking or anything. It was more because I didn't feel like getting in and out of another taxicab. Sometimes you get tired of riding in taxicabs the same way you get tired riding in elevators. All of a sudden, you have to walk, no matter how far or how high up. When I was a kid, I used to walk all the way up to our apartment very frequently. Twelve stories.

You wouldn't even have known it had snowed at all. There was hardly any snow on the sidewalks. But it was freezing cold, and I took my red hunting hat out of my pocket and put it on – I didn't give a damn how I looked. I even put the earlaps down. I wished I knew who'd swiped my gloves at Pencey, because my hands were freezing. Not that I'd have done much about it even if I had known. I'm one of these very yellow guys. I try not to show it, but I am. For instance, if I'd found out at Pencey who'd stolen my gloves, I probably would've gone down to the crook's room and said, 'Okay. How 'bout handing over those gloves?' Then the crook that had stolen them probably would've said, his voice very innocent and all, 'What gloves?' Then what I probably would've done, I'd have gone in his closet and found the gloves somewhere. Hidden in his goddam galoshes or something, for instance. I'd have taken them out and showed them to the guy and said, 'I suppose these are *your* goddam gloves?' Then the crook probably would've given me this very phony, innocent look, and said, ‘I never saw those gloves before in my life. If they’re yours, take ’em. I don’t want the goddam things.’ Then I probably would’ve just stood there for about five minutes. I’d have the damn gloves right in my hand and all, but I’d feel I ought to sock the guy in the jaw or something – break his goddam jaw. Only, I wouldn’t have the guts to do it. I’d just *stand* there, trying to look tough. What I might do, I might say something very cutting and snotty, to rile him up – *instead* of socking him in the jaw. Anyway, if I did say something very cutting and snotty, he’d probably get up and come over to me and say, ‘Listen, Caulfield. Are you calling me a crook?’ *Then*, instead of saying, ‘You’re goddam right I am, you dirty crooked bastard!’ all I probably would’ve said would be, ‘All I know is my goddam gloves were in *your* goddam galoshes.’ Right away then, the guy would know for sure that I wasn’t going to take a sock at him, and he probably would’ve said, ‘Listen. Let’s get this straight. Are you calling me a thief?’ Then I probably would’ve said, ‘Nobody’s calling anybody a thief. All I know is my gloves were in your goddam galoshes.’ It could go on like that for *hours*. Finally, though, I’d leave his room without even taking a sock at him. I’d probably go down to the can and sneak a cigarette and watch myself getting tough in the mirror. Anyway, that’s what I thought about the whole way back to the hotel. It’s no fun to be yellow. Maybe I’m not *all* yellow. I don’t know. I think maybe I’m just partly yellow and partly the type that doesn’t give much of a damn if they lose their gloves. One of my troubles is, I never care too much when I lose something – it used to drive my mother crazy when I was a kid. Some guys spend *days* looking for something they lost. I never seem to have anything that if I lost it I’d care too much. Maybe that’s why I’m partly yellow. It’s no excuse, though. It really isn’t. What you should be is not yellow at all. If you're supposed to sock somebody in the jaw, and you sort of feel like doing it, you should do it. I'm just no good at it, though. I'd rather push a guy out the window or chop his head off with an ax than sock him in the jaw. I hate fist fights. I don't mind getting hit so much – although I'm not crazy about it, naturally – but what scares me most in a fist fight is the guy's face. I can't stand looking at the other guy's face, is my trouble. It wouldn't be so bad if you could both be blindfolded or something. It's a funny kind of yellowness, when you come to think of it, but it's yellowness, all right. I'm not kidding myself.

The more I thought about my gloves and my yellowness, the more depressed I got, and I decided, while I was walking and all, to stop off and have a drink somewhere. I'd only had three drinks at Ernie's, and I didn't even finish the last one. One thing I have, it's a terrific capacity. I can drink all night and not even show it, if I'm in the mood. Once, at the Whooton School, this other boy, Raymond Goldfarb, and I bought a pint of Scotch and drank it in the chapel one Saturday night, where nobody'd see us. He got stinking, but I hardly didn't even show it. I just got very cool and nonchalant. I puked before I went to bed, but I didn't really have to – I forced myself.

Anyway, before I got to the hotel, I started to go in this dumpy-looking bar, but two guys came out, drunk as hell, and wanted to know where the subway was. One of them was this very Cuban-looking guy, and he kept breathing his stinking breath in my face while I gave him directions. I ended up not even going in the damn bar. I just went back to the hotel.

The whole lobby was empty. It smelled like fifty million dead cigars. It really did. I wasn't sleepy or anything, but I was feeling sort of lousy. Depressed and all. I almost wished I was dead.

Then, all of a sudden, I got in this big mess.

The first thing when I got in the elevator, the elevator guy said to me, 'Innarested in having a good time, fella? Or is it too late for you?'

'How do you mean?' I said. I didn't know what he was driving at or anything.

'Innarested in a little tail t'night?'

'Me?' I said. Which was a very dumb answer, but it's quite embarrassing when somebody comes right up and asks you a question like that.

'How old are you, chief?' the elevator guy said.

'Why?' I said. 'Twenty-two.'

'Uh huh. Well, how 'bout it? Y'innarested? Five bucks a throw. Fifteen bucks the whole night.' He looked at his wrist watch. 'Till noon. Five bucks a throw, fifteen bucks till noon.'

'Okay,' I said. It was against my principles and all, but I was feeling so depressed I didn't even *think*. That's the whole trouble. When you're feeling very depressed, you can't even think.

'Okay *what*? A throw, or till noon? I gotta know.'

'Just a throw.'

'Okay, what room ya in?'

I looked at the red thing with my number on it, on my key. 'Twelve twenty-two,' I said. I was already sort of sorry I'd let the thing start rolling, but it was too late now.

'Okay. I'll send a girl up in about fifteen minutes.' He opened the doors and I got out.

'Hey, is she good-looking?' I asked him. 'I don't want any old bag.'

'No old bag. Don't worry about it, chief.'

'Who do I pay?'

'Her,' he said. 'Let's go, chief.' He shut the doors, practically right in my face.

I went to my room and put some water on my hair, but you can't really comb a crew cut or anything. Then I tested to see if my breath stank from so many cigarettes and the Scotch and sodas I drank at Ernie's. All you do is hold your hand under your mouth and blow your breath up toward the old nostrils. It didn't seem to stink much, but I brushed my teeth anyway. Then I put on another clean shirt. I knew I didn't have to get all dolled up for a prostitute or anything, but it sort of gave me something to do. I was a little nervous. I was starting to feel pretty sexy and all, but I was a little nervous anyway. If you want to know the truth, I'm a virgin. I really am. I've had quite a few opportunities to lose my virginity and all, but I've never got around to it yet. Something always happens. For instance, if you're at a girl's house, her parents always come home at the wrong time – or you're afraid they will. Or if you're in the back seat of somebody's car, there's always somebody's date in the front seat – some girl, I mean – that always wants to know what's going on *all over* the whole goddam car. I mean some girl in front keeps turning around to see what the hell's going on. Anyway, something always happens. I came quite close to doing it a couple of times, though. One time in particular, I remember. Something went wrong, though – I don't even remember what any more. The thing is, most of the time when you're coming pretty close to doing it with a girl – a girl that isn't a prostitute or anything, I mean – she keeps telling you to stop. The trouble with me is, I stop. Most guys don't. I can't help it. You never know whether they really *want* you to stop, or whether they're just scared as hell, or whether they're just telling you to stop so that if you *do* go through with it, the blame'll be on *you*, not them. Anyway, I keep stopping. The trouble is, I get to feeling sorry for them. I mean most girls are so dumb and all. After you neck them for a while, you can really *watch* them losing their brains. You take a girl when she really gets passionate, she just hasn't any brains. I don't know. They tell me to stop, so I stop. I always wish I *hadn't*, after I take them home, but I keep doing it anyway.

Anyway, while I was putting on another clean shirt, I sort of figured this was my big chance, in a way. I figured if she was a prostitute and all, I could get in some practice on her, in case I ever get married or anything. I worry about that stuff sometimes. I read this book once, at the Whooton School, that had this very sophisticated, suave, sexy guy in it. Monsieur Blanchard was his name, I can still remember. It was a lousy book, but this Blanchard guy was pretty good. He had this big château and all on the Riviera, in Europe, and all he did in his spare time was beat women off with a club. He was a real rake and all, but he knocked women out. He said, in this one part, that a woman's body is like a violin and all, and that it takes a terrific musician to play it right. It was a very corny book – I realize that – but I couldn't get that violin stuff out of my mind anyway. In a way, that's why I sort of wanted to get some practice in, in case I ever get married. Caulfield and his Magic Violin, boy. It's corny, I realize, but it isn't *too* corny. I wouldn't mind being pretty good at that stuff. Half the time, if you really want to know the truth, when I'm horsing around with a girl, I have a helluva lot of trouble just *finding* what I'm looking for, for God's sake, if you know what I mean. Take this girl that I just missed having sexual intercourse with, that I told you about. It took me about an *hour* to just get her goddam brassiere off. By the time I did get it off, she was about ready to spit in my eye.

Anyway, I kept walking around the room, waiting for this prostitute to show up. I kept hoping she'd be good-looking. I didn't care too much, though. I sort of just wanted to get it over with. Finally, somebody knocked on the door, and when I went to open it, I had my suitcase right in the way and I fell over it and damn near broke my knee. I always pick a gorgeous time to fall over a suitcase or something.

When I opened the door, this prostitute was standing there. She had a polo coat on, and no hat. She was sort of a blonde, but you could tell she dyed her hair. She wasn't any old bag, though. 'How do you do,' I said. Suave as hell, boy.

'You the guy Maurice said?' she asked me. She didn't seem too goddam friendly.

'Is he the elevator boy?'

'Yeah,' she said.

'Yes, I am. Come in, won't you?' I said. I was getting more and more nonchalant as it went along. I really was.

She came in and took her coat off right away and sort of chucked it on the bed. She had on a green dress underneath. Then she sort of sat down sideways on the chair that went with the desk in the room and started jiggling her foot up and down. She crossed her legs and started jiggling this one foot up and down. She was very nervous, for a prostitute. She really was. I think it was because she was young as hell. She was around my age. I sat down in the big chair, next to her, and offered her a cigarette. 'I don't smoke,' she said. She had a tiny little wheeny-whiny voice. You could hardly hear her. She never said thank you, either, when you offered her something. She just didn't know any better.

'Allow me to introduce myself. My name is Jim Steele,' I said.

'Ya got a watch on ya?' she said. She didn't care what the hell my name was, naturally. 'Hey, how old are you, anyways?'

'Me? Twenty-two.'

'Like fun you are.'

It was a funny thing to say. It sounded like a real kid. You'd think a prostitute and all would say 'Like hell you are' or 'Cut the crap' instead of 'Like fun you are.'

'How old are *you*?' I asked her.

'Old enough to know better,' she said. She was really witty. 'Ya got a watch on ya?' she asked me again, and then she stood up and pulled her dress over her head.

I certainly felt peculiar when she did that. I mean she did it so *sudden* and all. I know you're supposed to feel pretty sexy when somebody gets up and pulls their dress over their head, but I didn't. Sexy was about the *last* thing I was feeling. I felt much more depressed than sexy.

'Ya got a watch on ya, hey?'

'No. No, I don't,' I said. *Boy*, was I feeling peculiar. 'What's your name?' I asked her. All she had on was this pink slip. It was really quite embarrassing. It really was.

'Sunny,' she said. 'Let's go, hey.'

'Don't you feel like talking for a while?' I asked her. It was a childish thing to say, but I was feeling so damn peculiar. 'Are you in a very big hurry?'

She looked at me like I was a madman. 'What the heck ya wanna talk about?' she said.

'I don't know. Nothing special. I just thought perhaps you might care to chat for a while.'

She sat down in the chair next to the desk again. She didn't like it, though, you could tell. She started jiggling her foot again – boy, she was a nervous girl.

'Would you care for a cigarette now?' I said. I forgot she didn't smoke.

'I don't smoke. Listen, if you're gonna talk, *do* it. I got things to do.'

I couldn't think of anything to talk about, though. I thought of asking her how she got to be a prostitute and all, but I was scared to ask her. She probably wouldn't've told me anyway.

'You don't come from New York, do you?' I said finally. That's all I could think of.

'Hollywood,' she said. Then she got up and went over to where she'd put her dress down, on the bed. 'Ya got a hanger? I don't want to get my dress all wrinkly. It's brand-clean.'

'Sure,' I said right away. I was only too glad to get up and do something. I took her dress over to the closet and hung it up for her. It was funny. It made me feel sort of sad when I hung it up. I thought of her going in a store and buying it, and nobody in the store knowing she was a prostitute and all. The salesman probably just thought she was a regular girl when she bought it. It made me feel sad as hell – I don't know why exactly.

I sat down again and tried to keep the old conversation going. She was a lousy conversationalist. 'Do you work every night?' I asked her – it sounded sort of awful, after I'd said it.

'Yeah.' She was walking all around the room. She picked up the menu off the desk and read it.

'What do you do during the day?'

She sort of shrugged her shoulders. She was pretty skinny. 'Sleep. Go to the show.' She put down the menu and looked at me. 'Let's go, hey. I haven't got all –'

'Look,' I said. 'I don't feel very much like myself tonight. I've had a rough night. Honest to God. I'll pay you and all, but do you mind very much if we don't do it? Do you mind very much?' The trouble was, I just didn't want to do it. I felt more depressed than sexy, if you want to know the truth. *She* was depressing. Her green dress hanging in the closet and all. And besides, I don't think I could *ever* do it with somebody that sits in a stupid movie all day long. I really don't think I could.

She came over to me, with this funny look on her face, like as if she didn't believe me. 'What'sa matter?' she said.

'Nothing's the matter.' Boy, was I getting nervous. 'The thing is, I had an operation very recently.'

'Yeah? Where?'

'On my wuddayacallit – my clavichord.'

'Yeah? Where the hell's that?'

'The clavichord?' I said. 'Well, actually, it's in the spinal canal. I mean it's quite a ways down in the spinal canal.'

'Yeah?' she said. 'That's tough.' Then she sat down on my goddam lap. 'You're cute.'

She made me so nervous, I just kept on lying my head off. 'I'm still recuperating,' I told her.

'You look like a guy in the movies. You know. Whosis. *You* know who I mean. What the heck's his name?'

'I don't know,' I said. She wouldn't get off my goddam lap.

'Sure you know. He was in that pitcher with Mel-vine Douglas? The one that was Mel-vine Douglas's kid brother? That falls off this boat? *You* know who I mean.'

'No, I don't. I go to the movies as seldom as I can.'

Then she started getting funny. Crude and all.

'Do you mind cutting it out?' I said. 'I'm not in the mood, I just told you. I just had an operation.'

She didn't get up from my lap or anything, but she gave me this terrifically dirty look. 'Listen,' she said. 'I was *sleep*in' when that crazy Maurice woke me up. If you think I'm –'

'I *said* I'd pay you for coming and all. I really will. I have plenty of dough. It's just that I'm practically just recovering from a very serious –'

'What the heck did you tell that crazy Maurice you wanted a *girl* for, then? If you just had a goddam operation on your goddam wuddayacallit. *Huh?*'

'I thought I'd be feeling a lot better than I do. I was a little premature in my calculations. No kidding. I'm sorry. If you'll just get up a second, I'll get my wallet. I mean it.'

She was sore as hell, but she got up off my goddam lap so that I could go over and get my wallet off the chiffonier. I took out a five-dollar bill and handed it to her. 'Thanks a lot,' I told her. 'Thanks a million.'

'This is a five. It costs ten.'

She was getting funny, you could tell. I was afraid something like that would happen – I really was.

'Maurice said five,' I told her. 'He said fifteen till noon and only five for a throw.'

'Ten for a throw.'

'He said five. I'm sorry – I really am – but that's all I'm gonna shell out.'

She sort of shrugged her shoulders, the way she did before, and then she said, very cold, 'Do you mind getting me my frock? Or would it be too much trouble?' She was a pretty spooky kid. Even with that little bitty voice she had, she could sort of scare you a little bit. If she'd been a big old prostitute, with a lot of makeup on her face and all, she wouldn't have been half as spooky.

I went and got her dress for her. She put it on and all, and then she picked up her polo coat off the bed. 'So long, crumb-bum,' she said.

'So long,' I said. I didn't thank her or anything. I'm glad I didn't.

14

After old Sunny was gone, I sat in the chair for a while and smoked a couple of cigarettes. It was getting daylight outside. Boy, I felt miserable. I felt so depressed, you can't imagine. What I did, I started talking, sort of out loud, to Allie. I do that sometimes when I get very depressed. I keep telling him to go home and get his bike and meet me in front of Bobby Fallon's house. Bobby Fallon used to live quite near us in Maine – this is, years ago. Anyway, what happened was, one day Bobby and I were going over to Lake Sedebego on our bikes. We were going to take our lunches and all, and our BB guns – we were kids and all, and we thought we could shoot something with our BB guns. Anyway, Allie heard us talking about it, and he wanted to go, and I wouldn't let him. I told him he was a child. So once in a while, now, when I get very depressed, I keep saying to him, 'Okay. Go home and get your bike and meet me in front of Bobby's house. Hurry up.' It wasn't that I didn't use to take him with me when I went somewhere. I did. But that one day, I didn't. He didn't get sore about it – he never got sore about anything – but I keep thinking about it anyway, when I get very depressed.

Finally, though, I got undressed and got in bed. I felt like praying or something, when I was in bed, but I couldn't do it. I can't always pray when I feel like it. In the first place, I'm sort of an atheist. I like Jesus and all, but I don't care too much for most of the other stuff in the Bible. Take the Disciples, for instance.

They annoy the hell out of me, if you want to know the truth. They were all right after Jesus was dead and all, but while He was alive, they were about as much use to Him as a hole in the head. All they did was keep letting Him down. I like almost anybody in the Bible better than the Disciples. If you want to know the truth, the guy I like best in the Bible, next to Jesus, was that lunatic and all, that lived in the tombs and kept cutting himself with stones. I like him ten times as much as the Disciples, that poor bastard. I used to get in quite a few arguments about it, when I was at the Whooton School, with this boy that lived down the corridor, Arthur Childs. Old Childs was a Quaker and all, and he read the Bible all the time. He was a very nice kid, and I liked him, but I could never see eye to eye with him on a lot of stuff in the Bible, especially the Disciples. He kept telling me if I didn't like the Disciples, then I didn't like Jesus and all. He said that because Jesus *picked* the Disciples, you were supposed to like them. I said I knew He picked them, but that He picked them at *random*. I said He didn't have time to go around analyzing everybody. I said I wasn't blaming Jesus or anything. It wasn't His fault that He didn't have any time. I remember I asked old Childs if he thought Judas, the one that betrayed Jesus and all, went to Hell after he committed suicide. Childs said certainly. That's exactly where I disagreed with him. I said I'd bet a thousand bucks that Jesus never sent old Judas to Hell. I still would, too, if I had a thousand bucks. I think any one of the Dis*cip*les would've sent him to Hell and all – and fast, too – but I'll bet anything Jesus didn't do it. Old Childs said the trouble with me was that I didn't go to church or anything. He was right about that, in a way. I don't. In the first place, my parents are different religions, and all the children in our family are atheists. If you want to know the truth, I can't even stand ministers. The ones they've had at every school I've gone to, they all have these Holy Joe voices when they start giving their sermons. God, I hate that. I don't see why the hell they can't talk in their natural voice. They sound so phony when they talk.

Anyway, when I was in bed, I couldn't pray worth a damn. Every time I got started, I kept picturing old Sunny calling me a crumb-bum. Finally, I sat up in bed and smoked another cigarette. It tasted lousy. I must've smoked around two packs since I left Pencey.

All of a sudden, while I was laying there smoking, somebody knocked on the door. I kept hoping it wasn't *my* door they were knocking on, but I knew damn well it was. I don't know *how* I knew, but I knew. I knew *who* it was, too. I'm psychic.

'Who's there?' I said. I was pretty scared. I'm very yellow about those things.

They just knocked again, though. Louder.

Finally I got out of bed, with just my pajamas on, and opened the door. I didn't even have to turn the light on in the room, because it was already daylight. Old Sunny and Maurice, the pimpy elevator guy, were standing there.

'What's the matter? Wuddaya want?' I said. Boy, my voice was shaking like hell.

'Nothin' much,' old Maurice said. 'Just five bucks.' He did all the talking for the two of them. Old Sunny just stood there next to him, with her mouth open and all.

'I paid her already. I gave her five bucks. Ask her,' I said. Boy, was my voice shaking.

'It's ten bucks, chief. I tole ya that. Ten bucks for a throw, fifteen bucks till noon. I tole ya that.'

'You did not tell me that. You said *five* bucks a throw. You said fifteen bucks till noon, all right, but I distinctly heard you –'

'Open up, chief.'

'What *for*?' I said. God, my old heart was damn near beating me out of the room. I wished I was *dressed* at least. It's terrible to be just in your pajamas when something like that happens.

'Let's go, chief,' old Maurice said. Then he gave me a big shove with his crumby hand. I damn near fell over on my can – he was a huge sonuvabitch. The next thing I knew, he and old Sunny were both in the room. They acted like they owned the damn place. Old Sunny sat down on the window sill. Old Maurice sat down in the big chair and loosened his collar and all – he wearing this elevator operator's uniform. *Boy*, was I nervous.

'All right, chief, let's have it. I gotta get back to work.'

'I told you about ten times, I don't owe you a cent. I already gave her the five –'

'Cut the crap, now. Let's have it.'

'Why should I give her another five bucks?' I said. My voice was cracking all over the place. 'You're trying to chisel me.'

Old Maurice unbuttoned his whole uniform coat. All he had on underneath was a phony shirt collar, but no shirt or anything. He had a big fat hairy stomach. 'Nobody's tryna chisel nobody,' he said. 'Let's have it, chief.'

'*No*.'

When I said that, he got up from his chair and started walking toward me and all. He looked like he was very, very tired or very, very bored. God, was I scared. I sort of had my arms folded, I remember. It wouldn't have been so bad, I don't think, if I hadn't had just my goddam *pajamas* on.

'Let's have it, chief.' He came right up to where I was standing. That's all he could say. 'Let's have it, chief.' He was a real moron.

'*No*.'

'Chief, you're gonna force me inna roughin' ya up a little bit. I don't wanna do it, but that's the way it looks,' he said. 'You owe us five bucks.'

'I *don't* owe you five bucks,' I said. 'If you rough me up, I'll yell like hell. I'll wake up everybody in the hotel. The police and all.' My voice was shaking like a bastard.

'Go ahead. Yell your goddam head off. Fine,' old Maurice said. 'Want your parents to know you spent the night with a whore? High-class kid like you?' He was pretty sharp, in his crumby way. He really was.

'Leave me alone. If you'd *said* ten, it'd be different. But you distinctly –'

'Are ya gonna let us have it?' He had me right up against the damn door. He was almost standing on top of me, his crumby old hairy stomach and all.

'Leave me alone. Get the hell out of my room,' I said. I still had my arms folded and all. God, what a jerk I was.

Then Sunny said something for the first time. 'Hey, Maurice. Want me to get his wallet?' she said. 'It's right on the wutchamacallit.'

'Yeah, get it.'

'Leave my wallet alone!'

'I awreddy got it,' Sunny said. She waved five bucks at me. 'See? All I'm takin' is the five you owe me. I'm no crook.'

All of a sudden I started to cry. I'd give anything if I hadn't, but I did. 'No, you're no crooks,' I said. 'You're just stealing five –'

'Shut up,' old Maurice said, and gave me a shove.

'Leave him alone, hey,' Sunny said. 'C'mon, hey. We got the dough he owes us. Let's go. C'mon, hey.'

'I'm comin',' old Maurice said. But he didn't.

'I mean it, Maurice, hey. Leave him alone.'

'Who's hurtin' anybody?' he said, innocent as hell. Then what he did, he snapped his finger very hard on my pajamas. I won't tell you *where* he snapped it, but it hurt like hell. I told him he was a goddam dirty moron. 'What's that?' he said. He put his hand behind his ear, like a deaf guy. 'What's that? What am I?'

I was still sort of crying. I was so damn mad and nervous and all. 'You're a dirty moron,' I said. 'You're a stupid chiseling moron, and in about two years you'll be one of those scraggy guys that come up to you on the street and ask for a dime for coffee. You'll have snot all over your dirty filthy overcoat, and you'll be –'

Then he smacked me. I didn't even try to get out of the way or duck or anything. All I felt was this terrific punch in my stomach.

I wasn't knocked out or anything, though, because I remember looking up from the floor and seeing them both go out the door and shut it. Then I stayed on the floor a fairly long time, sort of the way I did with Stradlater. Only, this time I thought I was dying. I really did. I thought I was drowning or something. The trouble was, I could hardly breathe. When I did finally get up, I had to walk to the bathroom all doubled up and holding onto my stomach and all.

But I'm crazy. I swear to God I am. About halfway to the bathroom, I sort of started pretending I had a bullet in my guts. Old Maurice had plugged me. Now I was on the way to the bathroom to get a good shot of bourbon or something to steady my nerves and help me *really* go into action. I pictured myself coming out of the goddam bathroom, dressed and all, with my automatic in my pocket, and staggering around a little bit. Then

I'd walk downstairs, instead of using the elevator. I'd hold onto the banister and all, with this blood trickling out of the side of my mouth a little at a time. What I'd do, I'd walk down a few floors – holding onto my guts, blood leaking all over the place – and then I'd ring the elevator bell. As soon as old Maurice opened the doors, he'd see me with the automatic in my hand and he'd start screaming at me, in this very high-pitched, yellow-belly voice, to leave him alone. But I'd plug him anyway. Six shots right through his fat hairy belly. Then I'd throw my automatic down the elevator shaft – after I'd wiped off all the finger prints and all. Then I'd crawl back to my room and call up Jane and have her come over and bandage up my guts. I pictured her holding a cigarette for me to smoke while I was bleeding and all.

The goddam movies. They can ruin you. I'm not kidding.

I stayed in the bathroom for about an hour, taking a bath and all. Then I got back in bed. It took me quite a while to get to sleep – I wasn't even tired – but finally I did. What I really felt like, though, was committing suicide. I felt like jumping out the window. I probably would've done it, too, if I'd been sure somebody'd cover me up as soon as I landed. I didn't want a bunch of stupid rubbernecks looking at me when I was all gory.

15

I didn't sleep too long, because I think it was only around ten o'clock when I woke up. I felt pretty hungry as soon as I had a cigarette. The last time I'd eaten was those two hamburgers I had with Brossard and Ackley when we went in to Agerstown to the movies. That was a long time ago. It seemed like fifty years ago. The phone was right next to me, and I started to call down and have them send up some breakfast, but I was sort of afraid they might send it up with old Maurice. If you think I was dying to see him again, you're crazy. So I just laid around in bed for a while and smoked another cigarette. I thought of giving old Jane a buzz, to see if she was home yet and all, but I wasn't in the mood.

What I did do, I gave old Sally Hayes a buzz. She went to Mary A. Woodruff, and I knew she was home because I'd had this letter from her a couple of weeks ago. I wasn't too crazy about her, but I'd known her for years. I used to think she was quite intelligent, in my stupidity. The reason I did was because she knew quite a lot about the theater and plays and literature and all that stuff. If somebody knows quite a lot about those things, it takes you quite a while to find out whether they're really stupid or not. It took me *years* to find it out, in old Sally's case. I think I'd have found it out a lot sooner if we hadn't necked so damn much. My big trouble is, I always sort of think whoever I'm necking is a pretty intelligent person. It hasn't got a goddam thing to do with it, but I keep thinking it anyway.

Anyway, I gave her a buzz. First the maid answered. Then her father. Then she got on. 'Sally?' I said.

'Yes – who is this?' she said. She was quite a little phony. I'd already told her father who it was.

'Holden Caulfield. How are ya?'

'Holden! I'm fine! How are you?'

'Swell. Listen. How are ya, anyway? I mean how's school?'

'Fine,' she said. 'I mean – you know.'

'Swell. Well, listen. I was wondering if you were busy today. It's Sunday, but there's always one or two matinees going on Sunday. Benefits and that stuff. Would you care to go?'

'I'd love to. Grand.'

Grand. If there's one word I hate, it's grand. It's so phony. For a second, I was tempted to tell her to forget about the matinee. But we chewed the fat for a while. That is, she chewed it. You couldn't get a word in edgewise. First she told me about some Harvard guy – it probably was a freshman, but she didn't say, naturally – that was rushing hell out of her. Calling her up *night and day*. Night and day – that killed me. Then she told me about some other guy, some West Point cadet, that was cutting his throat over her too. Big deal. I told her to meet me under the clock at the Biltmore at two o'clock, and not to be late, because the show probably started at two-thirty. She was always late. Then I hung up. She gave me a pain in the ass, but she was very good-looking.

After I made the date with old Sally, I got out of bed and got dressed and packed my bag. I took a look out the window before I left the room, though, to see how all the perverts were doing, but they all had their shades down. They were the height of modesty in the morning. Then I went down in the elevator and checked out. I didn't see old Maurice around anywhere. I didn't break my neck looking for him, naturally, the bastard.

I got a cab outside the hotel, but I didn't have the faintest damn idea where I was going. I had no place to go. It was only Sunday, and I couldn't go home till Wednesday – or Tuesday the *soon*est. And I certainly didn't feel like going to another hotel and getting my brains beat out. So what I did, I told the driver to take me to Grand Central Station. It was right near the Biltmore, where I was meeting Sally later, and I figured what I'd do, I'd check my bags in one of those strong boxes that they give you a key to, then get some breakfast. I was sort of hungry. While I was in the cab, I took out my wallet and sort of counted my money. I don't remember exactly what I had left, but it was no fortune or anything. I'd spent a king's ransom in about two lousy weeks. I really had. I'm a goddam spendthrift at heart. What I don't spend, I lose. Half the time I sort of even forget to pick up my change, at restaurants and night clubs and all. It drives my parents crazy. You can't blame them. My father's quite wealthy, though. I don't know how much he makes – he's never discussed that stuff with me – but I imagine quite a lot. He's a corporation lawyer. Those boys really haul it in. Another reason I know he's quite well off, he's always investing money in shows on Broadway. They always flop, though, and it drives my mother crazy when he does it. She hasn't felt too healthy since my brother Allie died. She's very nervous. That's another reason why I hated like hell for her to know I got the ax again.

After I put my bags in one of those strong boxes at the station, I went into this little sandwich bar and had breakfast. I had quite a large breakfast, for me – orange juice, bacon and eggs, toast and coffee. Usually I just drink some orange juice. I'm a very light eater. I really am. That's why I'm so damn skinny. I was supposed to be on this diet where you eat a lot of starches and crap, to gain weight and all, but I didn't ever do it. When

I'm out somewhere, I generally just eat a Swiss cheese sandwich and a malted milk. It isn't much, but you get quite a lot of vitamins in the malted milk. H. V. Caulfield. Holden Vitamin Caulfield.

While I was eating my eggs, these two nuns with suitcases and all – I guessed they were moving to another convent or something and were waiting for a train – came in and sat down next to me at the counter. They didn't seem to know what the hell to do with their suitcases, so I gave them a hand. They were these very inexpensive-looking suitcases – the ones that aren't genuine leather or anything. It isn't important, I know, but I hate it when somebody has cheap suitcases. It sounds terrible to say it, but I can even get to hate somebody, just *look*ing at them, if they have cheap suitcases with them. Something happened once. For a while when I was at Elkton Hills, I roomed with this boy, Dick Slagle, that had these very inexpensive suitcases. He used to keep them under the bed, instead of on the rack, so that nobody'd see them standing next to mine. It depressed holy hell out of me, and I kept wanting to throw mine out or something, or even *trade* with him. Mine came from Mark Cross, and they were genuine cowhide and all that crap, and I guess they cost quite a pretty penny. But it was a funny thing. Here's what happened. What I did, I finally put *my* suitcases under *my* bed, instead of on the rack, so that old Slagle wouldn't get a goddam inferiority complex about it. But here's what he did. The day after I put mine under my bed, he took them out and put them back on the rack. The reason he did it, it took me a while to find out, was because he wanted people to think my bags were his. He really did. He was a very funny guy, that way. He was always saying snotty things about them, my suitcases, for instance. He kept saying they were too new and bourgeois. That was his favorite goddam word. He read it somewhere or heard it somewhere. Everything I had was bourgeois as hell. Even my fountain pen was bourgeois. He borrowed it off me all the time, but it was bourgeois anyway. We only roomed together about two months. Then we both asked to be moved. And the funny thing was, I sort of missed him after we moved, because he had a helluva good sense of humor and we had a lot of fun sometimes. I wouldn't be surprised if he missed me, too. At first he only used to be kidding when he called my stuff bourgeois, and I didn't give a damn – it *was* sort of funny, in fact. Then, after a while, you could tell he wasn't kidding any more. The thing is, it's really hard to be roommates with people if your suitcases are much better than theirs – if yours are really *good* ones and theirs aren't. You think if they're intelligent and all, the other person, and have a good sense of humor, that they don't give a damn whose suitcases are better, but they do. They really do. It's one of the reasons why I roomed with a stupid bastard like Stradlater. At least his suitcases were as good as mine.

Anyway, these two nuns were sitting next to me, and we sort of struck up a conversation. The one right next to me had one of those straw baskets that you see nuns and Salvation Army babes collecting dough with around Christmas time. You see them standing on corners, especially on Fifth Avenue, in front of the big department stores and all. Anyway, the one next to me dropped hers on the floor and I reached down and picked it up for her. I asked her if she was out collecting money for charity and all. She said no. She said she couldn't get it in her suitcase when she was packing it and she was just carrying it. She had a pretty nice smile when she looked at you. She had a big nose, and she had on those glasses with sort of iron rims that aren't too attractive, but she had a helluva kind face. 'I thought if you were taking up a collection,' I told her, 'I could make a small contribution. You could keep the money for when you do take up a collection.'

'Oh, how very kind of you,' she said, and the other one, her friend, looked over at me. The other one was reading a little black book while she drank her coffee. It looked like a Bible, but it was too skinny. It was a Bible-type book, though. All the two of them were eating for breakfast was toast and coffee. That depressed me. I hate it if I'm eating bacon and eggs or something and somebody else is only eating toast and coffee.

They let me give them ten bucks as a contribution. They kept asking me if I was sure I could afford it and all. I told them I had quite a bit of money with me, but they didn't seem to believe me. They took it, though, finally. The both of them kept thanking me so much it was embarrassing. I swung the conversation around to general topics and asked them where they were going. They said they were schoolteachers and that they'd just come from Chicago and that they were going to start teaching at some convent on 168th Street or 186th Street or one of those streets way the hell uptown. The one next to me, with the iron glasses, said she taught English and her friend taught history and American government. Then I started wondering like a bastard what the one sitting next to me, that taught English, thought about, being a nun and all, when she read certain books for English. Books not necessarily with a lot of sexy stuff in them, but books with lovers and all in them. Take old Eustacia Vye, in *The Return of the Native* by Thomas Hardy. She wasn't too sexy or anything, but even so you can't help wondering what a nun maybe thinks about when she reads about old Eustacia. I didn't say anything, though, naturally. All I said was English was my best subject.

'Oh, really? Oh, I'm so glad!' the one with the glasses, that taught English, said. 'What have you read this year? I'd be very interested to know.' She was really nice.

'Well, most of the time we were on the Anglo-Saxons. Beowulf, and old Grendel, and Lord Randal My Son, and all those things. But we had to read outside books for extra credit once in a while. I read *The Return of the Native* by Thomas Hardy, and *Romeo and Juliet* and *Julius* –'

'Oh, *Romeo and Juliet*! Lovely! Didn't you just love it?' She certainly didn't sound much like a nun.

'Yes. I did. I liked it a lot. There were a few things I didn't like about it, but it was quite moving, on the whole.'

'What didn't you like about it? Can you remember?'

To tell you the truth, it was sort of embarrassing, in a way, to be talking about *Romeo and Juliet* with her. I mean that play gets pretty sexy in some parts, and she was a nun and all, but she *asked* me, so I discussed it with her for a while. 'Well, I'm not too crazy about Romeo and Juliet,' I said. 'I mean I like them, but – I don't know. They get pretty annoying sometimes. I mean I felt much sorrier when old Mercutio got killed than when Romeo and Juliet did. The thing is, I never liked Romeo too much after Mercutio gets stabbed by that other man – Juliet's cousin – what's his name?'

'Tybalt.'

'That's right. Tybalt,' I said – I always forget that guy's name. 'It was Romeo's fault. I mean I liked him the best in the play, old Mercutio. I don't know. All those Montagues and Capulets, they're all right – especially Juliet – but Mercutio, he was – it's hard to explain. He was very smart and entertaining and all. The thing is, it drives me crazy if somebody gets killed – especially somebody very smart and entertaining and all – and it's somebody else's fault. Romeo and Juliet, at least it was their own fault.'

'What school do you go to?' she asked me. She probably wanted to get off the subject of Romeo and Juliet.

I told her Pencey, and she'd heard of it. She said it was a very good school. I let it pass, though. Then the other one, the one that taught history and government, said they'd better be running along. I took their check off them, but they wouldn't let me pay it. The one with the glasses made me give it back to her.

'You've been more than generous,' she said. 'You're a very sweet boy.' She certainly was nice. She reminded me a little bit of old Ernest Morrow's mother, the one I met on the train. When she smiled, mostly. 'We've enjoyed talking to you *so* much,' she said.

I said I'd enjoyed talking to them a lot, too. I meant it, too. I'd have enjoyed it even more though, I think, if I hadn't been sort of afraid, the whole time I was talking to them, that they'd all of a sudden try to find out if I was a Catholic. Catholics are always trying to find out if you're a Catholic. It happens to me a lot, I know, partly because my last name is Irish, and most people of Irish descent are Catholics. As a matter of fact, my father *was* a Catholic once. He quit, though, when he married my mother. But Catholics are always trying to find out if you're a Catholic even if they don't know your last name. I knew this one Catholic boy, Louis Shaney, when I was at the Whooton School. He was the first boy I ever met there. He and I were sitting in the first two chairs outside the goddam infirmary, the day school opened, waiting for our physicals, and we sort of struck up this conversation about tennis. He was quite interested in tennis, and so was I. He told me he went to the Nationals at Forest Hills every summer, and I told him I did too, and then we talked about certain hot-shot tennis players for quite a while. He knew quite a lot about tennis, for a kid his age. He really did. Then, after a while, right in the middle of the goddam conversation, he asked me, 'Did you happen to notice where the Catholic church is in town, by any chance?' The thing was, you could tell by the way he asked me that he was trying to find out if I was a Catholic. He really was. Not that he was prejudiced or anything, but he just wanted to know. He was enjoying the conversation about tennis and all, but you could tell he would've enjoyed it *more* if I was a Catholic and all. That kind of stuff drives me crazy. I'm not saying it ruined our conversation or anything – it didn't – but it sure as hell didn't do it any good. That's why I was glad those two nuns didn't ask me if I was a Catholic. It wouldn't have *spoiled* the conversation if they had, but it would've been different, probably. I'm not saying I *blame* Catholics. I don't. I'd be the same way, probably, if I was a Catholic. It's just like those suitcases I was telling you about, in a way. All I'm saying is that it's no good for a nice conversation. That's all I'm saying.

When they got up to go, the two nuns, I did something very stupid and embarrassing. I was smoking a cigarette, and when I stood up to say good-by to them, by mistake I blew some smoke in their face. I didn't mean to, but I did it. I apologized like a madman, and they were very polite and nice about it, but it was very embarrassing anyway.

After they left, I started getting sorry that I'd only given them ten bucks for their collection. But the thing was, I'd made that date to go to a matinee with old Sally Hayes, and I needed to keep some dough for the tickets and stuff. I was sorry anyway, though. Goddam money. It always ends up making you blue as hell.

16

After I had my breakfast, it was only around noon, and I wasn't meeting old Sally till two o'clock, so I started taking this long walk. I couldn't stop thinking about those two nuns. I kept thinking about that beat-up old straw basket they went around collecting money with when they weren't teaching school. I kept trying to picture my mother or somebody, or my aunt, or Sally Hayes's crazy mother, standing outside some department store and collecting dough for poor people in a beat-up old straw basket. It was hard to picture. Not so much my mother, but those other two. My aunt's pretty charitable – she does a lot of Red Cross work and all – but she's very well-dressed and all, and when she does anything charitable she's always very well-dressed and has lipstick on and all that crap. I couldn't picture her doing anything for charity if she had to wear black clothes and no lipstick while she was doing it. And old Sally Hayes's mother. Jesus Christ. The only way *she* could go around with a basket collecting dough would be if everybody kissed her ass for her when they made a contribution. If they just dropped their dough in her basket, then walked away without saying anything to her, ignoring her and all, she'd quit in about an hour. She'd get bored. She'd hand in her basket and then go someplace swanky for lunch. That's what I liked about those nuns. You could tell, for one thing, that they never went anywhere swanky for lunch. It made me so damn sad when I thought about it, their never going anywhere swanky for lunch or anything. I knew it wasn't too important, but it made me sad anyway.

I started walking over toward Broadway, just for the hell of it, because I hadn't been over there in years. Besides, I wanted to find a record store that was open on Sunday. There was this record I wanted to get for Phoebe, called 'Little Shirley Beans.' It was a very hard record to get. It was about a little kid that wouldn't go out of the house because two of her front teeth were out and she was ashamed to. I heard it at Pencey. A boy that lived on the next floor had it, and I tried to buy it off him because I knew it would knock old Phoebe out, but he wouldn't sell it. It was a very old, terrific record that this colored girl singer, Estelle Fletcher, made about twenty years ago. She sings it very Dixieland and whorehouse, and it doesn't sound at all mushy. If a white girl was singing it, she'd make it sound *cute* as hell, but old Estelle Fletcher knew what the hell she was doing, and it was one of the best records I ever heard. I figured I'd buy it in some store that was open on Sunday and then I'd take it up to the park with me. It was Sunday and Phoebe goes roller-skating in the park on Sundays quite frequently. I knew where she hung out mostly.

It wasn't as cold as it was the day before, but the sun still wasn't out, and it wasn't too nice for walking. But there was one nice thing. This family that you could tell just came out of some church were walking right in front of me – a father, a mother, and a little kid about six years old. They looked sort of poor. The father had on one of those pearl-gray hats that poor guys wear a lot when they want to look sharp. He and his wife were just walking along, talking, not paying any attention to their kid. The kid was swell. He was walking in the street, instead of on the sidewalk, but right next to the curb. He was making out like he was walking a very straight line, the way kids do, and the whole time he kept singing and humming. I got up closer so I could hear what he was singing. He was singing that song, 'If a body catch a body coming through the rye.' He had a pretty little voice, too. He was just singing for the hell of it, you could tell. The cars zoomed by, brakes screeched all over the place, his parents paid no attention to him, and he kept on walking next to the curb and singing 'If a body catch a body coming through the rye.' It made me feel better. It made me feel not so depressed any more.

Broadway was mobbed and messy. It was Sunday, and only about twelve o'clock, but it was mobbed anyway. Everybody was on their way to the movies – the Paramount or the Astor or the Strand or the Capitol or one of those crazy places. Everybody was all dressed up, because it was Sunday, and that made it worse. But the worst part was that you could tell they all *wanted* to go to the movies. I couldn't stand looking at them. I can understand somebody going to the movies because there's nothing else to do, but when somebody really *wants* to go, and even walks fast so as to get there quicker, then it depresses hell out of me. Especially if I see millions of people standing in one of those long, terrible lines, all the way down the block, waiting with this terrific patience for seats and all. Boy, I couldn't get off that goddam Broadway fast enough. I was lucky. The first record store I went into had a copy of 'Little Shirley Beans.' They charged me five bucks for it, because it was so hard to get, but I didn't care. Boy, it made me so happy all of a sudden. I could hardly wait to get to the park to see if old Phoebe was around so that I could give it to her.

When I came out of the record store, I passed this drugstore, and I went in. I figured maybe I'd give old Jane a buzz and see if she was home for vacation yet. So I went in a phone booth and called her up. The only trouble was, her mother answered the phone, so I had to hang up. I didn't feel like getting involved in a long conversation and all with her. I'm not crazy about talking to girls' mothers on the phone anyway. I should've at *least* asked her if Jane was home yet, though. It wouldn't have killed me. But I didn't feel like it. You really have to be in the mood for that stuff.

I still had to get those damn theater tickets, so I bought a paper and looked up to see what shows were playing. On account of it was Sunday, there were only about three shows playing. So what I did was, I went over and bought two orchestra seats for *I Know My Love*. It was a benefit performance or something. I didn't much want to see it, but I knew old Sally, the queen of the phonies, would start drooling all over the place when I told her I had tickets for that, because the Lunts were in it and all. She liked shows that are supposed to be very sophisticated and dry and all, with the Lunts and all. I don't. I don't like any shows very much, if you want to know the truth. They're not as bad as movies, but they're certainly nothing to rave about. In the first place, I hate actors. They never act like people. They just think they do. Some of the good ones do, in a very slight way, but not in a way that's fun to watch. And if any actor's really good, you can always tell he *knows* he's good, and that spoils it. You take Sir Laurence Olivier, for example. I saw him in *Hamlet*. D.B. took Phoebe and I to see it last year. He treated us to lunch first, and then he took us. He'd already seen it, and the way he talked about it at lunch, I was anxious as hell to see it, too. But I didn't enjoy it much. I just don't see what's so marvelous about Sir Laurence Olivier, that's all. He has a terrific voice, and he's a helluva handsome guy, and he's very nice to watch when he's walking or dueling or something, but he wasn't at all the way D.B. said Hamlet was. He was too much like a goddam general, instead of a sad, screwed-up type guy. The best part in the whole picture was when old Ophelia's brother – the one that gets in the duel with Hamlet at the very end – was going away and his father was giving him a lot of advice. While the father kept giving him a lot of advice, old Ophelia was sort of horsing around with her brother, taking his dagger out of the holster, and teasing him and all while he was trying to look interested in the bull his father was shooting. That was nice. I got a big bang out of that. But you don't see that kind of stuff much. The only thing old Phoebe liked was when Hamlet patted this dog on the head. She thought that was funny and nice, and it was. What I'll have to do is, I'll have to read that play. The trouble with me is, I always have to read that stuff by myself. If an actor acts it out, I hardly listen. I keep worrying about whether he's going to do something phony every minute.

After I got the tickets to the Lunts' show, I took a cab up to the park. I should've taken a subway or something, because I was getting slightly low on dough, but I wanted to get off that damn Broadway as fast as I could.

It was lousy in the park. It wasn't too cold, but the sun still wasn't out, and there didn't look like there was anything in the park except dog crap and globs of spit and cigar butts from old men, and the benches all looked like they'd be wet if you sat down on them. It made you depressed, and every once in a while, for no reason, you got goose flesh while you walked. It didn't seem at all like Christmas was coming soon. It didn't seem like *any*thing was coming. But I kept walking over to the Mall anyway, because that's where Phoebe usually goes when she's in the park. She likes to skate near the bandstand. It's funny. That's the same place I used to like to skate when I was a kid.

When I got there, though, I didn't see her around anywhere. There were a few kids around, skating and all, and two boys were playing Flys Up with a soft ball, but no Phoebe. I saw one kid about her age, though, sitting on a bench all by herself, tightening her skate. I thought maybe she might know Phoebe and could tell me where she was or something, so I went over and sat down next to her and asked her, 'Do you know Phoebe Caulfield, by any chance?'

'Who?' she said. All she had on was jeans and about twenty sweaters. You could tell her mother made them for her, because they were lumpy as hell.

'Phoebe Caulfield. She lives on Seventy-first Street. She's in the fourth grade, over at –'

'You know Phoebe?'

'Yeah, I'm her brother. You know where she is?'

'She's in Miss Callon's class, isn't she?' the kid said.

'I don't know. Yes, I think she is.'

'She's prob'ly in the museum, then. *We* went last Saturday,' the kid said.

'Which museum?' I asked her.

She shrugged her shoulders, sort of. 'I don't know,' she said. 'The mu*se*um.'

'I know, but the one where the pictures are, or the one where the Indians are?'

'The one where the Indians.'

'Thanks a lot,' I said. I got up and started to go, but then I suddenly remembered it was Sunday. 'This is *Sun*day,' I told the kid.

She looked up at me. 'Oh. Then she isn't.'

She was having a helluva time tightening her skate. She didn't have any gloves on or anything and her hands were all red and cold. I gave her a hand with it. Boy, I hadn't had a skate key in my hand for years. It didn't feel funny, though. You could put a skate key in my hand fifty years from now, in pitch dark, and I'd still know what it is. She thanked me and all when I had it tightened for her. She was a very nice, polite little kid. God, I love it when a kid's nice and polite when you tighten their skate for them or something. Most kids are. They really are. I asked her if she'd care to have a hot chocolate or something with me, but she said no, thank you. She said she had to meet her friend. Kids always have to meet their friend. That kills me.

Even though it was Sunday and Phoebe wouldn't be there with her class or anything, and even though it was so damp and lousy out, I walked all the way through the park over to the Museum of Natural History. I knew that was the museum the kid with the skate key meant. I knew that whole museum routine like a book. Phoebe went to the same school I went to when I was a kid, and we used to go there all the time. We had this teacher, Miss Aigletinger, that took us there damn near every Saturday. Sometimes we looked at the animals and sometimes we looked at the stuff the Indians had made in ancient times. Pottery and straw baskets and all stuff like that. I get very happy when I think about it. Even now. I remember after we looked at all the Indian stuff, usually we went to see some movie in this big auditorium. Columbus. They were always showing Columbus discovering America, having one helluva time getting old Ferdinand and Isabella to lend him the dough to buy ships with, and then the sailors mutinying on him and all. Nobody gave too much of a damn about old Columbus, but you always had a lot of candy and gum and stuff with you, and the inside of that auditorium had such a nice smell. It always smelled like it was raining outside, even if it wasn't, and you were in the only nice, dry, cosy place in the world. I loved that damn museum. I remember you had to go through the Indian Room to get to the auditorium. It was a long, long room, and you were only supposed to whisper. The teacher would go first, then the class. You'd be two rows of kids, and you'd have a partner. Most of the time my partner was this girl named Gertrude Levine. She always wanted to hold your hand, and her hand was always sticky or sweaty or something. The floor was all stone, and if you had some marbles in your hand and you dropped them, they bounced like madmen all over the floor and made a helluva racket, and the teacher would hold up the class and go back and see what the hell was going on. She never got sore, though, Miss Aigletinger. Then you'd pass by this long, long Indian war canoe, about as long as three goddam Cadillacs in a row, with about twenty Indians in it, some of them paddling, some of them just standing around looking tough, and they all had war paint all over their faces. There was one very spooky guy in the back of the canoe, with a mask on. He was the witch doctor. He gave me the creeps, but I liked him anyway. Another thing, if you touched one of the paddles or anything while you were passing, one of the guards would say to you, 'Don't touch anything, children,' but he always said it in a nice voice, not like a goddam cop or anything. Then you'd pass by this big glass case, with Indians inside it rubbing sticks together to make a fire, and a squaw weaving a blanket. The squaw that was weaving the blanket was sort of bending over, and you could see her bosom and all. We all used to sneak a good look at it, even the girls, because they were only little kids and they didn't have any more bosom than *we* did. Then, just before you went inside the auditorium, right near the doors, you passed this Eskimo. He was sitting over a hole in this icy lake, and he was fishing through it. He had about two fish right next to the hole, that he'd already caught. Boy, that museum was full of glass cases. There were even more upstairs, with deer inside them drinking at water holes, and birds flying south for the winter. The birds nearest you were all stuffed and hung up on wires, and the ones in back were just painted on the wall, but they all looked like they were really flying south, and if you bent your head down and sort of looked at them upside down, they looked in an even bigger hurry to fly south. The best thing, though, in that museum was that everything always stayed right where it was. Nobody'd move. You could go there a hundred thousand times, and that Eskimo would still be just finished catching those two fish, the birds would still be on their way south, the deers would still be drinking out of that water hole, with their pretty antlers and their pretty, skinny legs, and that squaw with the naked bosom would still be weaving that same blanket. Nobody'd be different. The only thing that would be different would be *you*. Not that you'd be so much older or anything. It wouldn't be that, exactly. You'd just be different, that's all. You'd have an overcoat on this time. Or the kid that was your partner in line the last time had got scarlet fever and you'd have a new partner. Or you'd have a substitute taking the class, instead of Miss Aigletinger. Or you'd heard your mother and father having a terrific fight in the bathroom. Or you'd just passed by one of those puddles in the street with gasoline rainbows in them. I mean you'd be *dif*ferent in some way – I can't explain what I mean. And even if I could, I'm not sure I'd feel like it.

I took my old hunting hat out of my pocket while I walked, and put it on. I knew I wouldn't meet anybody that knew me, and it was pretty damp out. I kept walking and walking, and I kept thinking about old Phoebe going to that museum on Saturdays the way I used to. I thought how she'd see the same stuff I used to see, and how *she'd* be different every time she saw it. It didn't exactly depress me to think about it, but it didn't make me feel gay as hell, either. Certain things they should stay the way they are. You ought to be able to stick them in one of those big glass cases and just leave them alone. I know that's impossible, but it's too bad anyway. Anyway, I kept thinking about all that while I walked.

I passed by this playground and stopped and watched a couple of very tiny kids on a seesaw. One of them was sort of fat, and I put my hand on the skinny kid's end, to sort of even up the weight, but you could tell they didn't want me around, so I let them alone.

Then a funny thing happened. When I got to the museum, all of a sudden I wouldn't have gone inside for a million bucks. It just didn't appeal to me – and here I'd walked through the whole goddam park and looked forward to it and all. If Phoebe'd been there, I probably would have, but she wasn't. So all I did, in front of the museum, was get a cab and go down to the Biltmore. I didn't feel much like going. I'd made that damn date with Sally, though.

17

I was way early when I got there, so I just sat down on one of those leather couches right near the clock in the lobby and watched the girls. A lot of schools were home for vacation already, and there were about a million girls sitting and standing around waiting for their dates to show up. Girls with their legs crossed, girls with their legs not crossed, girls with terrific legs, girls with lousy legs, girls that looked like swell girls, girls that looked like they'd be bitches if you knew them. It was really nice, sightseeing, if you know what I mean. In a way, it was sort of depressing, too, because you kept wondering what the hell would *happen* to all of them. When they got out of school and college, I mean. You figured most of them would probably marry dopey guys. Guys that always talk about how many miles they get to a gallon in their goddam cars. Guys that get sore and childish as hell if you beat them at golf, or even just some stupid game like ping-pong. Guys that are very mean. Guys that never read books. Guys that are very boring – But I have to be careful about that. I mean about calling certain guys bores. I don't understand boring guys. I really don't. When I was at Elkton Hills, I roomed for about two months with this boy, Harris Macklin. He was very intelligent and all, but he was one of the biggest bores I ever met. He had one of these very raspy voices, and he never stopped talking, practically. He never stopped talking, and what was awful was, he never said anything you wanted to hear in the first place. But he could do one thing.

The sonuvabitch could whistle better than anybody I ever heard. He'd be making his bed, or hanging up stuff in the closet – he was always hanging up stuff in the closet – it drove me crazy – and he'd be whistling while he did it, if he wasn't talking in this raspy voice. He could even whistle classical stuff, but most of the time he just whistled jazz. He could take something very jazzy, like 'Tin Roof Blues,' and whistle it so nice and easy – right while he was hanging stuff up in the closet – that it could kill you. Naturally, I never *told* him I thought he was a terrific whistler. I mean you don't just go up to somebody and say, 'You're a terrific whistler.' But I roomed with him for about two whole months, even though he bored me till I was half crazy, just because he was such a terrific whistler, the best I ever heard. So I don't know about bores. Maybe you shouldn't feel too sorry if you see some swell girl getting married to them. They don't hurt anybody, most of them, and maybe they're secretly all terrific whistlers or something. Who the hell knows? Not me.

Finally, old Sally started coming up the stairs, and I started down to meet her. She looked terrific. She really did. She had on this black coat and sort of a black beret. She hardly ever wore a hat, but that beret looked nice. The funny part is, I felt like marrying her the minute I saw her. I'm crazy. I didn't even *like* her much, and yet all of a sudden I felt like I was in love with her and wanted to marry her. I swear to God I'm crazy. I admit it.

'Holden!' she said. 'It's marvelous to see you! It's been *ages*.' She had one of these very loud, embarrassing voices when you met her somewhere. She got away with it because she was so damn good-looking, but it always gave me a pain in the ass.

'Swell to see *you*,' I said. I meant it, too. 'How are ya, anyway?'

'Absolutely marvelous. Am I late?'

I told her no, but she was around ten minutes late, as a matter of fact. I didn't give a damn, though. All that crap they have in cartoons in the *Saturday Evening Post* and all, showing guys on street corners looking sore as hell because their dates are late – that's bunk. If a girl looks swell when she meets you, who gives a damn if she's late? Nobody. 'We better hurry,' I said. 'The show starts at two-forty.' We started going down the stairs to where the taxis are.

'What are we going to see?' she said.

'I don't know. The Lunts. It's all I could get tickets for.'

'The Lunts! Oh, marvelous!'

I told you she'd go mad when she heard it was for the Lunts.

We horsed around a little bit in the cab on the way over to the theater. At first she didn't want to, because she had her lipstick on and all, but I was being seductive as hell and she didn't have any alternative. Twice, when the goddam cab stopped short in traffic, I damn near fell off the seat. Those damn drivers never even look where they're going, I swear they don't. Then, just to show you how crazy I am, when we were coming out of this big clinch, I told her I loved her and all. It was a lie, of course, but the thing is, I *meant* it when I said it. I'm crazy. I swear to God I am.

'Oh, darling, I love you too,' she said. Then, right in the same damn breath, she said, 'Promise me you'll let your hair grow. Crew cuts are getting corny. And your hair's so lovely.'

Lovely my ass.

The show wasn't as bad as some I've seen. It was on the crappy side, though. It was about five hundred thousand years in the life of this one old couple. It starts out when they're young and all, and the girl's parents don't want her to marry the boy, but she marries him anyway. Then they keep getting older and older. The husband goes to war, and the wife has this brother that's a drunkard. I couldn't get very interested. I mean I didn't care too much when anybody in the family died or anything. They were all just a bunch of actors. The husband and wife were a pretty nice old couple – very witty and all – but I couldn't get too interested in them. For one thing, they kept drinking tea or some goddam thing all through the play. Every time you saw them, some butler was shoving some tea in front of them, or the wife was pouring it for somebody. And everybody kept coming *in* and going *out* all the time – you got dizzy watching people sit down and stand up. Alfred Lunt and Lynn Fontanne were the old couple, and they were very good, but I didn't like them much. They were different, though, I'll say that. They didn't act like people and they didn't act like actors. It's hard to explain. They acted more like they knew they were celebrities and all. I mean they were good, but they were *too* good. When one of them got finished making a speech, the other one said something very fast right after it. It was supposed to be like people really talking and interrupting each other and all. The trouble was, it was *too* much like people talking and interrupting each other. They acted a little bit the way old Ernie, down in the Village, plays the piano. If you do something *too* good, then, after a while, if you don't watch it, you start showing off. And then you're not as good any more. But anyway, they were the only ones in the show – the Lunts, I mean – that looked like they had any real brains. I have to admit it.

At the end of the first act we went out with all the other jerks for a cigarette. What a deal that was. You never saw so many phonies in all your life, everybody smoking their ears off and talking about the play so that everybody could hear and know how sharp they were. Some dopey movie actor was standing near us, having a cigarette. I don't know his name, but he always plays the part of a guy in a war movie that gets yellow before it's time to go over the top. He was with some gorgeous blonde, and the two of them were trying to be very blasé and all, like as if he didn't even know people were looking at him. Modest as hell. I got a big bang out of it. Old Sally didn't talk much, except to rave about the Lunts, because she was busy rubbering and being charming. Then all of a sudden, she saw some jerk she knew on the other side of the lobby. Some guy in one of those very dark gray flannel suits and one of those checkered vests. Strictly Ivy League. Big deal. He was standing next to the wall, smoking himself to death and looking bored as hell. Old Sally kept saying, 'I *know* that boy from somewhere.' She always *knew* somebody, any place you took her, or thought she did. She kept saying that till I got bored as hell, and I said to her, 'Why don't you go on over and give him a big soul kiss, if you know him? He'll enjoy it.' She got sore when I said that. Finally, though, the jerk noticed her and came over and said hello. You should've seen the way they said hello. You'd have thought they hadn't seen each other in twenty years. You'd have thought they'd taken baths in the same bathtub or something when they were little kids. Old buddyroos. It was nauseating. The funny part was, they probably met each other just *once*, at some phony party. Finally, when they were all done slobbering around, old Sally introduced us. His name was George something – I don't even remember – and he went to Andover. Big, big deal. You should've seen him when old Sally asked him how he liked the play. He was the kind of a phony that have to give themselves *room* when they answer somebody's question. He stepped back, and stepped right on the lady's foot behind him. He probably broke every toe in her body. He said the play *itself* was no masterpiece, but that the Lunts, of course, were absolute angels. Angels. For Chrissake. *Angels*. That killed me. Then he and old Sally started talking about a lot of people they both knew. It was the phoniest conversation you ever heard in your life. They both kept thinking of places as fast as they could, then they'd think of somebody that lived there and mention their name. I was all set to puke when it was time to go sit down again. I really was. And then, when the next act was over, they *continued* their goddam boring conversation. They kept thinking of more places and more names of people that lived there. The worst part was, the jerk had one of those very phony, Ivy League voices, one of those very tired, snobby voices. He sounded just like a girl. He didn't *hes*itate to horn in on my date, the bastard. I even thought for a minute that he was going to get in the goddam cab with us when the show was over, because he walked about two blocks with us, but he had to meet a bunch of phonies for cocktails, he said. I could see them all sitting around in some bar, with their goddam checkered vests, criticizing shows and books and women in those tired, snobby voices. They kill me, those guys.

I sort of hated old Sally by the time we got in the cab, after listening to that phony Andover bastard for about ten hours. I was all set to take her home and all – I really was – but she said, 'I have a marvelous idea!' She was always having a marvelous idea. 'Listen,' she said. 'What time do you have to be home for dinner? I mean are you in a terrible hurry or anything? Do you have to be home any special time?'

'Me? No. No special time,' I said. Truer word was never spoken, boy. 'Why?'

'Let's go ice-skating at Radio City!'

That's the kind of ideas she always had.

'Ice-skating at Radio City? You mean right now?'

'Just for an hour or so. Don't you want to? If you don't *want* to –'

'I didn't say I didn't want to,' I said. 'Sure. If you want to.'

'Do you mean it? Don't just *say* it if you don't mean it. I mean I don't *give* a darn, one way or the other.'

Not much she didn't.

'You can rent those darling little skating skirts,' old Sally said. 'Jeannette Cultz did it last week.'

That's why she was so hot to go. She wanted to see herself in one of those little skirts that just come down over their butt and all.

So we went, and after they gave us our skates, they gave Sally this little blue butt-twitcher of a dress to wear. She really did look damn good in it, though. I have to admit it. And don't think she didn't know it. She kept walking ahead of me, so that I'd see how cute her little ass looked. It did look pretty cute, too. I have to admit it.

The funny part was, though, we were the worst skaters on the whole goddam rink. I mean the *worst*. And there were some lulus, too. Old Sally's ankles kept bending in till they were practically on the ice. They not only looked stupid as hell, but they probably hurt like hell, too. I know mine did. Mine were killing me. We must've looked gorgeous. And what made it worse, there were at least a couple a hundred rubbernecks that didn't have anything better to do than stand around and watch everybody falling all over themselves.

'Do you want to get a table inside and have a drink or something?' I said to her finally.

'That's the most marvelous idea you've had all day,' she said. She was *killing* herself. It was brutal. I really felt sorry for her.

We took off our goddam skates and went inside this bar where you can get drinks and watch the skaters in just your stocking feet. As soon as we sat down, old Sally took off her gloves, and I gave her a cigarette. She wasn't looking too happy. The waiter came up, and I ordered a Coke for her – she didn't drink – and a Scotch and soda for myself, but the sonuvabitch wouldn't bring me one, so I had a Coke, too. Then I sort of started lighting matches. I do that quite a lot when I'm in a certain mood. I sort of let them burn down till I can't hold them any more, then I drop them in the ashtray. It's a nervous habit.

Then all of a sudden, out of a clear blue sky, old Sally said, 'Look. I have to know. Are you or aren't you coming over to help me trim the tree Christmas Eve? I have to know.' She was still being snotty on account of her ankles when she was skating.

'I wrote you I would. You've asked me that about twenty times. Sure, I am.'

'I mean I have to know,' she said. She started looking all around the goddam room.

All of a sudden I quit lighting matches, and sort of leaned nearer to her over the table. I had quite a few topics on my mind. 'Hey, Sally,' I said.

'What?' she said. She was looking at some girl on the other side of the room.

'Did you ever get fed up?' I said. 'I mean did you ever get scared that everything was going to go lousy unless you did something? I mean do you like school, and all that stuff?'

'It's a terrific *bore*.'

'I mean do you hate it? I know it's a terrific bore, but do you *hate* it, is what I mean.'

'Well, I don't exactly *hate* it. You always have to –'

'Well, *I* hate it. Boy, do I hate it,' I said. 'But it isn't just that. It's everything. I hate living in New York and all. Taxicabs, and Madison Avenue buses, with the drivers and all always yelling at you to get out at the rear door, and being introduced to phony guys that call the Lunts angels, and going up and down in elevators when you just want to go outside, and guys fitting your pants all the time at Brooks, and people always –'

'Don't shout, please,' old Sally said. Which was very funny, because I wasn't even shouting.

'Take cars,' I said. I said it in this very quiet voice. 'Take most people, they're crazy about cars. They worry if they get a little scratch on them, and they're always talking about how many miles they get to a gallon, and if they get a brand-new car already they start thinking about trading it in for one that's even newer. I don't even like *old* cars. I mean they don't even interest me. I'd rather have a goddam horse. A horse is at least *human*, for God's sake. A horse you can at least –'

'I don't know what you're even talking about,' old Sally said. 'You jump from one –'

'You know something?' I said. 'You're probably the only reason I'm in New York right now, or anywhere. If you weren't around, I'd probably be someplace way the hell off. In the woods or some goddam place. You're the only reason I'm around, practically.'

'You're sweet,' she said. But you could tell she wanted me to change the damn subject.

'You ought to go to a boys' school sometime. Try it sometime,' I said. 'It's full of phonies, and all you do is study so that you can learn enough to be smart enough to be able to buy a goddam Cadillac some day, and you have to keep making believe you give a damn if the football team loses, and all you do is talk about girls and liquor and sex all day, and everybody sticks together in these dirty little goddam cliques. The guys that are on the basketball team stick together, the Catholics stick together, the goddam intellectuals stick together, the guys that play bridge stick together. Even the guys that belong to the goddam Book-of-the-*Month* Club stick together. If you try to have a little intelligent –'

'Now, *lis*ten,' old Sally said. 'Lots of boys get more out of school than *that*.'

'I agree! I agree they do, some of them! But that's all *I* get out of it. See? That's my point. That's exactly my goddam point,' I said. 'I don't get hardly anything out of anything. I'm in bad shape. I'm in *lousy* shape.'

'You certainly are.'

Then, all of a sudden, I got this idea.

'Look,' I said. 'Here's my idea. How would you like to get the hell out of here? Here's my idea. I know this guy down in Greenwich Village that we can borrow his cab for a couple of weeks. He used to go to the same school I did and he still owes me ten bucks. What we could do is, tomorrow morning we could drive up to Massachusetts and Vermont, and all around there, see. It's beautiful as hell up there. It really is.' I was getting excited as hell, the more I thought about it, and I sort of reached over and took old Sally's goddam hand. What a goddam *fool* I was. 'No kidding,' I said. 'I have about a hundred and eighty bucks in the bank. I can take it out when it opens in the morning, and then I could go down and get this guy's car. No kidding. We'll stay in these cabin camps and stuff like that till the dough runs out. Then, when the dough runs out, I could get a job somewhere and we could live somewhere with a brook and all and, later on, we could get married or something. I could chop all our own wood in the wintertime and all. Honest to God, we could have a terrific time! Wuddaya say? C'mon! Wuddaya say? Will you do it with me? Please!'

'You can't just *do* something like that,' old Sally said. She sounded sore as hell.

'Why not? Why the hell not?'

'Stop screaming at me, please,' she said. Which was crap, because I wasn't even screaming at her.

'Why can'tcha? Why not?'

'Because you can't, that's all. In the first place, we're both practically *child*ren. And did you ever stop to think what you'd do if you *didn't* get a job when your money ran out? We'd *starve* to death. The whole thing's so fan*tas*tic, it isn't even –'

'It isn't fantastic. I'd get a job. Don't worry about that. You don't have to worry about that. What's the matter? Don't you want to go with me? *Say* so, if you don't.'

'It isn't *that*. It isn't that at *all*,' old Sally said. I was beginning to hate her, in a way. 'We'll have oodles of time to do those things – all those things. I mean after you go to college and all, and if we should get married and all. There'll be oodles of marvelous places to go to. You're just –'

'No, there wouldn't be. There wouldn't be oodles of places to go to at all. It'd be entirely different,' I said. I was getting depressed as hell again.

'What?' she said. 'I can't hear you. One minute you scream at me, and the next you –'

'I said no, there wouldn't be marvelous places to go to after I went to college and all. Open your ears. It'd be entirely different. We'd have to go downstairs in elevators with suitcases and stuff. We'd have to phone up everybody and tell 'em good-by and send 'em postcards from hotels and all. And I'd be working in some office, making a lot of dough, and riding to work in cabs and Madison Avenue buses, and reading newspapers, and playing bridge all the time, and going to the movies and seeing a lot of stupid shorts and coming attractions and newsreels. Newsreels. Christ almighty. There's always a dumb horse race, and some dame breaking a bottle over a ship, and some chimpanzee riding a goddam bicycle with pants on. It wouldn't be the same at all. You don't see what I mean at all.'

'Maybe I don't! Maybe *you* don't, either,' old Sally said. We both hated each other's guts by that time. You could see there wasn't any sense trying to have an intelligent conversation. I was sorry as hell I'd started it.

'C'mon, let's get outa here,' I said. 'You give me a royal pain in the ass, if you want to know the truth.'

Boy, did she hit the ceiling when I said that. I know I shouldn't've said it, and I probably wouldn't've ordinarily, but she was depressing the hell out of me. Usually I never say crude things like that to girls. *Boy*, did she hit the ceiling. I apologized like a madman, but she wouldn't accept my apology. She was even crying. Which scared me a little bit, because I was a little afraid she'd go home and tell her father I called her a pain in the ass. Her father was one of those big silent bastards, and he wasn't too crazy about me anyhow. He once told old Sally I was too goddam noisy.

'No kidding. I'm sorry,' I kept telling her.

'You're sorry. You're sorry. That's very funny,' she said. She was still sort of crying, and all of a sudden I *did* feel sort of sorry I'd said it.

'C'mon, I'll take ya home. No kidding.'

'I can go home by myself, thank you. If you think I'd let *you* take me home, you're mad. No boy ever said that to me in my entire life.'

The whole thing was sort of funny, in a way, if you thought about it, and all of a sudden I did something I shouldn't have. I laughed. And I have one of these very loud, stupid laughs. I mean if I ever sat behind myself in a movie or something, I'd probably lean over and tell myself to please shut up. It made old Sally madder than ever.

I stuck around for a while, apologizing and trying to get her to excuse me, but she wouldn't. She kept telling me to go away and leave her alone. So finally I did it. I went inside and got my shoes and stuff, and left without her. I shouldn't've, but I was pretty goddam fed up by that time.

If you want to know the truth, I don't even know why I started all that stuff with her. I mean about going away somewhere, to Massachusetts and Vermont and all. I probably wouldn't've taken her even if she'd wanted to go with me. She wouldn't have been anybody to go with. The terrible part, though, is that I *meant* it when I asked her. That's the terrible part. I swear to God I'm a madman.

18

When I left the skating rink I felt sort of hungry, so I went in this drugstore and had a Swiss cheese sandwich and a malted, and then I went in a phone booth. I thought maybe I might give old Jane another buzz and see if she was home yet. I mean I had the whole evening free, and I thought I'd give her a buzz and, if she was home yet, take her dancing or something somewhere. I never danced with her or anything the whole time I knew her. I saw her dancing once, though. She looked like a very good dancer. It was at this Fourth of July dance at the club. I didn't know her too well then, and I didn't think I ought to cut in on her date. She was dating this terrible guy, Al Pike, that went to Choate. I didn't know him too well, but he was always hanging around the swimming pool. He wore those white Lastex kind of swimming trunks, and he was always going off the high dive. He did the same lousy old half gainer all day long. It was the only dive he could do, but he thought he was very hot stuff. All muscles and no brains. Anyway, that's who Jane dated that night. I couldn't understand it. I swear I couldn't. After we started going around together, I asked her how come she could date a show-off bastard like Al Pike. Jane said he wasn't a show-off. She said he had an inferiority complex. She acted like she felt sorry for him or something, and she wasn't just putting it on. She meant it. It's a funny thing about girls. Every time you mention some guy that's strictly a bastard – very mean, or very conceited and all – and when you mention it to the girl, she'll tell you he has an inferiority complex. Maybe he *has*, but that still doesn't keep him from being a bastard, in my opinion. Girls. You never know what they're going to think. I once got this girl Roberta Walsh's roommate a date with a friend of mine. His name was Bob Robinson and he *really* had an inferiority complex. You could tell he was very ashamed of his parents and all, because they said 'he don't' and 'she don't' and stuff like that and they weren't very wealthy. But he wasn't a bastard or anything. He was a very nice guy. But this Roberta Walsh's roommate didn't like him at all. She told Roberta he was too conceited – and the *reason* she thought he was conceited was because he happened to mention to her that he was captain of the debating team. A little thing like that, and she thought he was conceited! The trouble with girls is, if they like a boy, no matter how big a bastard he is, they'll say he has an inferiority complex, and if they *don't* like him, no matter how nice a guy he is, or how big an inferiority complex he has, they'll say he's conceited. Even smart girls do it.

Anyway, I gave old Jane a buzz again, but her phone didn't answer, so I had to hang up. Then I had to look through my address book to see who the hell might be available for the evening. The trouble was, though, my address book only has about three people in it. Jane, and this man, Mr Antolini, that was my teacher at Elkton Hills, and my father's office number. I keep forgetting to put people's names in. So what I did finally, I gave old Carl Luce a buzz. He graduated from the Whooton School after I left. He was about three years older than I was, and I didn't like him too much, but he was one of these very intellectual guys – he had the highest I.Q. of any boy at Whooton – and I thought he might want to have dinner with me somewhere and have a slightly intellectual conversation. He was very enlightening sometimes. So I gave him a buzz. He went to Columbia now, but he lived on 65th Street and all, and I knew he'd be home. When I got him on the phone, he said he couldn't make it for dinner but that he'd meet me for a drink at ten o'clock at the Wicker Bar, on 54th. I think he was pretty surprised to hear from me. I once called him a fat-assed phony.

I had quite a bit of time to kill till ten o'clock, so what I did, I went to the movies at Radio City. It was probably the worst thing I could've done, but it was near, and I couldn't think of anything else.

I came in when the goddam stage show was on. The Rockettes were kicking their heads off, the way they do when they're all in line with their arms around each other's waist. The audience applauded like mad, and some guy behind me kept saying to his wife, 'You know what that is? That's precision.' He killed me. Then, after the Rockettes, a guy came out in a tuxedo and roller skates on, and started skating under a bunch of little tables, and telling jokes while he did it. He was a very good skater and all, but I couldn't enjoy it much because I kept picturing him *prac*ticing to be a guy that roller-skates on the stage. It seemed so stupid. I guess I just wasn't in the right mood. Then, after him, they had this Christmas thing they have at Radio City every year. All these angels start coming out of the boxes and everywhere, guys carrying crucifixes and stuff all over the place, and the whole bunch of them – *thousands* of them – singing 'Come All Ye Faithful!' like mad. Big deal. It's supposed to be religious as hell, I know, and very pretty and all, but I can't see anything religious or pretty, for God's sake, about a bunch of actors carrying crucifixes all over the stage. When they were all finished and started going out the boxes again, you could tell they could hardly wait to get a cigarette or something.

I saw it with old Sally Hayes the year before, and she kept saying how beautiful it was, the costumes and all. I said Jesus probably would've puked if He could see it – all those fancy costumes and all. Sally said I was a sacrilegious atheist. I probably am. The thing Jesus *really* would've liked would be the guy that plays the kettle drums in the orchestra. I've watched that guy since I was about eight years old. My brother Allie and I, if we were with our parents and all, we used to move our seats and go way down so we could watch him. He's the best drummer I ever saw. He only gets a chance to bang them a couple of times during a whole piece, but he never looks bored when he isn't doing it. Then when he does bang them, he does it so nice and sweet, with this nervous expression on his face. One time when we went to Washington with my father, Allie sent him a postcard, but I'll bet he never got it. We weren't too sure how to address it.

After the Christmas thing was over, the goddam picture started. It was so putrid I couldn't take my eyes off it. It was about this English guy, Alec something, that was in the war and loses his memory in the hospital and all. He comes out of the hospital carrying a cane and limping all over the place, all over London, not knowing who the hell he is. He's really a duke, but he doesn't know it. Then he meets this nice, homey, sincere girl getting on a bus. Her goddam hat blows off and he catches it, and then they go upstairs and sit down and start talking about Charles Dickens. He's both their favorite author and all. He's carrying this copy of *Oliver Twist* and so's she. I could've puked. Anyway, they fall in love right away, on account of they're both so nuts about Charles Dickens and all, and he helps her run her publishing business. She's a publisher, the girl. Only, she's not doing so hot, because her brother's a drunkard and he spends all their dough. He's a very bitter guy, the brother, because he was a doctor in the war and now he can't operate any more because his nerves are shot, so he boozes all the time, but he's pretty witty and all. Anyway, old Alec writes a book, and this girl publishes it, and they both make a hatful of dough on it. They're all set to get married when this other girl, old Marcia, shows up. Marcia was Alec's fiancée before he lost his memory, and she recognizes him when he's in this store autographing books. She tells old Alec he's really a duke and all, but he doesn't believe her and doesn't want to go with her to visit his mother and all. His mother's blind as a bat. But the other girl, the homey one, makes him go. She's very noble and all. So he goes. But he still doesn't get his memory back, even when his great Dane jumps all over him and his mother sticks her fingers all over his face and brings him this teddy bear he used to slobber around with when he was a kid. But then, one day, some kids are playing cricket on the lawn and he get smacked in the head with a cricket ball. Then right away he gets his goddam memory back and he goes in and kisses his mother on the forehead and all. Then he starts being a regular duke again, and he forgets all about the homey babe that has the publishing business. I'd tell you the rest of the story, but I might puke if I did. It isn't that I'd *spoil* it for you or anything. There isn't anything to *spoil*, for Chrissake. Anyway, it ends up with Alec and the homey babe getting married, and the brother that's a drunkard gets his nerves back and operates on Alec's mother so she can see again, and then the drunken brother and old Marcia go for each other. It ends up with everybody at this long dinner table laughing their asses off because the great Dane comes in with a bunch of puppies. Everybody thought it was a male, I suppose, or some goddam thing. All I can say is, don't see it if you don't want to puke all over yourself.

The part that got me was, there was a lady sitting next to me that cried all through the goddam picture. The phonier it got, the more she cried. You'd have thought she did it because she was kindhearted as hell, but I was sitting right next to her, and she wasn't. She had this little kid with her that was bored as hell and had to go to the bathroom, but she wouldn't take him. She kept telling him to sit still and behave himself. She was about as kindhearted as a goddam wolf. You take somebody that cries their goddam eyes out over phony stuff in the movies, and nine times out of ten they're mean bastards at heart. I'm not kidding.

After the movie was over, I started walking down to the Wicker Bar, where I was supposed to meet old Carl Luce, and while I walked I sort of thought about war and all. Those war movies always do that to me. I don't think I could stand it if I had to go to war. I really couldn't. It wouldn't be too bad if they'd just take you out and shoot you or something, but you have to stay in the *Army* so goddam long. That's the whole trouble. My brother D.B. was in the Army for four goddam years. He was in the war, too – he landed on D-Day and all – but I really think he hated the Army worse than the war. I was practically a child at the time, but I remember when he used to come home on furlough and all, all he did was lie on his bed, practically. He hardly ever even came in the living room. Later, when he went overseas and was in the war and all, he didn't get wounded or anything and he didn't have to shoot anybody. All he had to do was drive some cowboy general around all day in a command car. He once told Allie and I that if he'd had to shoot anybody, he wouldn't've known which direction to shoot in. He said the Army was practically as full of bastards as the Nazis were. I remember Allie once asked him wasn't it sort of good that he was in the war because he was a writer and it gave him a lot to write about and all. He made Allie go get his baseball mitt and then he asked him who was the best war poet, Rupert Brooke or Emily Dickinson. Allie said Emily Dickinson. I don't know too much about it myself, because I don't read much poetry, but I *do* know it'd drive me crazy if I had to be in the Army and be with a bunch of guys like Ackley and Stradlater and old Maurice all the time, marching with them and all. I was in the Boy Scouts once, for about a week, and I couldn't even stand looking at the back of the guy's neck in front of me. They kept telling you to look at the back of the guy's neck in front of you. I swear if there's ever another war, they better just take me out and stick me in front of a firing squad. I wouldn't object. What gets me about D.B., though, he hated the war so much, and yet he got me to read this book *A Farewell to Arms* last summer. He said it was so terrific. That's what I can't understand. It had this guy in it named Lieutenant Henry that was supposed to be a nice guy and all. I don't see how D.B. could hate the Army and war and all so much and still like a phony like that. I mean, for instance, I don't see how he could like a phony book like that and still like that one by Ring Lardner, or that other one he's so crazy about, *The Great Gatsby*. D.B. got sore when I said that, and said I was too young and all to appreciate it, but I don't think so. I told him I liked Ring Lardner and *The Great Gatsby* and all. I did, too. I was crazy about *The Great Gatsby*. Old Gatsby. Old sport. That killed me. Anyway, I'm sort of glad they've got the atomic bomb invented. If there's ever another war, I'm going to sit right the hell on top of it. I'll volunteer for it, I swear to God I will.

19

In case you don't live in New York, the Wicker Bar is in this sort of swanky hotel, the Seton Hotel. I used to go there quite a lot, but I don't any more. I gradually cut it out. It's one of those places that are supposed to be very sophisticated and all, and the phonies are coming in the window. They used to have these two French babes, Tina and Janine, come out and play the piano and sing about three times every night. One of them played the piano – strictly lousy – and the other one sang, and most of the songs were either pretty dirty or in French. The one that sang, old Janine, was always whispering into the goddam microphone before she sang. She'd say, 'And now we like to geeve you our impression of Vooly Voo Fransay. Eet ees the story of a leetle Fransh girl who comes to a beeg ceety, just like New York, and falls een love wees a leetle boy from Brookleen. We hope you like eet.' Then, when she was all done whispering and being cute as hell, she'd sing some dopey song, half in English and half in French, and drive all the phonies in the place mad with joy. If you sat around there long enough and heard all the phonies applauding and all, you got to hate everybody in the world, I swear you did. The bartender was a louse, too. He was a big snob. He didn't talk to you at all hardly unless you were a big shot or a celebrity or something. If you *were* a big shot or a celebrity or something, then he was even more nauseating. He'd go up to you and say, with this big charming smile, like he was a helluva swell guy if you knew him, 'Well! How's

Connecticut?' or 'How's Florida?' It was a terrible place, I'm not kidding. I cut out going there entirely, gradually.

It was pretty early when I got there. I sat down at the bar – it was pretty crowded – and had a couple of Scotch and sodas before old Luce even showed up. I stood up when I ordered them so they could see how tall I was and all and not think I was a goddam minor. Then I watched the phonies for a while. Some guy next to me was snowing hell out of the babe he was with. He kept telling her she had aristocratic hands. That killed me. The other end of the bar was full of flits. They weren't too flitty-looking – I mean they didn't have their hair too long or anything – but you could tell they were flits anyway. Finally old Luce showed up.

Old Luce. What a guy. He was supposed to be my Student Adviser when I was at Whooton. The only thing he ever did, though, was give these sex talks and all, late at night when there was a bunch of guys in his room. He knew quite a bit about sex, especially perverts and all. He was always telling us about a lot of creepy guys that go around having affairs with sheep, and guys that go around with girls' pants sewed in the lining of their hats and all. And flits and Lesbians. Old Luce knew who every flit and Lesbian in the United States was. All you had to do was mention somebody – *any*body – and old Luce'd tell you if he was a flit or not. Sometimes it was hard to believe, the people he said were flits and Lesbians and all, movie actors and like that. Some of the ones he said were flits were even married, for God's sake. You'd keep saying to him, 'You mean Joe Blow's a flit? Joe *Blow*? That big, tough guy that plays gangsters and cowboys all the time?' Old Luce'd say, 'Certainly.' He was always saying 'Certainly.' He said it didn't matter if a guy was married or not. He said half the married guys in the world were flits and didn't even know it. He said you could turn into one practically overnight, if you had all the traits and all. He used to scare the hell out of us. I kept waiting to turn into a flit or something. The funny thing about old Luce, I used to think he was sort of flitty himself, in a way. He was always saying, 'Try this for size,' and then he'd goose the hell out of you while you were going down the corridor. And whenever he went to the can, he always left the goddam door open and *talked* to you while you were brushing your teeth or something. That stuff's sort of flitty. It really is. I've known quite a few real flits, at schools and all, and they're always doing stuff like that, and that's why I always had my doubts about old Luce. He was a pretty intelligent guy, though. He really was.

He never said hello or anything when he met you. The first thing he said when he sat down was that he could only stay a couple of minutes. He said he had a date. Then he ordered a dry Martini. He told the bartender to make it very dry, and no olive.

'Hey, I got a flit for you,' I told him. 'At the end of the bar. Don't look now. I been saving him for ya.'

'Very funny,' he said. 'Same old Caulfield. When are you going to grow up?'

I bored him a lot. I really did. He amused me, though. He was one of those guys that sort of amuse me a lot.

'How's your sex life?' I asked him. He hated you to ask him stuff like that.

'Relax,' he said. 'Just sit back and relax, for Chrissake.'

'I'm relaxed,' I said. 'How's Columbia? Ya like it?'

'Certainly I like it. If I didn't like it I wouldn't have gone there,' he said. He could be pretty boring himself sometimes.

'What're you majoring in?' I asked him. 'Perverts?' I was only horsing around.

'What're you trying to be – funny?'

'No. I'm only kidding,' I said. 'Listen, hey, Luce. You're one of these intellectual guys. I need your advice. I'm in a terrific –'

He let out this big groan on me. '*Lis*ten, Caulfield. If you want to sit here and have a quiet, peaceful drink and a *quiet*, peaceful conver–'

'All right, all right,' I said. 'Relax.' You could tell he didn't feel like discussing anything serious with me. That's the trouble with these intellectual guys. They never want to discuss anything serious unless *they* feel like it. So all I did was, I started discussing topics in general with him. 'No kidding, how's your sex life?' I asked him. 'You still going around with that same babe you used to at Whooton? The one with the terrific –'

'Good God, no,' he said.

'How come? What happened to her?'

'I haven't the *faint*est idea. For all I know, since you ask, she's probably the Whore of New Hampshire by this time.'

'That isn't nice. If she was decent enough to let you get sexy with her all the time, you at least shouldn't talk about her that way.'

'Oh, God!' old Luce said. 'Is this going to be a typical Caulfield conversation? I want to know right now.'

'No,' I said, 'but it isn't nice anyway. If she was decent and nice enough to let you –'

'*Must* we pursue this horrible trend of thought?'

I didn't say anything. I was sort of afraid he'd get up and leave on me if I didn't shut up. So all I did was, I ordered another drink. I felt like getting stinking drunk.

'Who're you going around with now?' I asked him. 'You feel like telling me?'

'Nobody you know.'

'Yeah, but who? I might know her.'

'Girl lives in the Village. Sculptress. If you must know.'

'Yeah? No kidding? How old is she?'

'I've never *asked* her, for God's sake.'

'Well, around how old?'

'I should imagine she's in her late thirties,' old Luce said.

'In her late *thirt*ies? Yeah? You like that?' I asked him. 'You like 'em that old?' The reason I was asking was because he really knew quite a bit about sex and all. He was one of the few guys I knew that did. He lost his virginity when he was only fourteen, in Nantucket. He really did.

'I like a mature person, if that's what you mean. Certainly.'

'You do? Why? No kidding, they better for sex and all?'

'Listen. Let's get one thing straight. I refuse to answer any typical Caulfield questions tonight. When in *hell* are you going to grow up?'

I didn't say anything for a while. I let it drop for a while. Then old Luce ordered another Martini and told the bartender to make it a lot dryer.

'Listen. How long you been going around with her, this sculpture babe?' I asked him. I was really interested. 'Did you know her when you were at Whooton?'

'Hardly. She just arrived in this country a few months ago.'

'She did? Where's she from?'

'She happens to be from Shanghai.'

'No kidding! She Chi*nese*, for Chrissake?'

'Obviously.'

'No kidding! Do you like that? Her being Chinese?'

'Obviously.'

'Why? I'd be interested to know – I really would.'

'I simply happen to find Eastern philosophy more satisfactory than Western. Since you *ask*.'

'You do? Wuddaya mean "philosophy"? Ya mean sex and all? You mean it's better in China? That what you mean?'

'Not necessarily in *China*, for God's sake. The *East* I said. Must we go on with this inane conversation?'

'Listen, I'm serious,' I said. 'No kidding. Why's it better in the East?'

'It's too involved to go into, for God's sake,' old Luce said. 'They simply happen to regard sex as both a physical and a spiritual experience. If you think I'm –'

'So do I! So do I regard it as a wuddayacallit – a physical and spiritual experience and all. I really do. But it depends on who the hell I'm doing it with. If I'm doing it with somebody I don't even –'

'Not so *loud*, for God's sake, Caulfield. If you can't manage to keep your voice down, let's drop the whole –'

'All right, but listen,' I said. I was getting excited and I *was* talking a little too loud. Sometimes I talk a little loud when I get excited. 'This is what I mean, though,' I said. 'I know it's supposed to be physical and spiritual, and artistic and all. But what I mean is, you can't do it with *everybody* – every girl you neck with and all – and make it come out that way. Can you?'

'Let's drop it,' old Luce said. 'Do you mind?'

'All right, but listen. Take you and this Chinese babe. What's so good about you two?'

'*Drop* it, I said.'

I was getting a little too personal. I realize that. But that was one of the annoying things about Luce. When we were at Whooton, he'd make you describe the most personal stuff that happened to *you*, but if you started asking *him* questions about *him*self he got sore. These intellectual guys don't like to have an intellectual conversation with you unless they're running the whole thing. They always want you to shut up when *they* shut up, and go back to your room when they go back to *their* room. When I was at Whooton old Luce used to hate it – you really could tell he did – when after he was finished giving this sex talk to a bunch of us in his room we stuck around and chewed the fat by ourselves for a while. I mean the other guys and myself. In somebody else's room. Old Luce hated that. He always wanted everybody to go back to their own room and shut up when he was finished being the big shot. The thing he was afraid of, he was afraid somebody'd say something smarter than *he* had. He really amused me.

'Maybe I'll go to China. My sex life is lousy,' I said.

'Naturally. Your mind is immature.'

'It is. It really is. I know it,' I said. 'You know what the trouble with me is? I can never get really sexy – I mean *really* sexy – with a girl I don't like a lot. I mean I have to *like* her a lot. If I don't, I sort of lose my goddam desire for her and all. Boy, it really screws up my sex life something awful. My sex life stinks.'

'Naturally it does, for God's sake. I told you the last time I saw you what you need.'

'You mean to go to a psychoanalyst and all?' I said. That's what he'd told me I ought to do. His father was a psychoanalyst and all.

'It's up to you, for God's sake. It's none of my goddam business what you do with your life.'

I didn't say anything for a while. I was thinking.

'Supposing I went to your father and had him psychoanalyze me and all,' I said. 'What would he do to me? I mean what would he do to me?'

'He wouldn't do a goddam thing to you. He'd simply talk to

you, and you'd talk to him, for God's sake. For one thing, he'd help you to recognize the patterns of your mind.'

'That what?'

'The patterns of your mind. Your mind runs in – Listen. I'm not giving an elementary course in psychoanalysis. If you're interested, call him up and make an appointment. If you're not, don't. I couldn't care less, frankly.'

I put my hand on his shoulder. Boy, he amused me. 'You're a real friendly bastard,' I told him. 'You know that?'

He was looking at his wrist watch. 'I have to tear,' he said, and stood up. 'Nice seeing you.' He got the bartender and told him to bring him his check.

'Hey,' I said, just before he beat it. 'Did your father ever psychoanalyze you?'

'Me? Why do you ask?'

'No reason. Did he, though? Has he?'

'Not exactly. He's helped me to ad*just* myself to a certain extent, but an extensive analysis hasn't been necessary. Why do you ask?'

'No reason. I was just wondering.'

'Well. Take it easy,' he said. He was leaving his tip and all and he was starting to go.

'Have just one more drink,' I told him. 'Please. I'm lonesome as hell. No kidding.'

He said he couldn't do it, though. He said he was late now, and then he left.

Old Luce. He was strictly a pain in the ass, but he certainly had a good vocabulary. He had the largest vocabulary of any boy at Whooton when I was there. They gave us a test.

20

I kept sitting there getting drunk and waiting for old Tina and Janine to come out and do their stuff, but they weren't there. A flitty-looking guy with wavy hair came out and played the piano, and then this new babe, Valencia, came out and sang. She wasn't any good, but she was better than old Tina and Janine, and at least she sang good songs. The piano was right next to the bar where I was sitting and all, and old Valencia was standing practically right next to me. I sort of gave her the old eye, but she pretended she didn't even see me. I probably wouldn't have done it, but I was getting drunk as hell. When she was finished, she beat it out of the room so fast I didn't even get a chance to invite her to join me for a drink, so I called the head-waiter over. I told him to ask old Valencia if she'd care to join me for a drink. He said he would, but he probably didn't even give her my message. People never give your message to anybody.

Boy, I sat at that goddam bar till around one o'clock or so, getting drunk as a bastard. I could hardly see straight. The one thing I did, though, I was careful as hell not to get boisterous or anything. I didn't want anybody to notice me or anything or ask how old I was. But, boy, I could hardly see straight. When I was *really* drunk, I started that stupid business with the bullet in my guts again. I was the only guy at the bar with a bullet in their guts. I kept putting my hand under my jacket, on my stomach and all, to keep the blood from dripping all over the place. I didn't want anybody to know I was even wounded. I was con*ceal*ing the fact that I was a wounded sonuvabitch. Finally what I felt like, I felt like giving old Jane a buzz and see if she was home yet. So I paid my check and all. Then I left the bar and went out where the telephones were. I kept keeping my hand under my jacket to keep the blood from dripping. Boy, was I drunk.

But when I got inside this phone booth, I wasn't much in the mood any more to give old Jane a buzz. I was too drunk, I guess. So what I did, I gave old Sally Hayes a buzz.

I had to dial about twenty numbers before I got the right one. Boy, was I blind.

'Hello,' I said when somebody answered the goddam phone. I sort of yelled it, I was so drunk.

'Who is this?' this very cold lady's voice said.

'This is me. Holden Caulfield. Lemme speaka Sally, please.'

'Sally's a*sleep*. This is Sally's grandmother. Why are you calling at this hour, Holden? Do you know what time it is?'

'Yeah. Wanna talk a Sally. Very important. Put her on.'

'Sally's *asleep*, young man. Call her tomorrow. Good night.'

'Wake 'er up! Wake 'er up, hey. Attaboy.'

Then there was a different voice. 'Holden, this is me.' It was old Sally. 'What's the big idea?'

'Sally? That you?'

'Yes – stop screaming. Are you drunk?'

'Yeah. Listen. Listen, hey. I'll come over Christmas Eve. Okay? Trimma goddam tree for ya. Okay? Okay, hey, Sally?'

'Yes. You're drunk. Go to bed now. Where are you? Who's with you?'

'Sally? I'll come over and trimma tree for ya, okay? Okay, hey?'

'*Yes*. Go to bed now. Where are you? Who's with you?'

'Nobody. Me, myself and I.' Boy was I drunk. I was even still holding onto my guts. 'They got me. Rocky's mob got me. You know that? Sally, you know that?'

'I can't hear you. Go to bed now. I have to go. Call me tomorrow.'

'Hey, Sally! You want me trimma tree for ya? Ya want me to? *Huh?*'

'*Yes*. Good night. Go home and go to bed.'

She hung up on me.

'G'night. G'night, Sally baby. Sally sweetheart darling,' I said. Can you imagine how drunk I was? I hung up too, then. I figured she probably just came home from a date. I pictured her out with the Lunts and all somewhere, and that Andover jerk. All of them swimming around in a goddam pot of tea and saying sophisticated stuff to each other and being charming and phony. I wished to God I hadn't even phoned her. When I'm drunk, I'm a madman.

I stayed in the damn phone booth for quite a while. I kept holding onto the phone, sort of, so I wouldn't pass out. I wasn't feeling too marvelous, to tell you the truth. Finally, though, I came out and went in the men's room, staggering around like a moron, and filled one of the washbowls with cold water. Then I dunked my head in it, right up to the ears. I didn't even bother to dry it or anything. I just let the sonuvabitch drip. Then I walked over to this radiator by the window and sat down on it. It was nice and warm. It felt good because I was shivering like a bastard. It's a funny thing, I always shiver like hell when I'm drunk.

I didn't have anything else to do, so I kept sitting on the radiator and counting these little white squares on the floor. I was getting soaked. About a gallon of water was dripping down my neck, getting all over my collar and tie and all, but I didn't give a damn. I was too drunk to give a damn. Then, pretty soon, the guy that played the piano for old Valencia, this very wavy-haired, flitty-looking guy, came in to comb his golden locks. We sort of struck up a conversation while he was combing it, except that he wasn't too goddam friendly.

'Hey. You gonna see that Valencia babe when you go back in the bar?' I asked him.

'It's highly probable,' he said. Witty bastard. All I ever meet is witty bastards.

'Listen. Give her my compliments. Ask her if that goddam waiter gave her my message, willya?'

'Why don't you go home, Mac? How old are you, anyway?'

'Eighty-six. Listen. Give her my compliments. Okay?'

'Why don't you go home, Mac?'

'Not me. Boy, you can play that goddam piano,' I told him. I was just flattering him. He played the piano stinking, if you want to know the truth. 'You oughta go on the radio,' I said. 'Handsome chap like you. All those goddam golden locks. Ya need a manager?'

'Go home, Mac, like a good guy. Go home and hit the sack.'

'No home to go to. No kidding – you need a manager?'

He didn't answer me. He just went out. He was all through combing his hair and patting it and all, so he left. Like Stradlater. All these handsome guys are the same. When they're done combing their goddam hair, they beat it on you.

When I finally got down off the radiator and went out to the hat-check room, I was crying and all. I don't know why, but I was. I guess it was because I was feeling so damn depressed and lonesome. Then, when I went out to the checkroom, I couldn't find my goddam check. The hat-check girl was very nice about it, though. She gave me my coat anyway. And my 'Little Shirley Beans' record – I still had it with me and all. I gave her a buck for being so nice, but she wouldn't take it. She kept telling me to go home and go to bed. I sort of tried to make a date with her for when she got through working, but she wouldn't do it. She said she was old enough to be my mother and all. I showed her my goddam gray hair and told her I was forty-two – I was only horsing around, naturally. She was nice, though. I showed her my goddam red hunting hat, and she liked it. She made me put it on before I went out, because my hair was still pretty wet. She was all right.

I didn't feel too drunk any more when I went outside, but it was getting very cold out again, and my teeth started chattering like hell. I couldn't make them stop. I walked over to Madison Avenue and started to wait around for a bus because I didn't have hardly any money left and I had to start economizing on cabs and all. But I didn't feel like getting on a damn bus. And besides, I didn't even know where I was supposed to go. So what I did, I started walking over to the park. I figured I'd go by that little lake and see what the hell the ducks were doing, see if they were around or not. I still didn't know if they were around or not. It wasn't far over to the park, and I didn't have anyplace else special to go to – I didn't even know where I was going to *sleep* yet – so I went. I wasn't tired or anything. I just felt blue as hell.

Then something terrible happened just as I got in the park. I dropped old Phoebe's record. It broke into about fifty pieces. It was in a big envelope and all, but it broke anyway. I damn near cried, it made me feel so terrible, but all I did was, I took the pieces out of the envelope and put them in my coat pocket. They weren't any good for anything, but I didn't feel like just throwing them away. Then I went in the park. Boy, was it dark.

I've lived in New York all my life, and I know Central Park like the back of my hand, because I used to roller-skate there all the time and ride my bike when I was a kid, but I had the most terrific trouble finding that lagoon that night. I *knew* right where it was – it was right near Central Park South and all – but I still couldn't find it. I must've been drunker than I thought. I kept walking and walking, and it kept getting darker and darker and spookier and spookier. I didn't see one person the whole time I was in the park. I'm just as glad. I probably would've jumped about a mile if I had. Then, finally, I found it. What it was, it was partly frozen and partly not frozen. But I didn't see any ducks around. I walked all around the whole damn lake – I damn near fell *in* once, in fact – but I didn't see a single duck. I thought maybe if there *were* any around, they might be asleep or something near the edge of the water, near the grass and all. That's how I nearly fell in. But I couldn't find any.

Finally I sat down on this bench, where it wasn't so goddam dark. Boy, I was still shivering like a bastard, and the back of my hair, even though I had my hunting hat on, was sort of full of little hunks of ice. That worried me. I thought probably I'd get pneumonia and die. I started picturing millions of jerks coming to my funeral and all. My grandfather from Detroit, that keeps calling out the numbers of the streets when you ride on a goddam bus with him, and my aunts – I have about fifty aunts – and all my lousy cousins. What a mob'd be there. They all came when Allie died, the whole goddam stupid bunch of them. I have this one stupid aunt with halitosis that kept saying how *peace*ful he looked lying there, D.B. told me. I wasn't there. I was still in the hospital. I had to go to the hospital and all after I hurt my hand. Anyway, I kept worrying that I was getting pneumonia, with all those hunks of ice in my hair, and that I was going to die. I felt sorry as hell for my mother and father. Especially my mother, because she still isn't over my brother Allie yet. I kept picturing her not knowing what to do with all my suits and athletic equipment and all. The only good thing, I knew she wouldn't let old Phoebe come to my goddam funeral because she was only a little kid. That was the only good part. Then I thought about the whole bunch of them sticking me in a goddam cemetery and all, with my name on this tombstone and all. Surrounded by dead guys. Boy, when you're dead, they really fix you up. I hope to hell when I *do* die somebody has sense enough to just dump me in the river or something. Anything except sticking me in a goddam cemetery. People coming and putting a bunch of flowers on your stomach on Sunday, and all that crap. Who wants flowers when you're dead? Nobody.

When the weather's nice, my parents go out quite frequently and stick a bunch of flowers on old Allie's grave. I went with them a couple of times, but I cut it out. In the first place, I certainly don't enjoy seeing him in that crazy cemetery. Surrounded by dead guys and tombstones and all. It wasn't too bad when the sun was out, but twice – *twice* – we were there when it started to rain. It was awful. It rained on his lousy tombstone, and it rained on the grass on his stomach. It rained all over the place. All the visitors that were visiting the cemetery started running like hell over to their cars. That's what nearly drove me crazy. All the visitors could get in their cars and turn on their radios and all and then go someplace nice for dinner – everybody except Allie. I couldn't stand it. I know it's only his body and all that's in the cemetery, and his soul's in Heaven and all that crap, but I couldn't stand it anyway. I just wish he wasn't there. You didn't know him. If you'd known him, you'd know what I mean. It's not too bad when the sun's out, but the sun only comes out when it feels like coming out.

After a while, just to get my mind off getting pneumonia and all, I took out my dough and tried to count it in the lousy light from the street lamp. All I had was three singles and five quarters and a nickel left – boy, I spent a fortune since I left Pencey. Then what I did, I went down near the lagoon and I sort of skipped the quarters and the nickel across it, where it wasn't frozen. I don't know why I did it, but I did it. I guess I thought it'd take my mind off getting pneumonia and dying. It didn't though.

I started thinking how old Phoebe would feel if I got pneumonia and died. It was a childish way to think, but I couldn't stop myself. She'd feel pretty bad if something like that happened. She likes me a lot. I mean she's quite fond of me. She really is. Anyway, I couldn't get that off my mind, so finally what I figured I'd do, I figured I'd better sneak home and see her, in case I died and all. I had my door key with me and all, and I figured what I'd do, I'd sneak in the apartment, very quiet and all, and just sort of chew the fat with her for a while. The only thing that worried me was our front door. It creaks like a bastard. It's a pretty old apartment house, and the superintendent's a lazy bastard, and everything creaks and squeaks. I was afraid my parents might hear me sneaking in. But I decided I'd try it anyhow.

So I got the hell out of the park, and went home. I walked all the way. It wasn't too far, and I wasn't tired or even drunk any more. It was just very cold and nobody around anywhere.

21

The best break I had in years, when I got home the regular night elevator boy, Pete, wasn't on the car. Some new guy I'd never seen was on the car, so I figured that if I didn't bump smack into my parents and all I'd be able to say hello to old Phoebe and then beat it and nobody'd even know I'd been around. It was really a terrific break. What made it even better, the new elevator boy was sort of on the stupid side. I told him, in this very casual voice, to take me up to the Dicksteins'. The Dicksteins were these people that had the other apartment on our floor. I'd already taken off my hunting hat, so as not to look suspicious or anything. I went in the elevator like I was in a terrific hurry.

He had the elevator doors all shut and all, and was all set to take me up, and then he turned around and said, 'They ain't in. They're at a party on the fourteenth floor.'

'That's all right,' I said. 'I'm supposed to wait for them. I'm their nephew.'

He gave me this sort of stupid, suspicious look. 'You better wait in the lobby, fella,' he said.

'I'd like to – I really would,' I said. 'But I have a bad leg. I have to hold it in a certain position. I think I'd better sit down in the chair outside their door.'

He didn't know what the hell I was talking about, so all he said was 'Oh' and took me up. Not bad, boy. It's funny. All you have to do is say something nobody understands and they'll do practically anything you want them to.

I got off at our floor – limping like a bastard – and started walking over toward the Dicksteins' side. Then, when I heard the elevator doors shut, I turned around and went over to our side. I was doing all right. I didn't even feel drunk anymore. Then I took out my door key and opened our door, quiet as hell. Then, very, very carefully and all, I went inside and closed the door. I really should've been a crook.

It was dark as hell in the foyer, naturally, and naturally I couldn't turn on any lights. I had to be careful not to bump into anything and make a racket. I certainly knew I was home, though. Our foyer has a funny smell that doesn't smell like anyplace else. I don't know what the hell it is. It isn't cauliflower and it isn't perfume – I don't know what the hell it is – but you always know you're home. I started to take off my coat and hang it up in the foyer closet, but that closet's full of hangers that rattle like madmen when you open the door, so I left it on. Then I started walking very, very slowly back toward old Phoebe's room. I knew the maid wouldn't hear me because she had only one eardrum. She had this brother that stuck a straw down her ear when she was a kid, she once told me. She was pretty deaf and all. But my *par*ents, especially my mother, she has ears like a goddam bloodhound. So I took it very, very easy when I went past their door. I even held my breath, for God's sake. You can hit my father over the head with a chair and he won't wake up, but my mother, all you have to do to my mother is cough somewhere in Siberia and she'll hear you. She's nervous as hell. Half the time she's up all night smoking cigarettes.

Finally, after about an hour, I got to old Phoebe's room. She wasn't there, though. I forgot about that. I forgot she always sleeps in D.B.'s room when he's away in Hollywood or some place. She likes it because it's the biggest room in the house. Also because it has this big old madman desk in it that D.B. bought off some lady alcoholic in Philadelphia, and this big, gigantic bed that's about ten miles wide and ten miles long. I don't know where he bought that bed. Anyway, old Phoebe likes to sleep in D.B.'s room when he's away, and he lets her. You ought to see her doing her homework or something at that crazy desk. It's almost as big as the bed. You can hardly see her when she's doing her homework. That's the kind of stuff she likes, though. She doesn't like her own room because it's too little, she says. She says she likes to spread out. That kills me. What's old Phoebe got to spread out? Nothing.

Anyway, I went into D.B.'s room quiet as hell, and turned on the lamp on the desk. Old Phoebe didn't even wake up. When the light was on and all, I sort of looked at her for a while. She was laying there asleep, with her face sort of on the side of the pillow. She had her mouth way open. It's funny. You take adults, they look lousy when they're asleep and they have their mouths way open, but kids don't. Kids look all right. They can even have spit all over the pillow and they still look all right.

I went around the room, very quiet and all, looking at stuff for a while. I felt swell, for a change. I didn't even feel like I was getting pneumonia or anything any more. I just felt good, for a change. Old Phoebe's clothes were on this chair right next to the bed. She's very neat, for a child. I mean she doesn't just throw her stuff around, like some kids. She's no slob. She had the jacket to this tan suit my mother bought her in Canada hung up on the back of the chair. Then her blouse and stuff were on the seat. Her shoes and socks were on the floor, right underneath the chair, right next to each other. I never saw the shoes before. They were new. They were these dark brown loafers, sort of like this pair I have, and they went swell with that suit my mother bought her in Canada. My mother dresses her nice. She really does. My mother has terrific taste in some things. She's no good at buying ice skates or anything like that, but clothes, she's perfect. I mean Phoebe always has some dress on that can kill you. You take most little kids, even if their parents are wealthy and all, they usually have some terrible dress on. I wish you could see old Phoebe in that suit my mother bought her in Canada. I'm not kidding.

I sat down on old D.B.'s desk and looked at the stuff on it. It was mostly Phoebe's stuff, from school and all. Mostly books. The one on top was called *Arithmetic Is Fun!* I sort of opened the first page and took a look at it. This is what old Phoebe had on it:

PHOEBE WEATHERFIELD CAULFIELD

4B-1

That killed me. Her middle name is Josephine, for God's sake, not Weatherfield. She doesn't like it, though. Every time I see her she's got a new middle name for herself.

The book underneath the arithmetic was a geography, and the book under the geography was a speller. She's very good in spelling. She's very good in all her subjects, but she's best in spelling. Then, under the speller, there were a bunch of notebooks. She has about five thousand notebooks. You never saw a kid with so many notebooks. I opened the one on top and looked at the first page. It had on it:

Bernice meet me at recess I have something
very very important to tell you.

That was all there was on that page. The next one had on it:

Why has south eastern Alaska so many caning factories?
Because theres so much salmon
Why has it valuable forests?
because it has the right climate.
What has our government done to make
life easier for the alaskan eskimos?
look it up for tomorrow!!!

Phoebe Weatherfield Caulfield
Phoebe Weatherfield Caulfield
Phoebe Weatherfield Caulfield
Phoebe W. Caulfield
Phoebe Weatherfield Caulfield, Esq.

Please pass to Shirley!!!!
Shirley you said you were sagitarius
but your only taurus bring your skates
when you come over to my house

I sat there on D.B.'s desk and read the whole notebook. It didn't take me long, and I can read that kind of stuff, some kid's notebook, Phoebe's or anybody's, all day and all night long. Kids' notebooks kill me. Then I lit another cigarette – it was my last one. I must've smoked about three cartons that day. Then, finally, I woke her up. I mean I couldn't sit there on that desk for the rest of my life, and besides, I was afraid my parents might barge in on me all of a sudden and I wanted to at least say hello to her before they did. So I woke her up.

She wakes up very easily. I mean you don't have to yell at her or anything. All you have to do, practically, is sit down on the bed and say, 'Wake up, Phoeb,' and bingo, she's awake.

'*Hold*en!' she said right away. She put her arms around my neck and all. She's very affectionate. I mean she's quite affectionate, for a child. Sometimes she's even *too* affectionate. I sort of gave her a kiss, and she said, 'Whenja get *home*?' She was glad as hell to see me. You could tell.

'Not so loud. Just now. How are ya anyway?'

'I'm fine. Did you get my letter? I wrote you a five-page –'

'Yeah – not so loud. Thanks.'

She wrote me this letter. I didn't get a chance to answer it, though. It was all about this play she was in in school. She told me not to make any dates or anything for Friday so that I could come see it.

'How's the play?' I asked her. 'What'd you say the name of it was?'

' "A Christmas Pageant for Americans." It stinks, but I'm Benedict Arnold. I have practically the biggest part,' she said. Boy, was she wide-awake. She gets very excited when she tells you that stuff. 'It starts out when I'm dying. This ghost comes in on Christmas Eve and asks me if I'm ashamed and everything. You know. For betraying my country and everything. Are you coming to it?' She was sitting way the hell up in the bed and all. 'That's what I wrote you about. Are you?'

'Sure I'm coming. Certainly I'm coming.'

'Daddy can't come. He has to fly to California,' she said. Boy, was she wide-awake. It only takes her about two seconds to get wide-awake. She was sitting – sort of kneeling – way up in bed, and she was holding my goddam hand. 'Listen. Mother said you'd be home *Wednes*day,' she said. 'She said *Wednes*day.'

'I got out early. Not so loud. You'll wake everybody up.'

'What time is it? They won't be home till very late, Mother said. They went to a party in Norwalk, Connecticut,' old Phoebe said. 'Guess what I did this afternoon! What movie I saw. Guess!'

'I don't know – Listen. Didn't they say what time they'd –'

'*The Doctor*,' old Phoebe said. 'It's a special movie they had at the Lister Foundation. Just this one day they had it – today was the only day. It was all about this doctor in Kentucky and everything that sticks a blanket over this child's face that's a cripple and can't walk. Then they send him to jail and everything. It was excellent.'

'Listen a second. Didn't they say what time they'd –'

'He feels sorry for it, the doctor. That's why he sticks this blanket over her face and everything and makes her suffocate. Then they make him go to jail for life imprisonment, but this child that he stuck the blanket over its head comes to visit him all the time and thanks him for what he did. He was a mercy killer. Only, he knows he deserves to go to jail because a doctor isn't supposed to take things away from God. This girl in my class's mother took us. Alice Holmborg. She's my best friend. She's the only girl in the whole –'

'Wait a second, *will*ya?' I said. 'I'm asking you a question. Did they say what time they'd be back, or didn't they?'

'No, but not till very late. Daddy took the car and everything so they wouldn't have to worry about trains. We have a radio in it now! Except that Mother said nobody can play it when the car's in traffic.'

I began to relax, sort of. I mean I finally quit *wor*rying about whether they'd catch me home or not. I figured the hell with it. If they did, they did.

You should've seen old Phoebe. She had on these blue pajamas with red elephants on the collars. Elephants knock her out.

'So it was a good picture, huh?' I said.

'Swell, except Alice had a cold, and her mother kept asking her all the time if she felt grippy. Right in the middle of the *pic*ture. Always in the middle of something important, her mother'd lean all over me and everything and ask Alice if she felt grippy. It got on my nerves.'

Then I told her about the record. 'Listen, I bought you a record,' I told her. 'Only I broke it on the way home.' I took the pieces out of my coat pocket and showed her. 'I was plastered,' I said.

'Gimme the pieces,' she said. 'I'm saving them.' She took them right out of my hand and then she put them in the drawer of the night table. She kills me.

'D.B. coming home for Christmas?' I asked her.

'He may and he may not, Mother said. It all depends. He may have to stay in Hollywood and write a picture about Annapolis.'

'Annapolis, for God's sake!'

'It's a love story and everything. Guess who's going to be in it! What movie star. Guess!'

'I'm not interested. An*nap*olis, for God's sake. What's D.B. know about An*nap*olis, for God's sake? What's that got to do with the kind of stories he writes?' I said. Boy, that stuff drives me crazy. That goddam Hollywood. 'What'd you do to your arm?' I asked her. I noticed she had this big hunk of adhesive tape on her elbow. The reason I noticed it, her pajamas didn't have any sleeves.

'This boy, Curtis Weintraub, that's in my class, pushed me while I was going down the stairs in the park,' she said. 'Wanna see?' She started taking the crazy adhesive tape off her arm.

'Leave it alone. Why'd he push you down the stairs?'

'I don't know. I think he hates me,' old Phoebe said. 'This other girl and me, Selma Atterbury, put ink and stuff all over his wind-breaker.'

'That isn't nice. What are you – a child, for God's sake?'

'No, but every time I'm in the park, he follows me everywhere. He's always following me. He gets on my nerves.'

'He probably likes you. That's no reason to put ink all –'

'I don't want him to like me,' she said. Then she started looking at me funny. 'Holden,' she said, 'how come you're not home *Wednes*day?'

'What?'

Boy, you have to watch her every minute. If you don't think she's smart, you're mad.

'How come you're not home *Wednes*day?' she asked me. 'You didn't get kicked out or anything, did you?'

'I told you. They let us out early. They let the whole –'

'You did get kicked out! You did!' old Phoebe said. Then she hit me on the leg with her fist. She gets very fisty when she feels like it. 'You *did*! Oh, *Hol*den!' She had her hand on her mouth and all. She gets very emotional, I swear to God.

'Who said I got kicked out? Nobody said I –'

'You *did*. You *did*,' she said. Then she smacked me again with her fist. If you don't think that hurts, you're crazy. 'Daddy'll *kill* you!' she said. Then she flopped on her stomach on the bed and put the goddam pillow over her head. She does that quite frequently. She's a true madman sometimes.

'Cut it out, now,' I said. 'Nobody's gonna kill me. Nobody's gonna even – C'*mon*, Phoeb, take that goddam thing off your head. Nobody's gonna kill me.'

She wouldn't take it off, though. You can't make her do something if she doesn't want to. All she kept saying was, 'Daddy's gonna kill you.' You could hardly understand her with that goddam pillow over her head.

'Nobody's gonna kill me. Use your head. In the first place, I'm going away. What I may do, I may get a job on a ranch or something for a while. I know this guy whose grandfather's got a ranch in Colorado. I may get a job out there,' I said. 'I'll keep in touch with you and all when I'm gone, if I go. C'mon. Take that off your head. C'mon, hey, Phoeb. Please. Please, willya?'

She wouldn't take it off, though. I tried pulling it off, but she's strong as hell. You get tired fighting with her. Boy, if she wants to keep a pillow over her head, she *keeps* it. 'Phoebe, *please*. C'mon outa there,' I kept saying. 'C'mon, hey . . . Hey, Weatherfield. C'mon out.'

She wouldn't come out, though. You can't even reason with her sometimes. Finally, I got up and went out in the living room and got some cigarettes out of the box on the table and stuck some in my pocket. I was all out.

22

When I came back, she had the pillow off her head all right – I knew she would – but she still wouldn't look at me, even though she was laying on her back and all. When I came around the side of the bed and sat down again, she turned her crazy face the other way. She was ostracizing the hell out of me. Just like the fencing team at Pencey when I left all the goddam foils on the subway.

'How's old Hazel Weatherfield?' I said. 'You write any new stories about her? I got that one you sent me right in my suitcase. It's down at the station. It's very good.'

'Daddy'll *kill* you.'

Boy, she really gets something on her mind when she gets something on her mind.

'No, he won't. The worst he'll do, he'll give me hell again, and then he'll send me to that goddam military school. That's all he'll do to me. And in the *first* place, I won't even be around. I'll be away. I'll be – I'll probably be in Colorado on this ranch.'

'Don't make me laugh. You can't even ride a horse.'

'Who can't? Sure I can. Certainly I can. They can teach you in about two minutes,' I said. 'Stop picking at that.' She was picking at that adhesive tape on her arm. 'Who gave you that haircut?' I asked her. I just noticed what a stupid haircut somebody gave her. It was way too short.

'None of your business,' she said. She can be very snotty

sometimes. She can be quite snotty. 'I suppose you failed in every single subject again,' she said – very snotty. It was sort of funny, too, in a way. She sounds like a goddam schoolteacher sometimes, and she's only a little child.

'No, I didn't,' I said. 'I passed English.' Then, just for the hell of it, I gave her a pinch on the behind. It was sticking way out in the breeze, the way she was laying on her side. She had hardly any behind. I didn't do it hard, but she tried to hit my hand anyway, but she missed.

Then all of a sudden, she said, 'Oh, why did you *do* it?' She meant why did I get the ax again. It made me sort of sad, the way she said it.

'Oh, God, Phoebe, don't ask me. I'm sick of everybody asking me that,' I said. 'A million reasons why. It was one of the worst schools I ever went to. It was full of phonies. And mean guys. You never saw so many mean guys in your life. For instance, if you were having a bull session in somebody's room, and somebody wanted to come in, nobody'd let them in if they were some dopey, pimply guy. Everybody was always *lock*ing their door when somebody wanted to come in. And they had this goddam secret fraternity that I was too yellow not to join. There was this one pimply, boring guy, Robert Ackley, that wanted to get in. He kept trying to join, and they wouldn't let him. Just because he was boring and pimply. I don't even feel like talking about it. It was a stinking school. Take my word.'

Old Phoebe didn't say anything, but she was listening. I could tell by the back of her neck that she was listening. She always listens when you tell her something. And the funny part is she knows, half the time, what the hell you're talking about. She really does.

I kept talking about old Pencey. I sort of felt like it.

'Even the couple of *nice* teachers on the faculty, they were phonies, too,' I said. 'There was this one old guy, Mr Spencer. His wife was always giving you hot chocolate and all that stuff, and they were really pretty nice. But you should've seen him when the headmaster, old Thurmer, came in the history class and sat down in the back of the room. He was always coming in and sitting down in the back of the room for about a half an hour. He was supposed to be incognito or something. After a while, he'd be sitting back there and then he'd start interrupting what old Spencer was saying to crack a lot of corny jokes. Old Spencer'd practically kill himself chuckling and smiling and all, like as if Thurmer was a goddam prince or something.'

'Don't swear so much.'

'It would've made you puke, I swear it would,' I said. 'Then, on Veterans' Day. They have this day, Veterans' Day, that all the jerks that graduated from Pencey around 1776 come back and walk all over the place, with their wives and children and everybody. You should've seen this one old guy that was about fifty. What he did was, he came in our room and knocked on the door and asked us if we'd mind if he used the bathroom. The bathroom was at the end of the corridor – I don't know why the hell he asked *us*. You know what he said? He said he wanted to see if his initials were still in one of the can doors. What he did, he carved his goddam stupid sad old initials in one of the can doors about ninety years ago, and he wanted to see if they were still there. So my roommate and I walked him down to the bathroom and all, and we had to stand there while he looked for his initials in all the can doors. He kept talking to us the whole time, telling us how when he was at Pencey they were the happiest days of his life, and giving us a lot of advice for the future and all. Boy, did he depress me! I don't mean he was a bad guy – he wasn't. But you don't have to be a bad guy to depress somebody – you can be a *good* guy and do it. All you have to do to depress somebody is give them a lot of phony advice while you're looking for your initials in some can door – that's all you have to do. I don't know. Maybe it wouldn't have been so bad if he hadn't been all out of breath. He was all out of breath from just climbing up the stairs, and the whole time he was looking for his initials he kept breathing hard, with his nostrils all funny and sad, while he kept telling Stradlater and I to get all we could out of Pencey. God, Phoebe! I can't explain. I just didn't like anything that was *hap*pening at Pencey. I can't explain.'

Old Phoebe said something then, but I couldn't hear her. She had the side of her mouth right smack on the pillow, and I couldn't hear her.

'What?' I said. 'Take your mouth away. I can't hear you with your mouth that way.'

'You don't like *any*thing that's happening.'

It made me even more depressed when she said that.

'Yes I do. Yes I do. *Sure* I do. Don't say that. Why the hell do you say that?'

'Because you don't. You don't like any schools. You don't like a million things. You *don't*.'

'I do! That's where you're wrong – that's exactly where you're wrong! Why the hell do you have to say that?' I said. Boy, was she depressing me.

'Because you don't,' she said. 'Name one thing.'

'One thing? One thing I like?' I said. 'Okay.'

The trouble was, I couldn't concentrate too hot. Sometimes it's hard to concentrate.

'One thing I like a lot you mean?' I asked her.

She didn't answer me, though. She was in a cockeyed position way the hell over the other side of the bed. She was about a thousand miles away. 'C'mon, answer me,' I said. 'One thing I like a lot, or one thing I just like?'

'You like a lot.'

'All right,' I said. But the trouble was, I couldn't concentrate. About all I could think of were those two nuns that went around collecting dough in those beat-up old straw baskets. Especially the one with the glasses with those iron rims. And this boy I knew at Elkton Hills. There was this one boy at Elkton Hills, named James Castle, that wouldn't take back something he said about this very conceited boy, Phil Stabile. James Castle called him a very conceited guy, and one of Stabile's lousy friends went and squealed on him to Stabile. So Stabile, with about six other dirty bastards, went down to James Castle's room and went in and locked the goddam door and tried to make him take back what he said, but he wouldn't do it. So they started in on him. I won't even tell you what they did to him – it's too repulsive – but he *still* wouldn't take it back, old James Castle. And you should've seen him. He was a skinny little weak-looking guy, with wrists about as big as pencils. Finally, what he did, instead of taking back what he said, he jumped out the window. I was in the *shower* and all, and even *I* could hear him land outside. But I just thought something fell out the window, a radio or a desk or something, not a *boy* or anything. Then I heard everybody running through the corridor and down the stairs, so I put on my bathrobe and I ran downstairs too, and there was old James Castle laying right on the stone steps and all. He was dead, and his teeth, and blood, were all over the place, and nobody would even go near him. He had on this turtleneck sweater I'd lent him. All they did with the guys that were in the room with him was expel them. They didn't even go to jail.

That was about all I could think of, though. Those two nuns I saw at breakfast and this boy James Castle I knew at Elkton Hills. The funny part is, I hardly even knew James Castle, if you want to know the truth. He was one of these very quiet guys. He was in my math class, but he was way over on the other side of the room, and he hardly ever got up to recite or go to the blackboard or anything. Some guys in school hardly ever get up to recite or go to the blackboard. I think the only time I ever even had a conversation with him was that time he asked me if he could borrow this turtleneck sweater I had. I damn near dropped dead when he asked me, I was so surprised and all. I remember I was brushing my teeth, in the can, when he asked me. He said his cousin was coming up to take him for a drive and all. I didn't even know he knew I *had* a turtleneck sweater. All I knew about him was that his name was always right ahead of me at roll call. Cabel, R., Cabel, W., Castle, Caulfield – I can still remember it. If you want to know the truth, I almost didn't *lend* him my sweater. Just because I didn't know him too well.

'What?' I said to old Phoebe. She said something to me, but I didn't hear her.

'You can't even think of one thing.'

'Yes, I can. Yes, I can.'

'Well, do it, then.'

'I like Allie,' I said. 'And I like doing what I'm doing right now. Sitting here with you, and talking, and thinking about stuff, and –'

'Allie's *dead* – You always say that! If somebody's dead and everything, and in *Heaven*, then it isn't really –'

'I know he's dead! Don't you think I know that? I can still like him, though, can't I? Just because somebody's dead, you don't just stop liking them, for God's sake – especially if they were about a thousand times nicer than the people you know that're a*live* and all.'

Old Phoebe didn't say anything. When she can't think of anything to say, she doesn't say a goddam word.

'Anyway, I like it now,' I said. 'I mean right now. Sitting here with you and just chewing the fat and horsing –'

'That isn't anything *real*ly!'

'It is so something *real*ly! Certainly it is! Why the hell isn't it? People never think anything is anything *really*. I'm getting goddam sick of it.'

'Stop swearing. All right, name something else. Name something you'd like to *be*. Like a scientist. Or a *law*yer or something.'

'I couldn't be a scientist. I'm no good in science.'

'Well, a lawyer – like Daddy and all.'

'Lawyers are all right, I guess – but it doesn't appeal to me,' I said. 'I mean they're all right if they go around saving innocent guys' lives all the time, and like that, but you don't *do* that kind of stuff if you're a lawyer. All you do is make a lot of dough and play golf and play bridge and buy cars and drink Martinis and look like a hot-shot. And besides. Even if you *did* go around saving guys' lives and all, how would you know if you did it because you really *wanted* to save guys' lives, or because you did it because what you *real*ly wanted to do was be a terrific lawyer, with everybody slapping you on the back and congratulating you in court when the goddam trial was over, the reporters and everybody, the way it is in the dirty movies? How would you know you weren't being a phony? The trouble is, you *wouldn't*.'

I'm not too sure old Phoebe knew what the hell I was talking about. I mean she's only a little child and all. But she was listening, at least. If somebody at least listens, it's not too bad.

'Daddy's going to kill you. He's going to *kill* you,' she said.

I wasn't listening, though. I was thinking about something else – something crazy. 'You know what I'd like to be?' I said. 'You know what I'd like to be? I mean if I had my goddam choice?'

'What? Stop *swear*ing.'

'You know that song "If a body catch a body comin' through the rye"? I'd like –'

'It's "If a body *meet* a body coming through the rye"!' old Phoebe said. 'It's a poem. By Robert *Burns*.'

'I *know* it's a poem by Robert Burns.'

She was right, though. It *is* 'If a body meet a body coming through the rye.' I didn't know it then, though.

'I thought it was "If a body catch a body,"' I said. 'Anyway, I keep picturing all these little kids playing some game in this big field of rye and all. Thousands of little kids, and nobody's around – nobody big, I mean – except me. And I'm standing on the edge of some crazy cliff. What I have to do, I have to catch everybody if they start to go over the cliff – I mean if they're running and they don't look where they're going I have to come out from somewhere and *catch* them. That's all I'd do all day. I'd just be the catcher in the rye and all. I know it's crazy, but that's the only thing I'd really like to be. I know it's crazy.'

Old Phoebe didn't say anything for a long time. Then, when she said something, all she said was, 'Daddy's going to kill you.'

'I don't give a damn if he does,' I said. I got up from the bed then, because what I wanted to do, I wanted to phone up this guy that was my English teacher at Elkton Hills, Mr Antolini. He lived in New York now. He quit Elkton Hills. He took this job teaching English at N.Y.U. 'I have to make a phone call,' I told Phoebe. 'I'll be right back. Don't go to sleep.' I didn't want her to go to sleep while I was in the living room. I knew she wouldn't, but I said it anyway, just to make sure.

While I was walking toward the door, old Phoebe said, 'Holden!' and I turned around.

She was sitting way up in bed. She looked so pretty. 'I'm taking belching lessons from this girl, Phyllis Margulies,' she said. 'Listen.'

I listened, and I heard *some*thing, but it wasn't much. 'Good,' I said. Then I went out in the living room and called up this teacher I had, Mr Antolini.

23

I made it very snappy on the phone because I was afraid my parents would barge in on me right in the middle of it. They didn't, though. Mr Antolini was very nice. He said I could come right over if I wanted to. I think I probably woke he and his wife up, because it took them a helluva long time to answer the phone. The first thing he asked me was if anything was wrong, and I said no. I said I'd flunked out of Pencey, though. I thought I might as well tell him. He said 'Good God,' when I said that. He had a good sense of humor and all. He told me to come right over if I felt like it.

He was about the best teacher I ever had, Mr Antolini. He was a pretty young guy, not much older than my brother D.B., and you could kid around with him without losing your respect for him. He was the one that finally picked up that boy that jumped out the window I told you about, James Castle. Old Mr Antolini felt his pulse and all, and then he took off his coat and put it over James Castle and carried him all the way over to the infirmary. He didn't even give a damn if his coat got all bloody.

When I got back to D.B.'s room, old Phoebe'd turned the radio on. This dance music was coming out. She'd turned it on low, though, so the maid wouldn't hear it. You should've seen her. She was sitting smack in the middle of the bed, outside the covers, with her legs folded like one of those Yogi guys. She was listening to the music. She kills me.

'C'mon,' I said. 'You feel like dancing?' I taught her how to dance and all when she was a tiny little kid. She's a very good dancer. I mean I just taught her a few things. She learned it mostly by herself. You can't teach somebody how to *really* dance.

'You have shoes on,' she said.

'I'll take 'em off. C'mon.'

She practically jumped off the bed, and then she waited while I took my shoes off, and then I danced with her for a while. She's really damn good. I don't like people that dance with little kids, because most of the time it looks terrible. I mean if you're out at a restaurant somewhere and you see some old guy take his little kid out on the dance floor. Usually they keep yanking the kid's dress up in the back by mistake, and the kid can't dance worth a damn *any*way, and it looks terrible, but I don't do it out in public with Phoebe or anything. We just horse around in the house. It's different with her anyway, because she can *dance*. She can follow anything you do. I mean if you hold her in close as hell so that it doesn't matter that your legs are so much longer. She stays right with you. You can cross over, or do some corny dips, or even jitterbug a little, and she stays right with you. You can even *tango*, for God's sake.

We danced about four numbers. In between numbers she's funny as hell. She stays right in position. She won't even talk or anything. You both have to stay right in position and wait for the orchestra to start playing again. That kills me. You're not supposed to laugh or anything, either.

Anyway, we danced about four numbers, and then I turned off the radio. Old Phoebe jumped back in bed and got under the covers. 'I'm improving, aren't I?' she asked me.

'And how,' I said. I sat down next to her on the bed again. I was sort of out of breath. I was smoking so damn much, I had hardly any wind. She wasn't even out of breath.

'Feel my forehead,' she said all of a sudden.

'Why?'

'*Feel* it. Just feel it once.'

I felt it. I didn't feel anything, though.

'Does it feel very feverish?' she said.

'No. Is it supposed to?'

'Yes – I'm making it. Feel it again.'

I felt it again, and I still didn't feel anything, but I said, 'I think it's starting to, now.' I didn't want her to get a goddam inferiority complex.

She nodded. 'I can make it go up to over the thermoneter.'

'Ther*mom*eter. Who said so?'

'Alice Holmborg showed me how. You cross your legs and hold your breath and think of something very, very hot. A radiator or something. Then your whole forehead gets so hot you can burn somebody's hand.'

That killed me. I pulled my hand away from her forehead, like I was in terrific danger. 'Thanks for *tell*ing me,' I said.

'Oh, I wouldn't've burned *your* hand. I'd've stopped before it got too – *Shhh!*' Then, quick as hell, she sat way the hell up in bed.

She scared hell out of me when she did that. 'What's the matter?' I said.

'The front door!' she said in this loud whisper. 'It's them!'

I quickly jumped up and ran over and turned off the light over the desk. Then I jammed out my cigarette on my shoe and put it in my pocket. Then I fanned hell out of the air, to get the smoke out – I shouldn't even have been smoking, for God's sake. Then I grabbed my shoes and got in the closet and shut the door. Boy, my heart was beating like a bastard.

I heard my mother come in the room.

'Phoebe?' she said. 'Now, stop that. I saw the light, young lady.'

'Hello!' I heard old Phoebe say. 'I couldn't sleep. Did you have a good time?'

'Marvelous,' my mother said, but you could tell she didn't mean it. She doesn't enjoy herself much when she goes out. 'Why are you awake, may I ask? Were you warm enough?'

'I was warm enough, I just couldn't sleep.'

'Phoebe, have you been smoking a cigarette in here? Tell me the truth, please, young lady.'

'What?' old Phoebe said.

'You heard me.'

'I just lit one for one second. I just took *one puff*. Then I threw it out the window.'

'*Why*, may I ask?'

'I couldn't sleep.'

'I don't like that, Phoebe. I don't like that at all,' my mother said. 'Do you want another blanket?'

'No, thanks. G'night!' old Phoebe said. She was trying to get rid of her, you could tell.

'How was the movie?' my mother said.

'Excellent. Except Alice's mother. She kept leaning over and asking her if she felt grippy during the whole entire movie. We took a taxi home.'

'Let me feel your forehead.'

'I didn't catch anything. She didn't have anything. It was just her mother.'

'Well. Go to sleep now. How was your dinner?'

'Lousy,' Phoebe said.

'You heard what your father said about using that word. What was lousy about it? You had a lovely lamb chop. I walked all over Lexington Avenue just to –'

'The lamb chop was all right, but Charlene always *breathes* on me whenever she puts something down. She breathes all over the food and everything. She *breathes* on everything.'

'Well. Go to sleep. Give Mother a kiss. Did you say your prayers?'

'I said them in the bathroom. G'night!'

'Good night. Go right to sleep now. I have a splitting headache,' my mother said. She gets headaches quite frequently. She really does.

'Take a few aspirins,' old Phoebe said. 'Holden'll be home on Wednesday, won't he?'

'So far as I know. Get under there, now. Way down.'

I heard my mother go out and close the door. I waited a couple of minutes. Then I came out of the closet. I bumped smack into old Phoebe when I did it, because it was so dark and she was out of bed and coming to tell me. 'I hurt you?' I said. You had to whisper now, because they were both home. 'I gotta get a move on,' I said. I found the edge of the bed in the dark and sat down on it and started putting on my shoes. I was pretty nervous. I admit it.

'Don't go *now*,' Phoebe whispered. 'Wait'll they're asleep!'

'No. Now. Now's the best time,' I said. 'She'll be in the bathroom and Daddy'll turn on the news or something. Now's the best time.' I could hardly tie my shoelaces, I was so damn nervous. Not that they would've *killed* me or anything if they'd caught me home, but it would've been very unpleasant and all. 'Where the hell are ya?' I said to old Phoebe. It was so dark I couldn't see her.

'Here.' She was standing right next to me. I didn't even see her.

'I got my damn bags at the station,' I said. 'Listen. You got any dough, Phoeb? I'm practically broke.'

'Just my Christmas dough. For presents and all. I haven't done any shopping at *all* yet.'

'Oh.' I didn't want to take her Christmas dough.

'You want some?' she said.

'I don't want to take your Christmas dough.'

'I can lend you *some*,' she said. Then I heard her over at D.B.'s desk, opening a million drawers and feeling around with her hand. It was pitch-black, it was so dark in the room. 'If you go away, you won't see me in the play,' she said. Her voice sounded funny when she said it.

'Yes, I will. I won't go way before that. You think I wanna miss the play?' I said. 'What I'll do, I'll probably stay at Mr Antolini's house till maybe Tuesday night. Then I'll come home. If I get a chance, I'll phone ya.'

'Here,' old Phoebe said. She was trying to give me the dough, but she couldn't find my hand.

'Where?'

She put the dough in my hand.

'Hey, I don't need all this,' I said. 'Just give me two bucks, is all. No kidding – Here.' I tried to give it back to her, but she wouldn't take it.

'You can take it all. You can pay me back. Bring it to the play.'

'How much is it, for God's sake?'

'Eight dollars and eighty-five cents. *Six*ty-five cents. I spent some.'

Then, all of a sudden, I started to cry. I couldn't help it. I did it so nobody could hear me, but I did it. It scared hell out of old Phoebe when I started doing it, and she came over and tried to make me stop, but once you get started, you can't just stop on a goddam *dime*. I was still sitting on the edge of the bed when I did it, and she put her old arm around my neck, and I put my arm around her, too, but I still couldn't stop for a long time. I thought I was going to choke to death or something. Boy, I scared hell out of poor old Phoebe. The damn window was open and everything, and I could feel her shivering and all, because all she had on was her pajamas. I tried to make her get back in bed, but she wouldn't go. Finally I stopped. But it certainly took me a long, long time. Then I finished buttoning my coat and all. I told her I'd keep in touch with her. She told me I could sleep with her if I wanted to, but I said no, that I'd better beat it, that Mr. Antolini was waiting for me and all. Then I took my hunting hat out of my coat pocket and gave it to her. She likes those kind of crazy hats. She didn't want to take it, but I made her. I'll bet she slept with it on. She really likes those kind of hats. Then I told her again I'd give her a buzz if I got a chance, and then I left.

It was a helluva lot easier getting out of the house than it was getting in, for some reason. For one thing, I didn't give much of a damn any more if they caught me. I really didn't. I figured if they caught me, they caught me. I almost wished they did, in a way.

I walked all the way downstairs, instead of taking the elevator. I went down the back stairs. I nearly broke my neck on about ten million garbage pails, but I got out all right. The elevator boy didn't even see me. He probably *still* thinks I'm up at the Dicksteins'.

24

Mr and Mrs Antolini had this very swanky apartment over on Sutton Place, with two steps that you go down to get in the living room, and a bar and all. I'd been there quite a few times, because after I left Elkton Hills Mr Antolini came up to our house for dinner quite frequently to find out how I was getting along. He wasn't married then. Then when he got married, I used to play tennis with he and Mrs Antolini quite frequently, out at the West Side Tennis Club, in Forest Hills, Long Island. Mrs Antolini belonged there. She was lousy with dough. She was about sixty years older than Mr Antolini, but they seemed to get along quite well. For one thing, they were both very intellectual, especially Mr Antolini, except that he was more witty than intellectual when you were with him, sort of like D.B. Mrs Antolini was mostly serious. She had asthma pretty bad. They both read all D.B.'s stories – Mrs Antolini, too – and when D.B. went to Hollywood, Mr Antolini phoned him up and told him not to go. He went anyway, though. Mr Antolini said that anybody that could write like D.B. had no business going out to Hollywood. That's exactly what I said, practically.

I would have walked down to their house, because I didn't want to spend any of Phoebe's Christmas dough that I didn't have to, but I felt funny when I got outside. Sort of dizzy. So I took a cab. I didn't want to, but I did. I had a helluva time even *find*ing a cab.

Old Mr Antolini answered the door when I rang the

bell – after the elevator boy *fin*ally let me up, the bastard. He had on his bathrobe and slippers, and he had a highball in one hand. He was a pretty sophisticated guy, and he was a pretty heavy drinker. 'Holden, m'boy!' he said. 'My God, he's grown another twenty inches. Fine to see you.'

'How are you, Mr Antolini? How's Mrs Antolini?'

'We're both just dandy. Let's have that coat.' He took my coat off me and hung it up. 'I expected to see a day-old infant in your arms. Nowhere to turn. Snowflakes in your eyelashes.' He's a very witty guy sometimes. He turned around and yelled out to the kitchen, 'Lillian! How's the coffee coming?' Lillian was Mrs Antolini's first name.

'It's all ready,' she yelled back. 'Is that Holden? Hello, Holden!'

'Hello, Mrs Antolini!'

You were always yelling when you were there. That's because the both of them were never in the same room at the same time. It was sort of funny.

'Sit down, Holden,' Mr Antolini said. You could tell he was a little oiled up. The room looked like they'd just had a party. Glasses were all over the place, and dishes with peanuts in them. 'Excuse the appearance of the place,' he said. 'We've been entertaining some Buffalo friends of Mrs Antolini's . . . Some buffaloes, as a matter of fact.'

I laughed, and Mrs Antolini yelled something in to me from the kitchen, but I couldn't hear her. 'What'd she say?' I asked Mr Antolini.

'She said not to look at her when she comes in. She just arose from the sack. Have a cigarette. Are you smoking now?'

'Thanks,' I said. I took a cigarette from this box he offered me. 'Just once in a while. I'm a moderate smoker.'

'I'll bet you are,' he said. He gave me a light from this big lighter off the table. 'So. You and Pencey are no longer one,' he said. He always said things that way. Sometimes it amused me a lot and sometimes it didn't. He sort of did it a little bit *too* much. I don't mean he wasn't witty or anything – he was – but sometimes it gets on your nerves when somebody's *al*ways saying things like 'So you and Pencey are no longer one.' D.B. does it too much sometimes, too.

'What was the trouble?' Mr Antolini asked me. 'How'd you do in English? I'll show you the door in short order if you flunked English, you little ace composition writer.'

'Oh, I passed English all right. It was mostly literature, though. I only wrote about two compositions the whole term,' I said. 'I flunked Oral Expression, though. They had this course you had to take, Oral Expression. *That* I flunked.'

'Why?'

'Oh, I don't know.' I didn't feel much like going into it. I was still feeling sort of dizzy or something, and I had a helluva headache all of a sudden. I really did. But you could tell he was interested, so I told him a little bit about it. 'It's this course where each boy in class has to get up in class and make a speech. You know. Spontaneous and all. And if the boy digresses at all, you're supposed to yell "Digression!" at him as fast as you can. It just about drove me crazy. I got an *F* in it.'

'Why?'

'Oh, I don't know. That digression business got on my nerves. I don't know. The trouble with me is, I *like* it when somebody digresses. It's more *in*teresting and all.'

'You don't care to have somebody stick to the point when he tells you something?'

'Oh, sure! I like somebody to stick to the point and all. But I don't like them to stick *too* much to the point. I don't know.

I guess I don't like it when somebody sticks to the point *all* the time. The boys that got the best marks in Oral Expression were the ones that stuck to the point all the time – I admit it. But there was this one boy, Richard Kinsella. He didn't stick to the point too much, and they were always yelling "Digression!" at him. It was terrible, because in the first place, he was a very nervous guy – I mean he was a very nervous guy – and his lips were always shaking whenever it was his time to make a speech, and you could hardly hear him if you were sitting way in the back of the room. When his lips sort of quit shaking a little bit, though, I liked his speeches better than anybody else's. He practically flunked the course, though, too. He got a *D* plus because they kept yelling "Digression!" at him all the time. For instance, he made this speech about this farm his father bought in Vermont. They kept yelling "Digression!" at him the whole time he was making it, and this teacher, Mr Vinson, gave him an *F* on it because he hadn't told what kind of animals and vegetables and stuff grew on the farm and all. What he did was, Richard Kinsella, he'd *start* telling you all about that stuff – then all of a sudden he'd start telling you about this letter his mother got from his uncle, and how his uncle got polio and all when he was forty-two years old, and how he wouldn't let anybody come to see him in the hospital because he didn't want anybody to see him with a brace on. It didn't have much to do with the farm – I admit it – but it was *nice*. It's nice when somebody tells you about their uncle. Especially when they start out telling you about their father's farm and then all of a sudden get more interested in their uncle. I mean it's dirty to keep yelling "Digression!" at him when he's all nice and excited . . . I don't know. It's hard to explain.' I didn't feel too much like trying, either. For one thing, I had this terrific headache all of a sudden. I wished to God old Mrs Antolini would come in with the coffee. That's something that annoys hell out of me – I mean if somebody *says* the coffee's all ready and it isn't.

'Holden . . . One short, faintly stuffy, pedagogical question. Don't you think there's a time and place for everything? Don't you think if someone starts out to tell you about his father's farm, he should stick to his guns, *then* get around to telling you about his uncle's brace? *Or*, if his uncle's brace is such a provocative subject, shouldn't he have selected it in the first place as his subject – not the farm?'

I didn't feel much like thinking and answering and all. I had a headache and I felt lousy. I even had sort of a stomach-ache, if you want to know the truth.

'Yes – I don't know. I guess he should. I mean I guess he should've picked his uncle as a subject, instead of the farm, if that interested him most. But what I mean is, lots of time you don't *know* what interests you most till you start talking about something that *doesn't* interest you most. I mean you can't help it sometimes. What I think is, you're supposed to leave somebody alone if he's at least being interesting and he's getting all excited about something. I like it when somebody gets excited about something. It's nice. You just didn't know this teacher, Mr Vinson. He could drive you crazy sometimes, him and the goddam class. I mean he'd keep telling you to *un*ify and *simp*lify all the time. Some things you just can't *do* that to. I mean you can't hardly ever simplify and unify something just because somebody *wants* you to. You didn't know this guy, Mr Vinson. I mean he was very intelligent and all, but you could tell he didn't have too much brains.'

'Coffee, gentlemen, *fin*ally,' Mrs Antolini said. She came in carrying this tray with coffee and cakes and stuff on it. 'Holden, don't you even peek at me. I'm a mess.'

'Hello, Mrs Antolini,' I said. I started to get up and all, but Mr Antolini got hold of my jacket and pulled me back down. Old Mrs Antolini's hair was full of those iron curler jobs, and she didn't have any lipstick or anything on. She didn't look too gorgeous. She looked pretty old and all.

'I'll leave this right here. Just dive in, you two,' she said. She put the tray down on the cigarette table, pushing all these glasses out of the way. 'How's your mother, Holden?'

'She's fine, thanks. I haven't seen her too recently, but the last I –'

'Darling, if Holden needs anything, everything's in the linen closet. The top shelf. I'm going to bed. I'm exhausted,' Mrs Antolini said. She looked it, too. 'Can you boys make up the couch by yourselves?'

'We'll take care of everything. You run along to bed,' Mr Antolini said. He gave Mrs Antolini a kiss and she said good-by to me and went in the bedroom. They were always kissing each other a lot in public.

I had part of a cup of coffee and about half of some cake that was about as hard as a rock. All old Mr Antolini had was another highball, though. He makes them very strong, too, you could tell. He may get to be an alcoholic if he doesn't watch his step.

'I had lunch with your dad a couple of weeks ago,' he said all of a sudden. 'Did you know that?'

'No, I didn't.'

'You're aware, of course, that he's terribly concerned about you.'

'I know it. I know he is,' I said.

'Apparently before he phoned me he'd just had a long, rather harrowing letter from your latest headmaster, to the effect that you were making absolutely no effort at all. Cutting classes.

Coming unprepared to all your classes. In general, being an all-around –'

'I didn't cut any classes. You weren't allowed to cut any. There were a couple of them I didn't attend once in a while, like that Oral Expression I told you about, but I didn't cut any.'

I didn't feel at all like discussing it. The coffee made my stomach feel a little better, but I still had this awful headache.

Mr Antolini lit another cigarette. He smoked like a fiend. Then he said, 'Frankly, I don't know what the hell to say to you, Holden.'

'I know. I'm very hard to talk to. I realize that.'

'I have a feeling that you're riding for some kind of a terrible, terrible fall. But I don't honestly know what kind . . . Are you listening to me?'

'Yes.'

You could tell he was trying to concentrate and all.

'It may be the kind where, at the age of thirty, you sit in some bar hating everybody who comes in looking as if he might have played football in college. Then again, you may pick up just enough education to hate people who say, "It's a secret between he and I." Or you may end up in some business office, throwing paper clips at the nearest stenographer. I just don't know. But do you know what I'm driving at, at all?'

'Yes. Sure,' I said. I did, too. 'But you're wrong about that hating business. I mean about hating football players and all. You really are. I don't hate too many guys. What I may do, I may hate them for a *little* while, like this guy Stradlater I knew at Pencey, and this other boy, Robert Ackley. I hated *them* once in a while – I admit it – but it doesn't last too long, is what I mean. After a while, if I didn't see them, if they didn't come in the room, or if I didn't see them in the dining room for a couple of meals, I sort of missed them. I mean I sort of missed them.'

Mr Antolini didn't say anything for a while. He got up and got another hunk of ice and put it in his drink, then he sat down again. You could tell he was thinking. I kept wishing, though, that he'd continue the conversation in the morning, instead of now, but he was hot. People are mostly hot to have a discussion when you're not.

'All right. Listen to me a minute now . . . I may not word this as memorably as I'd like to, but I'll write you a letter about it in a day or two. Then you can get it all straight. But listen now, anyway.' He started concentrating again. Then he said, 'This fall I think you're riding for – it's a special kind of fall, a horrible kind. The man falling isn't permitted to feel or hear himself hit bottom. He just keeps falling and falling. The whole arrangement's designed for men who, at some time or other in their lives, were looking for something their own environment couldn't supply them with. Or they thought their own environment couldn't supply them with. So they gave up looking. They gave it up before they ever really even got started. You follow me?'

'Yes, sir.'

'Sure?'

'Yes.'

He got up and poured some more booze in his glass. Then he sat down again. He didn't say anything for quite a long time.

'I don't want to scare you,' he said, 'but I can very clearly see you dying nobly, one way or another, for some highly unworthy cause.' He gave me a funny look. 'If I write something down for you, will you read it carefully? And keep it?'

'Yes. Sure,' I said. I did, too. I still have the paper he gave me.

He went over to this desk on the other side of the room, and without sitting down wrote something on a piece of paper. Then he came back and sat down with the paper in his hand. 'Oddly enough, this wasn't written by a practicing poet. It was written by a psychoanalyst named Wilhelm Stekel. Here's what he – Are you still with me?'

'Yes, sure I am.'

'Here's what he said: "The mark of the immature man is that he wants to die nobly for a cause, while the mark of the mature man is that he wants to live humbly for one." '

He leaned over and handed it to me. I read it right when he gave it to me, and then I thanked him and all and put it in my pocket. It was nice of him to go to all that trouble. It really was. The thing was, though, I didn't feel much like concentrating. Boy, I felt so damn *tired* all of a sudden.

You could tell he wasn't tired at all, though. He was pretty oiled up, for one thing. 'I think that one of these days,' he said, 'you're going to have to find out where you want to go. And then you've got to start going there. But immediately. You can't afford to lose a minute. Not you.'

I nodded, because he was looking right at me and all, but I wasn't too sure what he was talking about. I was *pretty* sure I knew, but I wasn't too positive at the time. I was too damn tired.

'And I hate to tell you,' he said, 'but I think that once you have a fair idea where you want to go, your first move will be to apply yourself in school. You'll have to. You're a student – whether the idea appeals to you or not. You're in love with knowledge. And I think you'll find, once you get past all the Mr Vineses and their Oral Comp– '

'Mr Vinsons,' I said. He meant all the Mr Vinsons, not all the Mr Vineses. I shouldn't have interrupted him, though.

'All right – the Mr Vinsons. Once you get past all the Mr Vinsons, you're going to start getting closer and closer – that is, if you *want* to, and if you look for it and wait for it – to the kind of information that will be very, very dear to your heart. Among other things, you'll find that you're not the first person who was ever confused and frightened and even sickened by human behavior. You're by no means alone on that score, you'll be excited and *stimulated* to know. Many, many men have been just as troubled morally and spiritually as you are right now. Happily, some of them kept records of their troubles. You'll learn from them – if you want to. Just as someday, if you have something to offer, someone will learn something from you. It's a beautiful reciprocal arrangement. And it isn't education. It's history. It's poetry.' He stopped and took a big drink out of his highball. Then he started again. Boy, he was really hot. I was glad I didn't try to stop him or anything. 'I'm not trying to tell you,' he said, 'that only educated and scholarly men are able to contribute something valuable to the world. It's not so. But I do say that educated and scholarly men, if they're brilliant and creative to begin with – which, unfortunately, is rarely the case – tend to leave infinitely more valuable records behind them than men do who are *mere*ly brilliant and creative. They tend to express themselves more clearly, and they usually have a passion for following their thoughts through to the end. And – most important – nine times out of ten they have more humility than the unscholarly thinker. Do you follow me at all?'

'Yes, sir.'

He didn't say anything again for quite a while. I don't know if you've ever done it, but it's sort of hard to sit around waiting for somebody to say something when they're thinking and all. It really is. I kept trying not to yawn. It wasn't that I was bored or anything – I wasn't – but I was so damn sleepy all of a sudden.

'Something else an academic education will do for you. If you go along with it any considerable distance, it'll begin to give you an idea what size mind you have. What it'll fit and, maybe, what it won't. After a while, you'll have an idea what kind of thoughts your particular size mind should be wearing. For one thing, it may save you an extraordinary amount of time trying on ideas that don't suit you, aren't becoming to you. You'll begin to know your true measurements and dress your mind accordingly.'

Then, all of a sudden, I yawned. What a *rude bastard*, but I couldn't help it!

Mr Antolini just laughed, though. 'C'mon,' he said, and got up. 'We'll fix up the couch for you.'

I followed him and he went over to this closet and tried to take down some sheets and blankets and stuff that was on the top shelf, but he couldn't do it with this highball glass in his hand. So he drank it and then put the glass down on the floor and *then* he took the stuff down. I helped him bring it over to the couch. We both made the bed together. He wasn't too hot at it. He didn't tuck anything in very tight. I didn't care, though. I could've slept standing up I was so tired.

'How're all your women?'

'They're okay.' I was being a lousy conversationalist, but I didn't feel like it.

'How's Sally?' He knew old Sally Hayes. I introduced him once.

'She's all right. I had a date with her this afternoon.' Boy, it seemed like twenty years ago! 'We don't have too much in common any more.'

'Helluva pretty girl. What about that other girl? The one you told me about, in Maine?'

'Oh – Jane Gallagher. She's all right. I'm probably gonna give her a buzz tomorrow.'

We were all done making up the couch then. 'It's all yours,' Mr Antolini said. 'I don't know what the hell you're going to do with those legs of yours.'

'That's all right. I'm used to short beds,' I said. 'Thanks a lot, sir. You and Mrs Antolini really saved my life tonight.'

'You know where the bathroom is. If there's anything you want, just holler. I'll be in the kitchen for a while – will the light bother you?'

'No – heck, no. Thanks a lot.'

'All right. Good night, handsome.'

'G'night, sir. Thanks a lot.'

He went out in the kitchen and I went in the bathroom and got undressed and all. I couldn't brush my teeth because I didn't have any toothbrush with me. I didn't have any pajamas either and Mr Antolini forgot to lend me some. So I just went back in the living room and turned off this little lamp next to the couch, and then I got in bed with just my shorts on. It was way too short for me, the couch, but I really could've slept standing up without batting an eyelash. I laid awake for just a couple of seconds thinking about all that stuff Mr Antolini'd told me. About finding out the size of your mind and all. He was really a pretty smart guy. But I couldn't keep my goddam eyes open, and I fell asleep.

Then something happened. I don't even like to *talk* about it.

I woke up all of a sudden. I don't know what time it was or anything, but I woke up. I felt something on my head, some guy's hand. Boy, it really scared hell out of me. What it was, it was Mr Antolini's hand. What he was doing was, he was sitting on the floor right next to the couch, in the dark and all, and he was sort of petting me or patting me on the goddam head. Boy, I'll bet I jumped about a thousand feet.

'What the hellya *do*ing?' I said.

'Nothing! I'm simply sitting here, admiring – '

'What're ya *do*ing, anyway?' I said over again. I didn't know *what* the hell to say – I mean I was embarrassed as hell.

'How 'bout keeping your voice down? I'm simply sitting here –'

'I have to go, anyway,' I said – boy, was I nervous! I started putting on my damn pants in the dark. I could hardly get them on I was so damn nervous. I know more damn perverts, at schools and all, than anybody you ever met, and they're always being perverty when *I'm* around.

'You have to go *where*?' Mr Antolini said. He was trying to act very goddam casual and cool and all, but he wasn't any too goddam cool. Take my word.

'I left my bags and all at the station. I think maybe I'd better go down and get them. I have all my stuff in them.'

'They'll be there in the morning. Now, go back to bed. I'm going to bed myself. What's the matter with you?'

'Nothing's the matter, it's just that all my money and stuff's in one of my bags. I'll be right back. I'll get a cab and be right back,' I said. Boy, I was falling all over myself in the dark. 'The thing is, it isn't mine, the money. It's my mother's, and I –'

'Don't be ridiculous, Holden. Get back in that bed. I'm going to bed myself. The money will be there safe and sound in the morn –'

'No, no kidding. I gotta get going. I really do.' I was damn near all dressed already, except that I couldn't find my tie. I couldn't remember where I'd put my tie. I put on my jacket and all without it. Old Mr Antolini was sitting now in the big chair a little ways away from me, watching me. It was dark and all and I couldn't see him so hot, but I knew he was watching me, all right. He was still boozing, too. I could see his trusty highball glass in his hand.

'You're a very, very strange boy.'

'I know it,' I said. I didn't even look around much for my tie. So I went without it. 'Good-by, sir,' I said. 'Thanks a lot. No kidding.'

He kept walking right behind me when I went to the front door, and when I rang the elevator bell he stayed in the damn doorway. All he said was that business about my being a 'very, very strange boy' again. Strange, my ass. Then he waited in the doorway and all till the goddam elevator came. I never waited so long for an elevator in my whole goddam life. I swear.

I didn't know what the hell to talk about while I was waiting for the elevator, and he kept standing there, so I said, 'I'm gonna start reading some good books. I really am.' I mean you had to say *some*thing. It was very embarrassing.

'You grab your bags and scoot right on back here again. I'll leave the door unlatched.'

'Thanks a lot,' I said. 'G'by!' The elevator was finally there. I got in and went down. Boy, I was shaking like a madman. I was sweating, too. When something perverty like that happens, I start sweating like a bastard. That kind of stuff's happened to me about twenty times since I was a kid. I can't stand it.

25

When I got outside, it was just getting light out. It was pretty cold, too, but it felt good because I was sweating so much.

I didn't know where the hell to go. I didn't want to go to another hotel and spend all Phoebe's dough. So finally all I did was I walked over to Lexington and took the subway down to Grand Central. My bags were there and all, and I figured I'd sleep in that crazy waiting room where all the benches are. So that's what I did. It wasn't too bad for a while because there weren't many people around and I could stick my feet up. But I don't feel much like discussing it. It wasn't too nice. Don't ever try it. I mean it. It'll depress you.

I only slept till around nine o'clock because a million people started coming in the waiting room and I had to take my feet down. I can't sleep so hot if I have to keep my feet on the floor. So I sat up. I still had that headache. It was even worse. And I think I was more depressed than I ever was in my whole life.

I didn't want to, but I started thinking about old Mr Antolini and I wondered what he'd tell Mrs Antolini when she saw I hadn't slept there or anything. That part didn't worry me too much, though, because I knew Mr Antolini was very smart and that he could make up something to tell her. He could tell her I'd gone home or something. That part didn't worry me much. But what *did* worry me was the part about how I'd woke up and found him patting me on the head and all. I mean I wondered if just maybe I was wrong about thinking he was making a flitty pass at me. I wondered if maybe he just liked to pat guys on the head when they're asleep. I mean how can you tell about that stuff for sure? You can't. I even started wondering if maybe I should've got my bags and gone back to his house, the way I'd said I would. I mean I started thinking that even if he was a flit he certainly'd been very nice to me. I thought how he hadn't minded it when I'd called him up so late, and how he'd told me to come right over if I felt like it. And how he went to all that trouble giving me that advice about finding out the size of your mind and all, and how he was the only guy that'd even gone *near* that boy James Castle I told you about when he was dead. I thought about all that stuff. And the more I thought about it, the more depressed I got. I mean I started thinking maybe I *should've* gone back to his house. Maybe he *was* only patting my head just for the hell of it. The more I thought about it, though, the more depressed and screwed up about it I got. What made it even worse, my eyes were sore as hell. They felt all sore and burny from not getting too much sleep. Besides that, I was getting sort of a cold, and I didn't even have a goddam handkerchief with me. I had some in my suitcase, but I didn't feel like taking it out of that strong box and opening it up right in public and all.

There was this magazine that somebody'd left on the bench next to me, so I started reading it, thinking it'd make me stop thinking about Mr Antolini and a million other things for at least a little while. But this damn article I started reading made me feel almost worse. It was all about hormones. It described how you should look, your face and eyes and all, if your hormones were in good shape, and I didn't look that way at all. I looked exactly like the guy in the article with lousy hormones. So I started getting worried about my hormones. Then I read this other article about how you can tell if you have cancer or not. It said if you had any sores in your mouth that didn't heal pretty quickly, it was a sign that you probably had cancer. I'd had this sore on the inside of my lip for about *two weeks*. So figured I was getting cancer. That magazine was some little cheerer upper. I finally quit reading it and went outside for a walk. I figured I'd be dead in a couple of months because I had cancer. I really did. I was even positive I would be. It certainly didn't make me feel too gorgeous.

It sort of looked like it was going to rain, but I went for this walk anyway. For one thing, I figured I ought to get some breakfast. I wasn't at all hungry, but I figured I ought to at least eat something. I mean at least get something with some vitamins in it. So I started walking way over east, where the pretty cheap restaurants are, because I didn't want to spend a lot of dough.

While I was walking, I passed these two guys that were unloading this big Christmas tree off a truck. One guy kept saying to the other guy, 'Hold the sonuvabitch *up*! Hold it *up*, for Chrissake!' It certainly was a gorgeous way to talk about a Christmas tree. It was sort of funny, though, in an awful way, and I started to sort of laugh. It was about the *worst* thing I could've done, because the minute I started to laugh I thought I was going to vomit. I really did. I even started to, but it went away. I don't know why. I mean I hadn't eaten anything unsanitary or like that and usually I have quite a strong stomach. Anyway, I got over it, and I figured I'd feel better if I had something to eat. So I went in this very cheap-looking restaurant and had doughnuts and coffee. Only, I didn't eat the doughnuts. I couldn't swallow them too well. The thing is, if you get very depressed about something, it's hard as hell to swallow.

The waiter was very nice, though. He took them back without charging me. I just drank the coffee. Then I left and started walking over toward Fifth Avenue.

It was Monday and all, and pretty near Christmas, and all the stores were open. So it wasn't too bad walking on Fifth Avenue. It was fairly Christmasy. All those scraggy-looking Santa Clauses were standing on corners ringing those bells, and the Salvation Army girls, the ones that don't wear any lipstick or anything, were ringing bells too. I sort of kept looking around for those two nuns I'd met at breakfast the day before, but I didn't see them. I knew I wouldn't, because they'd told me they'd come to New York to be schoolteachers, but I kept looking for them anyway. Anyway, it was pretty Christmasy all of a sudden. A million little kids were downtown with their mothers, getting on and off buses and coming in and out of stores. I wished old Phoebe was around. She's not little enough any more to go stark staring mad in the toy department, but she enjoys horsing around and looking at the people. The Christmas before last I took her downtown shopping with me. We had a helluva time. I think it was in Bloomingdale's. We went in the shoe department and we pretended she – old Phoebe – wanted to get a pair of those very high storm shoes, the kind that have about a million holes to lace up. We had the poor salesman guy going crazy. Old Phoebe tried on about twenty pairs, and each time the poor guy had to lace one shoe all the way up. It was a dirty trick, but it killed old Phoebe. We finally bought a pair of moccasins and charged them. The salesman was very nice about it. I think he knew we were horsing around, because old Phoebe always starts giggling.

Anyway, I kept walking and walking up Fifth Avenue, without any tie on or anything. Then all of a sudden, something very spooky started happening. Every time I came to the end of a block and stepped off the goddam curb, I had this feeling that I'd never get to the other side of the street. I thought I'd just go down, down, down, and nobody'd ever see me again. Boy, did it scare me. You can't imagine. I started sweating like a bastard – my whole shirt and underwear and everything. Then I started doing something else. Every time I'd get to the end of a block I'd make believe I was talking to my brother Allie. I'd say to him, 'Allie, don't let me disappear. Allie, don't let me disappear. Allie, don't let me disappear. Please, Allie.' And then when I'd reach the other side of the street without disappearing, I'd *thank* him. Then it would start all over again as soon as I got to the next corner. But I kept going and all. I was sort of afraid to stop, I think – I don't remember, to tell you the truth. I know I didn't stop till I was way up in the Sixties, past the zoo and all. Then I sat down on this bench. I could hardly get my breath, and I was still sweating like a bastard. I sat there, I guess, for about an hour. Finally, what I decided I'd do, I decided I'd go away. I decided I'd never go home again and I'd never go away to another school again. I decided I'd just see old Phoebe and sort of say good-by to her and all, and give her back her Christmas dough, and then I'd start hitchhiking my way out West. What I'd do, I figured, I'd go down to the Holland Tunnel and bum a ride, and then I'd bum another one, and another one, and another one, and in a few days I'd be somewhere out West where it was very pretty and sunny and where nobody'd know me and I'd get a job. I figured I could get a job at a filling station somewhere, putting gas and oil in people's cars. I didn't care what kind of a job it was, though. Just so people didn't know me and I didn't know anybody. I thought what I'd do was, I'd pretend I was one of those deaf-mutes. That way I wouldn't have to have any goddam stupid useless conversations with anybody. If anybody wanted to tell me something, they'd have to write it on a piece of paper and shove it over to me. They'd get bored as hell doing that after a while, and then I'd be through with having conversations for the rest of my life. Everybody'd think I was just a poor deaf-mute bastard and they'd leave me alone. They'd let me put gas and oil in their stupid cars, and they'd pay me a salary and all for it, and I'd build me a little cabin somewhere with the dough I made and live there for the rest of my life. I'd build it right near the woods, but not right *in* them, because I'd want it to be sunny as hell all the time. I'd cook all my own food, and later on, if I wanted to get married or something, I'd meet this beautiful girl that was also a deaf-mute and we'd get married. She'd come and live in my cabin with me, and if she wanted to say anything to me, she'd have to write it on a goddam piece of paper, like everybody else. If we had any children, we'd hide them somewhere. We could buy them a lot of books and teach them how to read and write by ourselves.

I got excited as hell thinking about it. I really did. I knew the part about pretending I was a deaf-mute was crazy, but I liked thinking about it anyway. But I really decided to go out West and all. All I wanted to do first was say good-by to old Phoebe. So all of a sudden, I ran like a madman across the street – I damn near got killed doing it, if you want to know the truth – and went in this stationery store and bought a pad and pencil. I figured I'd write her a note telling her where to meet me so I could say good-by to her and give her back her Christmas dough, and then I'd take the note up to her school and get somebody in the principal's office to give it to her. But I just put the pad and pencil in my pocket and started walking fast as hell up to her school – I was too excited to write the note right in the stationery store. I walked fast because I wanted her to get the note before she went home for lunch, and I didn't have any too much time.

I knew where her school was, naturally, because I went there myself when I was a kid. When I got there, it felt funny. I wasn't sure I'd remember what it was like inside, but I did. It was exactly the same as it was when I went there. They had that same big yard inside, that was always sort of dark, with those cages around the light bulbs so they wouldn't break if they got hit with a ball. They had those same white circles painted all over the floor, for games and stuff. And those same old basketball rings without any nets – just the backboards and the rings.

Nobody was around at all, probably because it wasn't recess period, and it wasn't lunchtime yet. All I saw was one little kid, a colored kid, on his way to the bathroom. He had one of those wooden passes sticking out of his hip pocket, the same way we used to have, to show he had permission and all to go to the bathroom.

I was still sweating, but not so bad any more. I went over to the stairs and sat down on the first step and took out the pad and pencil I'd bought. The stairs had the same smell they used to have when I went there. Like somebody'd just taken a leak on them. School stairs always smell like that. Anyway, I sat there and wrote this note:

DEAR PHOEBE,

I can't wait around till Wednesday any more so I will probably hitch hike out west this afternoon. Meet me at the Museum of art near the door at quarter past 12 if you can and I will give you your Christmas dough back. I didn't spend much.

Love,

HOLDEN

Her school was practically right near the museum, and she had to pass it on her way home for lunch anyway, so I knew she could meet me all right.

Then I started walking up the stairs to the principal's office so I could give the note to somebody that would bring it to her in her classroom. I folded it about ten times so nobody'd open it. You can't trust anybody in a goddam school. But I knew they'd give it to her if I was her brother and all.

While I was walking up the stairs, though, all of a sudden I thought I was going to puke again. Only, I didn't. I sat down for a second, and then I felt better. But while I was sitting down, I saw something that drove me crazy. Somebody'd written 'Fuck you' on the wall. It drove me damn near crazy. I thought how Phoebe and all the other little kids would see it, and how they'd wonder what the hell it meant, and then finally some dirty kid would tell them – all cockeyed, naturally – what it meant, and how they'd all *think* about it and maybe even *worry* about it for a couple of days. I kept wanting to kill whoever'd written it. I figured it was some perverty bum that'd sneaked in the school late at night to take a leak or something and then wrote it on the wall. I kept picturing myself catching him at it, and how I'd smash his head on the stone steps till he was good and goddam dead and bloody. But I knew, too, I wouldn't have the guts to do it. I knew that. That made me even more depressed. I hardly even had the guts to rub it off the wall with my *hand*, if you want to know the truth. I was afraid some teacher would catch me rubbing it off and would think *I'd* written it. But I rubbed it out anyway, finally. Then I went on up to the principal's office.

The principal didn't seem to be around, but some old lady around a hundred years old was sitting at a typewriter. I told her I was Phoebe Caulfield's brother, in 4B-1, and I asked her to please give Phoebe the note. I said it was very important because my mother was sick and wouldn't have lunch ready for Phoebe and that she'd have to meet me and have lunch in a drugstore. She was very nice about it, the old lady. She took the note off me and called some other lady, from the next office, and the other lady went to give it to Phoebe. Then the old lady that was around a hundred years old and I shot the breeze for a while. She was pretty nice, and I told her how I'd gone there to school, too, and my brothers. She asked me where I went to school now, and I told her Pencey, and she said Pencey was a very good school. Even if I'd wanted to, I wouldn't have had the strength to straighten her out. Besides, if she thought Pencey was a very good school, let her think it. You hate to tell *new* stuff to somebody around a hundred years old. They don't like to hear it. Then, after a while, I left. It was funny. She yelled 'Good luck!' at me the same way old Spencer did when I left Pencey. God, how I hate it when somebody yells 'Good luck!' at me when I'm leaving somewhere. It's depressing.

I went down by a different staircase, and I saw another 'Fuck you' on the wall. I tried to rub it off with my hand again, but this one was *scratched* on, with a knife or something. It wouldn't come off. It's hopeless, anyway. If you had a million years to do it in, you couldn't rub out even *half* the 'Fuck you' signs in the world. It's impossible.

I looked at the clock in the recess yard, and it was only twenty to twelve, so I had quite a lot of time to kill before I met old Phoebe. But I just walked over to the museum anyway. There wasn't anyplace else to go. I thought maybe I might stop in a phone booth and give old Jane Gallagher a buzz before I started bumming my way West, but I wasn't in the mood. For one thing, I wasn't even sure she was home for vacation yet. So I just went over to the museum, and hung around.

While I was waiting around for Phoebe in the museum, right inside the doors and all, these two little kids came up to me and asked me if I knew where the mummies were. The one little kid, the one that asked me, had his pants open. I told him about it. So he buttoned them up right where he was standing talking to me – he didn't even bother to go behind a post or anything. He killed me. I would've laughed, but I was afraid I'd feel like vomiting again, so I didn't. 'Where're the mummies, fella?' the kid said again. 'Ya know?'

I horsed around with the two of them a little bit. 'The mummies? What're they?' I asked the one kid.

'You know. The *mum*mies – them dead guys. That get buried in them toons and all.'

Toons. That killed me. He meant tombs.

'How come you two guys aren't in school?' I said.

'No school t'day,' the kid that did all the talking said. He was lying, sure as I'm alive, the little bastard. I didn't have anything to do, though, till old Phoebe showed up, so I helped them find the place where the mummies were. Boy, I used to know exactly where they were, but I hadn't been in that museum in years.

'You two guys so interested in mummies?' I said.

'Yeah.'

'Can't your friend talk?' I said.

'He ain't my friend. He's my brudda.'

'Can't he talk?' I looked at the one that wasn't doing any talking. 'Can't you talk at all?' I asked him.

'Yeah,' he said. 'I don't feel like it.'

Finally we found the place where the mummies were, and we went in.

'You know how the Egyptians buried their dead?' I asked the one kid.

'Naa.'

'Well, you should. It's very interesting. They wrapped their faces up in these cloths that were treated with some secret chemical. That way they could be buried in their tombs for thousands of years and their faces wouldn't rot or anything. Nobody knows how to do it except the Egyptians. Even modern science.'

To get to where the mummies were, you had to go down this very narrow sort of hall with stones on the side that they'd taken right out of this Pharaoh's tomb and all. It was pretty spooky, and you could tell the two hot-shots I was with weren't enjoying it too much. They stuck close as hell to me, and the one that didn't talk at all practically was holding onto my sleeve. 'Let's go,' he said to his brother. 'I seen 'em awreddy. C'mon, hey.' He turned around and beat it.

'He's got a yella streak a mile wide,' the other one said. 'So long!' He beat it too.

I was the only one left in the tomb then. I sort of liked it, in a way. It was so nice and peaceful. Then, all of a sudden, you'd never guess what I saw on the wall. Another 'Fuck you.' It was written with a red crayon or something, right under the glass part of the wall, under the stones.

That's the whole trouble. You can't ever find a place that's nice and peaceful, because there isn't any. You may *think* there is, but once you get there, when you're not looking, somebody'll sneak up and write 'Fuck you' right under your nose. Try it sometime. I think, even, if I ever die, and they stick me in a cemetery, and I have a tombstone and all, it'll say 'Holden Caulfield' on it, and then what year I was born and what year I died, and then right under that it'll say 'Fuck you.' I'm positive, in fact.

After I came out of the place where the mummies were, I had to go to the bathroom. I sort of had diarrhea, if you want to know the truth. I didn't mind the diarrhea part too much, but something else happened. When I was coming out of the can, right before I got to the door, I sort of passed out. I was lucky, though. I mean I could've killed myself when I hit the floor, but all I did was sort of land on my side. It was a funny thing, though. I felt better after I passed out. I really did. My arm sort of hurt, from where I fell, but I didn't feel so damn dizzy any more.

It was about ten after twelve or so then, and so I went back and stood by the door and waited for old Phoebe. I thought how it might be the last time I'd ever see her again. Any of my relatives, I mean. I figured I'd probably see them again, but not for years. I might come home when I was about thirty-five, I figured, in case somebody got sick and wanted to see me before they died, but that would be the only reason I'd leave my cabin and come back. I even started picturing how it would be when I came back. I knew my mother'd get nervous as hell and start to cry and beg me to stay home and not go back to my cabin, but I'd go anyway. I'd be casual as hell. I'd make her calm down, and then I'd go over to the other side of the living room and take out this cigarette case and light a cigarette, cool as all hell. I'd ask them all to visit me sometime if they wanted to, but I wouldn't insist or anything. What I'd do, I'd let old Phoebe come out and visit me in the summertime and on Christmas vacation and Easter vacation. And I'd let D.B. come out and visit me for a while if he wanted a nice, quiet place for his writing, but he couldn't write any movies in my cabin, only stories and books. I'd have this rule that nobody could do anything phony when they visited me. If anybody tried to do anything phony, they couldn't stay.

All of a sudden I looked at the clock in the checkroom and it was twenty-five of one. I began to get scared that maybe that old lady in the school had told that other lady not to give old Phoebe my message. I began to get scared that maybe she'd told her to burn it or something. It really scared hell out of me. I really wanted to see old Phoebe before I hit the road. I mean I had her Christmas dough and all.

Finally, I saw her. I saw her through the glass part of the door. The reason I saw her, she had my crazy hunting hat on – you could see that hat about ten miles away.

I went out the doors and started down these stone stairs to meet her. The thing I couldn't understand, she had this big suitcase with her. She was just coming across Fifth Avenue, and she was dragging this goddam big suitcase with her. She could hardly drag it. When I got up closer, I saw it was my old suitcase, the one I used to use when I was at Whooton. I couldn't figure out what the hell she was doing with it. 'Hi,' she said when she got up close. She was all out of breath from that crazy suitcase.

'I thought maybe you weren't coming,' I said. 'What the hell's in that bag? I don't need anything. I'm just going the way I am. I'm not even taking the bags I got at the station. What the hellya *got* in there?'

She put the suitcase down. 'My clothes,' she said. 'I'm going with you. Can I? Okay?'

'What?' I said. I almost fell over when she said that. I swear to God I did. I got sort of dizzy and I thought I was going to pass out or something again.

'I took them down the back elevator so Charlene wouldn't see me. It isn't heavy. All I have in it is two dresses and my moccasins and my underwear and socks and some other things. Feel it. It isn't heavy. Feel it once . . . Can't I go with you? Holden? Can't I? *Please*.'

'No. Shut up.'

I thought I was going to pass out cold. I mean I didn't mean to tell her to shut up and all, but I thought I was going to pass out again.

'Why can't I? *Please*, Holden! I won't do anything – I'll just go with you, that's all! I won't even take my clothes with me if you don't want me to – I'll just take my –'

'You can't take anything. Because you're not going. I'm going alone. So shut up.'

'*Please*, Holden. *Please* let me go. I'll be very, very, very – You won't even –'

'You're not *going*. Now, shut up! Gimme that bag,' I said. I took the bag off her. I was almost all set to hit her. I thought I was going to smack her for a second. I really did.

She started to cry.

'I thought you were supposed to be in a play at school and all. I thought you were supposed to be Benedict Arnold in that play and all,' I said. I said it very nasty. 'Wuddaya want to do? Not be in the play, for God's sake?' That made her cry even harder. I was glad. All of a sudden I wanted her to cry till her eyes practically dropped out. I almost hated her. I think I hated her most because she wouldn't be in that play any more if she went away with me.

'Come on,' I said. I started up the steps to the museum again. I figured what I'd do was, I'd check the crazy suitcase she'd brought in the checkroom, and then she could get it again at three o'clock, after school. I knew she couldn't take it back to school with her. 'Come on, now,' I said.

She didn't go up the steps with me, though. She wouldn't come with me. I went up anyway, though, and brought the bag in the checkroom and checked it, and then I came down again. She was still standing there on the sidewalk, but she turned her back on me when I came up to her. She can do that. She can turn her back on you when she feels like it. 'I'm not going away anywhere. I changed my mind. So stop crying and shut up,' I said. The funny part was, she wasn't even crying when I said that. I said it anyway, though. 'C'mon, now. I'll walk you back to school. C'mon, now. You'll be late.'

She wouldn't answer me or anything. I sort of tried to get hold of her old hand, but she wouldn't let me. She kept turning around on me.

'Didja have your lunch? Ya had your lunch yet?' I asked her.

She wouldn't answer me. All she did was, she took off my red hunting hat – the one I gave her – and practically chucked it right in my face. Then she turned her back on me again. It nearly killed me, but I didn't say anything. I just picked it up and stuck it in my coat pocket.

'Come on, hey. I'll walk you back to school,' I said.

'I'm not *go*ing back to school.'

I didn't know what to say when she said that. I just stood there for a couple of minutes.

'You *have* to go back to school. You want to be in that play, don't you? You want to be Benedict Arnold, don't you?'

'No.'

'Sure you do. Certainly you do. C'mon, now, let's go,' I said. 'In the first place, I'm not going away anywhere, I told you. I'm going home. I'm going home as soon as you go back to school.

First I'm gonna go down to the station and get my bags, and then I'm gonna go straight –'

'I said I'm not *go*ing back to school. You can do what *you* want to do, but I'm not going back to school,' she said. 'So shut up.' It was the first time she ever told me to shut up. It sounded terrible. God, it sounded terrible. It sounded worse than swearing. She still wouldn't look at me either, and every time I sort of put my hand on her shoulder or something, she wouldn't let me.

'Listen, do you want to go for a walk?' I asked her. 'Do you want to take a walk down to the zoo? If I let you not go back to school this afternoon and go for a walk, will you cut out this crazy stuff?'

She wouldn't answer me, so I said it over again. 'If I let you skip school this afternoon and go for a little walk, will you cut out the crazy stuff? Will you go back to school tomorrow like a good girl?'

'I may and I may not,' she said. Then she ran right the hell across the street, without even looking to see if any cars were coming. She's a madman sometimes.

I didn't follow her, though. I knew she'd follow *me*, so I started walking downtown toward the zoo, on the park side of the street, and she started walking downtown on the *other* goddam side of the street. She wouldn't look over at me at all, but I could tell she was probably watching me out of the corner of her crazy eye to see where I was going and all. Anyway, we kept walking that way all the way to the zoo. The only thing that bothered me was when a double-decker bus came along because then I couldn't see across the street and I couldn't see where the hell she was. But when we got to the zoo, I yelled over to her, 'Phoebe! I'm going in the zoo! C'mon, now!' She wouldn't look at me, but I could tell she heard me, and when I started down the steps to the zoo I turned around and saw she was crossing the street and following me and all.

There weren't too many people in the zoo because it was sort of a lousy day, but there were a few around the sea lions' swimming pool and all. I started to go by it, but old Phoebe stopped and made out she was watching the sea lions getting fed – a guy was throwing fish at them – so I went back. I figured it was a good chance to catch up with her and all. I went up and sort of stood behind her and sort of put my hands on her shoulders, but she bent her knees and slid out from me – she can certainly be very snotty when she wants to. She kept standing there while the sea lions were getting fed and I stood right behind her. I didn't put my hands on her shoulders again or anything because if I had she *really* would've beat it on me. Kids are funny. You have to watch what you're doing.

She wouldn't walk right next to me when we left the sea lions, but she didn't walk too far away. She sort of walked on one side of the sidewalk and I walked on the other side. It wasn't too gorgeous, but it was better than having her walk about a mile away from me, like before. We went up and watched the bears, on that little hill, for a while, but there wasn't much to watch. Only one of the bears was out, the polar bear. The other one, the brown one, was in his goddam cave and wouldn't come out. All you could see was his rear end. There was a little kid standing next to me, with a cowboy hat on practically over his ears, and he kept telling his father, 'Make him come out, Daddy. Make him come *out*.' I looked at old Phoebe, but she wouldn't laugh. You know kids when they're sore at you. They won't laugh or anything.

After we left the bears, we left the zoo and crossed over this little street in the park, and then we went through one of those little tunnels that always smell from somebody's taking a leak. It was on the way to the carrousel. Old Phoebe still wouldn't talk to me or anything, but she was sort of walking next to me now. I took a hold of the belt at the back of her coat, just for the hell of it, but she wouldn't let me. She said, 'Keep your hands to yourself, if you don't mind.' She was still sore at me. But not as sore as she was before. Anyway, we kept getting closer and closer to the carrousel and you could start to hear that nutty music it always plays. It was playing 'Oh, Marie!' It played that same song about fifty years ago when *I* was a little kid. That's one nice thing about carrousels, they always play the same songs.

'I thought the carrousel was *closed* in the wintertime,' old Phoebe said. It was the first time she practically said anything. She probably forgot she was supposed to be sore at me.

'Maybe because it's around Christmas,' I said.

She didn't say anything when I said that. She probably remembered she was supposed to be sore at me.

'Do you want to go for a ride on it?' I said. I knew she probably did. When she was a tiny little kid, and Allie and D.B. and I used to go to the park with her, she was mad about the carrousel. You couldn't get her off the goddam thing.

'I'm too big,' she said. I thought she wasn't going to answer me, but she did.

'No, you're not. Go on. I'll wait for ya. Go on,' I said. We were right there then. There were a few kids riding on it, mostly very little kids, and a few parents were waiting around outside, sitting on the benches and all. What I did was, I went up to the window where they sell the tickets and bought old Phoebe a ticket. Then I gave it to her. She was standing right next to me.

'Here,' I said. 'Wait a second – take the rest of your dough, too.' I started giving her the rest of the dough she'd lent me.

'You keep it. Keep it for me,' she said. Then she said right afterward – 'Please.'

That's depressing, when somebody says 'please' to you. I mean if it's Phoebe or somebody. That depressed the hell out of me. But I put the dough back in my pocket.

'Aren't you gonna ride, too?' she asked me. She was looking at me sort of funny. You could tell she wasn't *too* sore at me any more.

'Maybe I will the next time. I'll watch ya,' I said. 'Got your ticket?'

'Yes.'

'Go ahead, then – I'll be on this bench right over here. I'll watch ya.' I went over and sat down on this bench, and she went and got on the carrousel. She walked all around it. I mean she walked once all the way around it. Then she sat down on this big, brown, beat-up-looking old horse. Then the carrousel started, and I watched her go around and around. There were only about five or six other kids on the ride, and the song the carrousel was playing was 'Smoke Gets in Your Eyes.' It was playing it very jazzy and funny. All the kids kept trying to grab for the gold ring, and so was old Phoebe, and I was sort of afraid she'd fall off the goddam horse, but I didn't say anything or do anything. The thing with kids is, if they want to grab for the gold ring, you have to let them do it, and not say anything. If they fall off, they fall off, but it's bad if you say anything to them.

When the ride was over she got off her horse and came over to me. 'You ride once, too, this time,' she said.

'No, I'll just watch ya. I think I'll just watch,' I said. I gave her some more of her dough. 'Here. Get some more tickets.'

She took the dough off me. 'I'm not mad at you any more,' she said.

'I know. Hurry up – the thing's gonna start again.'

Then all of a sudden she gave me a kiss. Then she held her hand out, and said, 'It's raining. It's starting to rain.'

'I know.'

Then what she did – it damn near killed me – she reached in my coat pocket and took out my red hunting hat and put it on my head.

'Don't *you* want it?' I said.

'You can wear it a while.'

'Okay. Hurry up, though, now. You're gonna miss your ride. You won't get your own horse or anything.'

She kept hanging around, though.

'Did you mean it what you said? You really aren't going away anywhere? Are you really going home afterwards?' she asked me.

'Yeah,' I said. I meant it, too. I wasn't lying to her. I really did go home afterwards. 'Hurry *up*, now,' I said. 'The thing's starting.'

She ran and bought her ticket and got back on the goddam carrousel just in time. Then she walked all the way around it till she got her own horse back. Then she got on it. She waved to me and I waved back.

Boy, it began to rain like a bastard. In *buckets*, I swear to God. All the parents and mothers and everybody went over and stood right under the roof of the carrousel, so they wouldn't get soaked to the skin or anything, but I stuck around on the bench for quite a while. I got pretty soaking wet, especially my neck and my pants. My hunting hat really gave me quite a lot of protection, in a way, but I got soaked anyway. I didn't care, though.

I felt so damn happy all of a sudden, the way old Phoebe kept going around and around. I was damn near bawling, I felt so damn happy, if you want to know the truth. I don't know why. It was just that she looked so damn *nice*, the way she kept going around and around, in her blue coat and all. God, I wish you could've been there.

26

That's all I'm going to tell about. I could probably tell you what I did after I went home, and how I got sick and all, and what school I'm supposed to go to next fall, after I get out of here, but I don't feel like it. I really don't. That stuff doesn't interest me too much right now.

A lot of people, especially this one psychoanalyst guy they have here, keeps asking me if I'm going to apply myself when I go back to school next September. It's such a stupid question, in my opinion. I mean how do you know what you're going to do till you *do* it? The answer is, you don't. I *think* I am, but how do I know? I swear it's a stupid question.

D.B. isn't as bad as the rest of them, but he keeps asking me a lot of questions, too. He drove over last Saturday with this English babe that's in this new picture he's writing. She was pretty affected, but very good-looking. Anyway, one time when she went to the ladies' room way the hell down in the other wing, D.B. asked me what I thought about all this stuff I just finished telling you about. I didn't know what the hell to say. If you want to know the truth, I don't *know* what I think about it. I'm sorry I told so many people about it. About all I know is, I sort of *miss* everybody I told about. Even old Stradlater and Ackley, for instance. I think I even miss that goddam Maurice. It's funny. Don't ever tell anybody anything. If you do, you start missing everybody.